BOOK OF L.O.F.I.

COREY L SIMMINS

ISBN: 1500437107
ISBN 13: 9781500437107

CHAPTER I

"Yea, though I walk through the valley of the shadow of death, I will fear no evil: for thou art with me; thy rod and thy staff they comfort me."
Psalm 23

Sam Wolfe fell, bounced, spun, settled, then dropped. The soft spongy sod of Guam absorbed the blow of the newly deposited convict gently but only for a second. Wolfe unclipped the ankle straps attached to his legs then jumped into a crouching position. While reconnoitering the immediate area, he became instantly possessed by a rush of visceral trepidation. Glancing up quickly, Wolfe regarded the expulsion device as it retracted the bungee cord. The twenty-five foot wall which protected the military airbase towered over the clearing much like its namesake in Northern England over seventeen hundred years ago. All who gathered on the Hadrian's Wall gandered into the open field as the two convicts thrown into the penal colony immediately ahead of him bolted for the tree line. Glancing back, Wolfe became painfully aware that all looked upon the scene with quizzical expectation. He learned in school only a couple of years ago that Lord of the Flies Island, so society called it, proved to be America's greatest societal petri dish. Sam Wolfe scowled. "Bastards," he muttered under his breath, quickly realizing he had no time for those atop the security wall and began to move while crouching. Ahead of Wolfe, the other two condemned, expelled from society along with him, had already moved toward the tree-line when two gangs emerged. Quickly analyzing the situation, Wolfe knew he must immediately choose. His light brown skin gave him

1

latitude in making the decision. The two convicts in front of him, one a rare white male, the other a typical swarthy hue, stopped shoulder-to-shoulder. Whether they discussed teaming up or not, Wolfe did not know. It did not matter; he knew that on the United States Penal Colony of Guam in 2075, life proved cheap and fleeting.

Looking south from Andersen Air Force Base, Wolfe knew that the island contained three villages inhabited by hostile groups who generally slaughtered one another all to the sociological and psychological delight of the United States military and the government agencies which studied society's refuse. Their citizenship revoked for criminality, the last contact with America for some came with an individual's unceremonious expulsion from civilization. With military precision, hordes of murderers, rapists, child molesters, drug dealers, larcenists, and all other forms of human offal found themselves entering through a massive gate on the other side of the island. A select few were ceremonially projected into the abyss of Guam to fight for survival or succumb to a quick death. Wolfe noticed the group which emerged from the eastern edge of the clearing consisted of all dark skinned men with any manner of crude weaponry. The group on the right, which emerged from the western edge of the woods, seemed to be of a brown yet more Hispanic hue. This would prove advantageous for Sam Wolfe who knew that skin color mattered greatly on this island. The two men hurled over the wall before him, Starke and Neyer as he recalled, stood stone still. Neyer, clearly a dark brown mix of black and white parents, surveyed the situation and quickly surmised that the Hispanic group may not welcome him with open arms. Judging from his head swinging hither and thither, Neyer attempted to gather an inkling of approbation from either group. Wolfe continued to observe but began to slink toward the woods.

In the dark brown group stood a solid-looking fully black man, a rarity for society in the United States with its nearly 90% brown skin color among the younger generations but common on L.O.F.I. Wolfe noticed that the pure black man resonated an air of authority over his brown comrades. As he drifted toward the edge of the woods, Wolfe observed the black man with the rounded face nod a look of approval as he turned and walked away. The convict named Neyer, who Sam got to know minimally at the detention center, bolted toward the brown group. Wolfe stood steadfast and indecisive, observing from a distance. Starke, white, understood his fate. Both groups looked toward Wolfe as Starke spread his arms open as if he prepared to take flight—though Wolfe recognized the resignation. Four of the Hispanic men approached Starke and without a word ran a spear through his abdomen. Starke doubled over, fell to his knees, and collapsed, his hands barely holding him up and head hung low. Wolfe quickly glanced up to the top of Hadrian's Wall—so named by the smug politicians playing on the Roman reference—and he felt a powerful revulsion. This daily routine of citizen expulsions onto Guam resulted in this quotidian carnage whether en masse at the main gate or independently at the wall. The group made quick work of Starke; Wolfe bolted into the brush followed by the sounds of shouting.

───────

Sam Wolfe had studied the island of Guam along with America's penal colony and its history in high school, which ended abruptly for him only last year. After receiving his first felony conviction right before his eighteenth birthday, his parole officer, upon reminding Sam that minority status did not matter for juvenile records were no longer expunged, offered him this advice, "Study a map of Guam, son." He disregarded the officer's guidance until he found himself with a second felony drug charge and wound up in a rehabilitation center in Mayfield, Ohio under court order. Having dropped out of school, his future in modern American society seemed doomed. His former country's intolerance of felons left no room for the criminal in 2075. He studied the map for he knew a third strike meant revocation of citizenship and a one-way flight to L.O.F.I.—America's Penal Colony on Guam. Wolfe knew of two methods. The first through the main gate. The second occurred via the bungee into the abyss of anarchy. This process proved a delight for the new administrators, followed by the heinous welcoming committee who either accosted the new villains, killed them, or fought over them. Wolfe knew if he found himself expelled in this manner onto L.O.F.I., he would not leave his fate to chance. He ran, knowing just south of Andersen Air Force Base and through the woods, the road to Yigo still existed, if only as a trail after decades of nothing but foot travel.

Moving steadily and silently, Wolfe found the main road, crossed it into the woods, then headed south toward the town when he heard the snap of a branch. His fear realized, Sam stopped, scurried up a tree, and scouted to find his pursuer. Grim. Two Hispanic males stepped out onto the road from the brush, one armed with a type of homemade club, the other a spear. Wolfe regretted that he had nothing. He knew the fate of those accepted by the groups: bottom of the pecking order, initiations, feared sodomy, incessant trials, murderous raids on the other colonies. He wanted no part of that type of life. Truthfully, Sam Wolfe wanted no part of L.O.F.I. Now fully in fight-or-flight mode, he chose to stay put, hoping the men would pass by, oblivious to his presence. The foliage provided coverage as the men spoke, pointed about, then decided to split momentarily before heading northwest on the road in the opposite direction Wolfe wished to proceed. After waiting for what seemed an adequately safe amount of time, Sam Wolfe descended the tree and moved quickly and quietly toward Yigo in search of any type of weapon and food followed by a safe shelter.

He felt like an animal—a hunted animal in fact. It reminded him of the time he first encountered a bully walking home from school. His assailant jumped out of a stairwell, made a false accusation about him, then proceeded to push him around. Here as then, Sam Wolfe resolved to follow the same course of action; he fled. He ran as a kid due to fear; today would be no different as a near crippling terror seized him. He bolted much like startled prey but ruefully whispered to himself, "I am not an animal." That would remain to be seen.

On the outskirts of Yigo, Sam Wolfe discovered an abandoned and half-razed Church of Jesus Christ of Latter-day Saints. Clearly evident through the vines and other plant life covering the building and protruding through the windows, the modest structure had been sacked years ago. Moving surreptitiously, Wolfe sprinted from the cover of the woods into the doorway, stumbled through weeds growing out from the cracks, nudged aside a tattered chair, and entered the building hoping to avoid being noticed. He felt confident that he had eluded his pursuers but also realized he possessed no expertise in this cat-and-mouse game. Sam had no idea whether the Hispanic group would continue to pursue him, give up on him, or fight the brown group led by the black man for him. He knew his learning curve would need to be quick in order to survive. As he pushed through the shattered remains of the Mormon church searching in vain for anything remotely useful as a weapon, he soon realized that of the many doors ripped off the hinges, or windows broken, one particular door seemed to be well-guarded by a pile of desks. Fearing a type of trap, he moved away from the door and into the area he suspected once held the Mormon faithful for worship when he heard a vibrant and terrifying scream. Turning, seeing a charging man in rags with weapon raised, Sam Wolfe did not have time to appreciate the basic karate classes he took in the rehabilitation center; he could only react.

As the charging man brought down the weapon, Wolfe raised his left arm to absorb the blow as he crouched down on his right knee. The defensive move—perfected during hours of practice in the dojo trying to break his narcotic addiction—worked to perfection. As the weapon came crashing down, his subtle move caused the assailant to miss with the now apparent hammer and only strike Sam's forearm with his fist. From the kneeling position, his enemy's chest fully exposed and Sam's right arm instinctively cocked and twisted for attack, Wolfe let his arm extend swiftly, corkscrewing with a brutal thrust, knuckles-first, into the solar plexus. Sam Wolfe heard the weapon drop as the attacker exhaled every ounce of breath, staggering from the blow. Quickly assessing the situation, realizing that L.O.F.I. represented a kill-or-be-killed world, Sam looked for the hammer to delivery at the very least an incapacitating blow to his would-be killer. At that moment he noticed a shank-like claw made from a garden tool dangling from the hand of the stunned assailant. Wolfe stood in a crouched position to keep his center of gravity low and delivered a stunning blow to the exposed kidney of his now victim, who dropped to his hands and knees releasing the shank. In a swift motion, Sam Wolfe grabbed the claw in his right hand, the hair of his crazed assailant in the other. Lifting with his left hand, tilting the gasping attacker's head back, he swung the shank upwards, lodging it into the neck. The man, rolling in agony from the terrifying blows, leaned over as Wolfe removed the claw and swung again. This time the shank hit the jugular and spouted black blood violently into the air. As Sam let out a boisterous open mouth yell, an uncontrolled verbal release of adrenaline, the stream of blood filled his mouth with a strange bit of irony causing him to choke, swallow, gag, then puke. His unnamed attacker became the first life young Sam Wolfe ever took.

Sam Wolfe surveyed the situation, a tad embarrassed by the vomiting. Though no one had witnessed his apparent weakness, he rationalized the incident as a result of the blood and not the act itself. In the days awaiting the shipment to L.O.F.I., he knew he would have to kill on this island in order to survive. Of the millions of convicts shipped to Lord of the Flies Island since its inception post-Great Compromise, the publically disclosed population of the island had remained relatively steady at an estimated couple hundred thousand. These men and women shipped to the Penal Colony of Guam represented the worst forms of human depravity. When conducting the obligatory research in middle school on the penal colony that every American did in order to comprehend the fate of criminality, Wolfe remembered learning of America's rapid improvement beginning in 2025. For every criminal, drug addict, and social deviant shipped out for a lifetime of banishment, a productive immigrant would be granted an invite and citizenship to the United States. Violence and slovenliness had been replaced by productivity. With mild prestidigitation concerning the Bill of Rights and Constitution, the United States had moved toward a social utopia. Consequently, with the vicious removed from society, Sam learned in high school that only the decisive and brutal survived on Lord of the Flies Island. He knew he would have to kill. Admittedly, it proved easy.

Sam Wolfe walked around the man who had finally stopped twitching and moving since bleeding out. Glancing down at the man, Wolfe felt a swelling of compunction. The morality of it all. Right or wrong did not matter; it had proven necessary. Lost most of his young life on spirituality, Sam stood momentarily perplexed as how to feel about his act of taking another person's life. He quickly suppressed the thoughts citing internally that he did not have time for ethics. Wolfe grabbed the claw and picked up the weapon, which proved to be a mini sledgehammer. Feeling good that the blunt head did not crush his arm, Wolfe reflected upon his karate. He took the classes offered in the rehabilitation center to get his mind off the drugs and defend himself against the perverts. Karate proved efficacious in jail and deadly on the island already. Only advancing two belt levels served as all the time he needed, for as his sensei often taught them, the early defense moves would save a person in any fight with an opponent not trained in martial arts. So far his journey on the island met his expectations—unparalleled violence. In just under a couple hours, two people brutally killed. Not feeling at risk any longer, Wolfe realized he may have stumbled across a loner's hovel. He removed the barrier to the door he originally considered a trap. The irrational and sudden attack, the clearly-protected door, all led Wolfe to feel he had encountered a less than intelligent hermit. The little room turned out to be a closet with a bit of food stowed away. Wolfe gathered two military MREs, his new weapons, scurried to the door, then headed for the woods; for in order to exact his retribution for his expulsion to L.O.F.I., he needed to embark immediately for the city of Barrigada.

CHAPTER 2

"In another moment down went Alice after it, never once considering how in the world she would get out again."
Alice in Wonderland – Lewis Carroll

Sam Wolfe woke with a start. Spooked, he jumped, rolled over, and attempted to comprehend his situation. As the nebulous haze of sleep wore off, Wolfe remembered his last waking strategy—sleep until dark and move from Yigo to Barrigada, a treacherous nine miles through what used to be the white section of Guam before American demographics melded into a swarthy hue. Prior to dropping out of school due to drug use, Sam retained only a paucity of facts concerning Guam though he remembered his two favorite instructors hammering away at the importance of the penal colony. Mr. Murray Mallory Moore, his language arts instructor, loved the sobriquet of L.O.F.I. since he seemed obsessed with the Golding novel. Mr. Jacob Wilde, the government teacher, pounded the pulpit at school about the societal significance of the prison. However, Sam's interest in Guam piqued after his second felony when, during his drug rehabilitation, the clinic forced them to view countless films on L.O.F.I. almost in the same fashion as Burgess's Alex without the eye clips. The instructors constantly reiterated the necessity of knowing the geography for most Americans who obtain two felonies had a 78% chance of obtaining their third. Though Wolfe felt sure the third felony would never occur, for he felt he had turned the proverbial corner on his addiction and criminality, he studied the map nonetheless. Therefore, knowing that Yigo had once been the hotbed of the white supremacist of the island prior to the amalgamation of the races in America, Wolfe's plan, while awaiting expulsion from society, hinged upon the fact that he would slip past Yigo and head toward the center of the island virtually razed during the Guam Race War of 2026-2032. Being brown, the fascinating history of the once dominant racial groups in America—blacks, whites, and Hispanics—slaughtering each other simply over color seemed absurd since he grew up in a mostly "chocolate" world.

Coming from his reverie and shaking off the thoughts of home and school, Sam's nebulous haze evaporated into complete lucidity regarding his plan and task at hand. Sam scanned the broken-down barn as he sat in an apparently abandoned farm on the outskirts of Yigo. Though dark, the moon cast an eerie glow, which enabled him to investigate the origin of the sound which had awoken him. In the cracked doorway, he could see the dim shadow cast by the moon silhouetting through the aperture. As the door pushed open, Sam Wolfe gripped his hammer and shank and resolved himself to kill again. A head peered in, accompanied by a hushed whisper. As the door slid open, in crept a middle-aged man followed by a similarly aged woman.

"Hello?" Sam Wolfe said nothing. At twenty, wise beyond his years, he realized that these two more than likely posed little to no danger. In fact, it seemed odd for a couple to be walking together on this island, which certainly had to be as safe for a woman's chastity as Viking Europe a thousand years ago.

"What do you want?" Wolfe spoke, rising. Aghast, the couple seemed horrified, especially upon seeing the weapons in this shadowy figure's hands.

"Oh....uh...we don't want no trouble mister."

"Good. We have something in common." Wolfe observed as the woman backed out; the man following. "Hey, where you going?"

"Sorry. We want no trouble." They bolted. Cursing, Sam moved quickly toward the door preparing to chase them down. Sam advanced to the door, foolishly whipped it open, and gazed into the dark. At first he wanted to avoid contact; however, the timidity of these two characters inadvertently lowered his guard. He hissed a muffled "wait" at the mysterious couple only to hear, "We must run. God bless you." He started to pursue, then allowed a cooler head to prevail—knowing little about the island, not wanting to hunt down and corner any type of animal, human or not. The mystery would remain unsolved. Sam gave the couple a head start seeing them push west into the darkness. Wolfe found himself perplexed. "God bless you" had stunned him. He expected to find no religious people on Guam. In fact it proved quite odd, for Sam grew up absent of religion mostly. He found it oddly coincidental that since his incarceration religion had come up a couple of times. Mr. Moore, his teacher, brought up the subject, and he had been visited by a priest prior to expulsion. The recent juxtaposition of faith proved incongruous given his predicament. Shrugging off morality again due to survival needs, he crept out of the barn and headed through the woods along the road toward the ruined city of Barrigada.

———

The destroyed remnants of Barrigada stood a solid nine miles from Sam's current location, and he realized that traveling in the dark would make that a two-day hike. Remembering his studies from the drug rehabilitation center, Sam Wolfe had memorized the road names and directions in hopes of quickly making it to the destroyed city-center of Barrigada or Agana Heights to find a safe abode, hook up with a group for protection, then began to enact his plan. During the time period between his second felony and that fateful day he erroneously acquired his third, Sam Wolfe had dedicated himself to the studying of all of the items he should have studied in class prior to his dropping out. He remembered the day that Mr. Moore and Mr. Wilde had visited him as he went through detoxification in the rehabilitation center; both entered in bow ties as if it were a graduation party.

Wolfe remembered the two blasting into the visiting area with books in hand, the one trying to out-swagger the other. Those books sustained him during his drying out; furthermore, after the third strike felony and the seemingly endless detention until expulsion from civilization, Sam Wolfe had read them all.

"Anything shaking?" Mr. Wilde opened with, displaying a level of frivolity unbecoming of a drug rehabilitation center.

"You dolt! This look like the hallway to you?" Mr. Moore rebuked Mr. Wilde. "Display a modicum of decorum please. People are trying to convalesce."

"Don't worry Mr. Moore," Wolfe had interjected. "I appreciate the visit."

"Yeah, besides, I wanted to cheer him up. Looks like a zombie lunch room in here. Minus the brain eating of course."

"Jacob," Mr. Moore continued the attack, "shall we keep this professional?" As a distinguished member of society, Moore puffed out his chest looking respectable in his anachronistic bow tie and school jacket. "Besides, your attempts at humor fail regularly."

"Relax, Murray." Mr. Wilde looked at Wolfe, "So, Sammie, anything shaking?" Feeling abandoned by his parents and friends, it seemed only fitting that his only visitors proved to be the only teachers to have made any impact upon him in school. Naturally, Mr. Wilde brought him a book of the Federalist Papers and great speeches of American history. He read them all. Mr. Moore, in his typical romantic and heroic fashion, brought him a book on Ernest Shackleton and the inspiration for his middle name, George Mallory.

"Paper?" Wolfe, befuddled by the gift, inquired.

"Yes, paper." In the digitized world, paper books had nearly been extinct for forty years. "Remember, we monk teachers have our ways." Moore informed Sam.

"Actually," interjected Mr. Jacob Wilde, "a group of monks around the country run old-fashioned print-on-demand presses. We can get anything."

"You guys are awesome!" Even though Murray Mallory Moore and Jacob Wilde delivered the typical "you can do it" speech filled with all the usual platitudes, their very presence exemplified the monk teaching practice. They lived for their students. To Sam, public education's philosophy of paying teachers to remain unmarried and live in school, obliged to live a priestly existence, seemed the most prudent form of pedagogy. Sam had determined not to fail them in his recovery, and he had not. Unfortunately, his penchant for flare, inspired by the king of chutzpah, Mr. Moore, had led him to his ultimate mistake and third-strike downfall. This mistake and his subsequent expulsion from society, along with his citizenship revocation, would motivate his survival on Guam. His two days of sleeping in barns and creeping via the night passed by uneventfully with the thoughts of his mission occupying his mind and military meals ready-to-eat sustaining his body.

———

As the luminescence of dawn began to enlighten the eastern horizon, Sam Wolfe knew he needed to get indoors before the savages were loose on the island. His successful march of nine miles to Barrigada increased his confidence. Scanning Purple Heart Highway, he decided to skitter down onto an unknown backstreet, scooting through a Catholic Church parking lot. Most of the houses seemed to be dilapidated and ruinous—windows long gone, doors ripped off, roofs disintegrating from forty years of neglect, sun, and weather. Barrigada manifested all that school had taught him in regards to Guam history. The remnants of the early days of the penal colony, a viciously violent race and convict war waged here until prison yard lines of demarcation had been engendered. This city, where much of the fighting had occurred, had been pillaged and plundered after the carnage. Wolfe moved quickly down the street, an unsettling panic effusing, knowing he must get inside until he could further assess the situation, gather some allies, then commence with his plan. Then, a building caught his eye, only because the windows were boarded and the front door still seemed intact. A quick squint of the eyes in the dim dawn revealed the nature of the building—Barrigada Library. An odd sight in all of this destruction, the library seemed in better shape than the rest of the abandoned neighborhood; furthermore, the irony, he thought of his high school classes where he learned that in Nazi Germany books were torched and how in the Muslim expansion across the Middle East, the great library of Alexandria had been burned. Strangely though, here, the library seemed to survive while all else did not.

Like Time Traveler, and against his better judgment for he felt sure it reflected a sign of habitation, the domiciliary nature of civilization served as a siren song; Sam Wolfe entered the seemingly unscathed edifice. He remembered reading H.G. Wells's *Time Machine* with Mr. Moore in high school, or at least, he remembered not reading it but rather simply listening to the lectures. Mr. Moore talked about the value of the public library in Western Civilization. He remembered the lesson, for it brought together the only two teachers in the building he felt made any logical sense.

"Think of it people," bellowed Mr. Moore as Sam reminisced, "the entire compendium of human knowledge, all at the average citizen's fingertips. All they had to do in order to obtain knowledge, just walk in and grab a book." Moore constantly droned on about the Founding Fathers, the development of public libraries and school systems, and the emphasis on education.

"You can applaud the liberals and taxes for that, thank you." Mr. Wilde, the other teacher, would frequently barge into Mr. Moore's room, and oftentimes vice a versa, interrupting each other's class, but continuing the lesson as if they planned it. Knowing those two, Sam figured they did.

"Yes, yes. But why? The reason," he always paused, "ignorance did not reflect strength!" Mr. Moore always stated, "The ignorant will always be conquered."

With thoughts of his only high school influences rattling around in his mind, against his better judgment, Sam Wolfe continued through the entry way and into the main floor of the library, quickly ascertaining that the building, at least, currently housed someone. The place seemed organized, untouched, and unpilfered. Judging by the state of most of the structures in town, this place too should reflect a few decades worth of thrashings. Not the case. With clawed shank in left hand and hammer in his right, Sam Wolfe moved surreptitiously through the library skirting the wall, hoping that the inhabitant reflected the manner of the mysterious couple he met briefly the other evening and not the deranged man he slaughtered his first night.

After circling the small area of the local neighborhood library and determining that someone did occupy the space, Wolfe determined to continue the search, for clues in his mind elicited images of a tremulous hermit. The fact that books seemed to be on the shelves in a clean order could not be a coincidence. At the very least, the various titles should be covered with dust. The limited chairs were orderly; the air did not smell stagnant. People circulated through here. Given the vacated open space, the culprit occupying this redoubt against anarchy must be in the restrooms. It seemed to be the only place to hide. Wolfe grabbed a chair and headed for the two restroom doors located on either side of a defunct water fountain. The door opened inwardly, so Sam leaned the chair at a forty-five degree angle; therefore, if while he explored the men's and someone exited the women's, he would be alerted by the falling seat. In a bold move, Sam Wolfe violently flung open the door slamming it against the wall. Figuring the denizen of the library knew of his intrusion, there seemed little sense in clandestine movements; fright would be his weapon. The slamming door reverberated in the two-stall bathroom. A brisk opening of the doors quickly demonstrated the vacant nature of the room. Wolfe quickly went out and removed the warning chair. Upon entering the women's room, a similarly disappointing vacancy greeted him. The library seemed empty.

Wolfe moved out, walked around the library floor, slid back into the women's room, then the men's. Epiphany. Though he could not place it immediately, in the back of his mind Sam Wolfe recognized a difference in the identical bathrooms: each with two stalls, two sinks, and two small windows. Quickly moving back into the women's restroom, the difference manifested itself, a small janitor's closet. Testing the knob, determining it unlocked, Sam Wolfe knew the resident must be inside for it could only be locked from his side. Pulling the door open with his left hand with hammer raised in his right, Sam Wolfe eased into the dark closet, pushing the door outwardly, hoping for natural light to illuminate the space. Empty. The contents: an old bucket, a moth eaten mop, an ancient hot water heater, a few discarded rags seemed to be the only contents. Wolfe exited the closet into the toilet area. Concentrating on what he must be missing, he reviewed the facts. Clean library area, orderly, unmolested. No dust. Nothing out of place. Fresh, non-stagnant air throughout. Exactly! Sam Wolfe briskly moved back into the closet and reconnoitered the area again noticing the fresh air, the dustless environment, and orderliness of the janitor's closet, which due to neglect should have been filled with cobwebs and dust, elements of abandonment. Something existed here—benevolence or malevolence yet to be determined.

Sam Wolfe moved toward the hot water heater, which could not have been utilized in over a half century, noticing the cleanliness of the thing. Holding on to the heater, he eased around to see if a clue could be ascertained to discover the whereabouts of the library's denizen. Nothing. Neither behind the water heater nor around the narrow space, the closet too seemed utterly deserted. He stepped back exasperated, exhaled a long drawn breath, then frustratedly leaned on the heater. It moved, tipped, and Sam Wolfe lost his balance and toppled toward the floor, landing by a hole at the base as the faux water heater rested at a forty-five degree angle, which allowed a small space for a person to enter—a veritable portal into the underworld. What could all of this mean? Questions whirled about Sam's mind. A warmth of spirit effusively overcame Sam. A confidence. A calling. Sam couldn't explain the ephemeral rush which caused him to feel confident in this library and in this closet. He felt no trepidation; he sensed no danger. On this island of terror and murder, Sam felt oddly safe. Consequently, without hesitation, like Alice, Sam Wolfe descended into the rabbit hole never once considering how in the world he would get out again.

CHAPTER 3

"Never attempt to win by force what can be won by deception."
The Prince – Niccolo Machiavelli

With incredulous recklessness, Sam Wolfe descended into the pit located under the carefully crafted hatch constructed with the hot water heater. The library now above him and the dimly lit passage before him, his incautious journey continued. Hammer in the right hand at the ready to hurl if need be, clawed shank in reserve in the left and determined to see this adventure through, Sam Wolfe, completely cocksure, proceeded into the unknown. The tunnel, cut ruggedly from the earth, wound in an arc preventing him from seeing around the corner; however, dim light penetrated from some unknown region. Slowly moving along a wall and listening intently, Sam could hear a steady drip of water but nothing else. As the tunnel turned the corner, it straightened out, opening into an underground room, which produced the dripping water. The space quickly expanded into an area of equal size to the library's small, book display room. In the four corners, if you would call them corners in this less than geometrically square room, rather large tubs sat under shafts of light into which the water steadily dripped. Stepping into the center of the room, Sam surveyed, noticing the tubs filled with the overhead runoff. The collection, he suspected, purposefully for the sustenance of life by some dweller or dwellers. Off of this room, beckoning into the further unknown, four tunnels, in addition to the one from which he had emerged, sat dark and foreboding. Determined to continue, Sam Wolfe began to move.

"Far enough son! Stop where you are!" A voice bellowed from behind. Sam Wolfe whirled around to see a great bear of a man emerge from the shadows brandishing a sword, probably a claymore, which rendered his hammer and clawed shank futile. The barrel-chested man, an octogenarian, sauntered toward him truculently exclaiming, "You are not wanted down here. Drop the weapon. You are surrounded." Without a sound, the other tunnel entryways filled with young ladies all wielding weapons of antiquated warfare—rapiers and cutlasses. The steel-toting ladies all ranged from their mid-teens to their mid-twenties. Sam Wolfe thought something smelled rotten in Denmark.

"Just what are you doing down here grandpa?"

"You are trespassing. Punishable by death in these parts. Mind your tongue. If you won't respect your elders, you will damn well respect your betters!" The old, yet John Waynish figure, glanced over Sam Wolfe's shoulder, "Becky! Megan! Show this punk some manners." Before Sam could locate the pair being addressed, two audible snaps followed by smart blows to his left hand and right arm stung him causing him to drop the clawed shank. Sam Wolfe never saw the shooters. As he attempted to hold onto the hammer, another blow struck him on the hand followed by one in the forehead. The final shot to the face proved the coup de grace as he reacted instinctively, dropping the hammer to protect his head.

"Damn man! Alright! Alright. You got me." Wolfe reeled in pain with stinging hands, thumping arm, and bruising forehead. He knew resistance would prove superfluous.

"When you break into a man's castle, you best expect to defend yourself." From behind two of the rapier-wielding girls, emerging from the dark, two teens aiming slingshots stalked toward Sam Wolfe, loaded for bear and ready to hit him again. Added to the mix, a third young lady with a slingshot appeared from the shadows next to the elder also ready to strike Sam down.

"Look man! I don't know what you got going on down here, but it looks pretty sick."

"Lauryn, shut him up." The girl next to the man pulled back on the sling and stepped forward.

"Alright! Don't shoot dammit!"

"Mind your manners then you foul-minded, jackanapes." The man covered the room with a circular glance at his Amazonian militia, "If he moves, Lauryn, Becky, and Megan put him down. When down, Kayla, Sarah, Nicole move in and cut him to shreds." The girls remained disconsolately silent. "Now you know your predicament. You going to cooperate?"

"Yes." Wolfe glanced around the room befuddled as to the nature of this octogenarian with this armed harem protecting a labyrinth under a pristine library on a penal colony of anarchy. He realized that on this island, all things considered, he could indeed have stumbled into a worse hornet's nest of armed combatants. "Yes. I will cooperate. I apologize for intruding. I want no trouble."

"Why did you find us?"

"No offense, but you made it easy." Wolfe gazed upon the countenance of the bruiser of a man hoping to obtain a sense of his emotions. "Following a few clues, common sense, deductive reasoning, and relying on myriad tales from Sir Arthur Conan Doyle, well, it proved elementary."

"I didn't ask you how. I asked you why?"

"Excuse me." Sam Wolfe answered, flummoxed.

"In all of my forty plus years on this island and nearly all here in this library, not one of these convicts has ventured into my oasis." The big man lowered his sword onto his shoulder, resting it much like a bat by a baseball player's neck in the on-deck circle. "You are educated even though young. I suppose you just landed here on L.O.F.I."

"Yes, sir."

"So, why did you find us?"

"Well, I researched the island prior to coming here. I knew I didn't want to venture into the camps. No man's land down south seemed too nebulous. I had hoped that the razed city here would provide me access to a group of loners which could give me some protection while I enact my plan."

"Enact your plan? You researched coming here. By God you are intelligent." The big man presented Sam with a smile of approbation. "Explain your plan."

"Well, I plan on getting off this island."

———

After his proclamation of escaping the island, the giant man instructed him to follow his warrior women down the left hall about one hundred feet into a small room with a table surrounded by a mismatched group of chairs. The girls surrounded the room still armed. The older leader indicated for Sam Wolfe to sit on the far end before he spoke.

"I am Kellas Somervell. I have been on the United States Penal Colony here at Guam since 2035. I came just after the Race War—though I still saw a tremendous amount of killing in my day, none quite like those first years when the colony opened in '25." Kellas Somervell sat down. "These here are my girls. More like my aides if you will. I have had them since they were babies. You met Becky and Megan via the slingshot. Though they rarely agree philosophically, they both can shoot. Lauryn, the third shooter, does a better job painting than shooting. I will show you her work a bit later."

"The others?"

"Well, standing by the door there with the cutlass would be Kayla. She alerted me to your presence being on guard duty in the library. She bolted down here, told me, doubled back behind you to cover your escape. The other quiet ones, Nicole and Sarah, rarely talk, though Nicole tends to giggle at everything said." At this comment a snicker occurred. "Finally, the one I sent to get us some water, Hamilton, though a diligent worker and curious thinker, tends to never shut up." At that, all of the girls in the room smiled.

"Here! The water. Just like you requested." Hamilton entered the room with a pitcher and a few cups. "I got them. Do you need me to…"

"No." Somervell cut her off. "Thanks Hamilton, I have it." Somervell smiled; Hamilton poured. "I used to call her Sarah, but due to her fascination at a young age with everything about running this operation, I changed her name after that Founding Father, Alexander Hamilton. Then she came," pointing toward the quiet girl on the side of the room, "So I called her Sarah. I like the name. Biblical you know." Somervell smiled. "How long have you been here?"

"My expulsion occurred two days ago. Like I said, I figured my best shot of survival lay in this part of town. Looks like I struck gold."

"Meet anyone on the way here?" Somervell inquired.

"A deranged lunatic who attacked me and a creepy couple who found me in a barn."

"What happened?"

"Well, unfortunately, the deranged man tried to kill me. Him or me, you know. I am here."

"Understood. Killing happens to be a way of life on this island tragically." Somervell drank the water deeply. "What about the couple?"

"Well, they caught me in a barn, saw me, said they wanted no trouble, then ran. I didn't follow."

"Mike and Sally."

"How do you know?"

"Well, I have known them for twenty-plus years. A tragic couple. Got hooked on drugs and had their three kids taken from them. You know the law for three strikes. A felony for each kid permanently removed and made a ward of the state. They arrived in L.O.F.I. devastated—never to see their kids again. So besides going through withdrawal, suffering from detoxification, they had to cope with the loss of their family. I reckon they loved their children, but the drugs were too much."

"So what do they do now? Just wander through the night dropping into barns on sleeping men?"

"Nope. They could best be described as Guam's social services. They find young baby girls and bring them to me to raise."

"That doesn't sound good," Sam responded hesitantly.

"Well son, this island represents one of the worse places on earth to be a woman." Kellas Somervell looked sullenly around the room at his gaggle of girls. "With a twenty or thirty to one ratio of men to women, the life of a lady consists of rape and rape. Young girls can be purchased by the quasi-warlords on the island for slaves of the most ignominious nature."

"How does that affect you and Mike and Sally?"

"Well, these two benevolent criminals now patrol the island in the dead of night, looking for girls to rescue before they reach puberty and attract the eye of the tens of thousands of lonely criminals on this oasis of hell."

"I think I understand." And indeed the manifestation of reality began to settle in on Sam Wolfe.

"Mike and Sally brought me all the girls they could find. I have twelve here. They help me in my work, and I protect them from the irascible nature of humanity's worst forms of life."

"They stole these girls from their parents?" At this question, Sam Wolfe seemed troubled.

"Not usually. For the most part, they hunt down the young mothers, make contact with them when they are away from their tribe, then offer to 'steal' them in the dead of night. Most often the mothers are cooperative for they wish to save their daughters from the same sexual violence which more than likely brought the innocent children onto this island."

"So, these girls represent children born on this island? They committed no crimes? No murder? Does that seem right they are trapped here? They did not commit a crime!" Sam Wolfe's indignant voice felt palpable to the entire room. Though his plans did not account for the injustice presented before him, nevertheless, a sense of duty had been aroused within him. An obligation to assist.

"Why do you think we try to protect them?"

"Well, I apologize for ever implying that….well…I apologize that I assumed something nefarious on your part happened to be going on here with you and these girls."

"No worries, son. Given the nature of this Godforsaken island, I can understand why you suspected the worst." Kellas Somervell looked around admiringly at his delegation of damsels. "I loathe contemplating what these savage bastards would do to my girls if it were not for the exploits of Mike and Sally. Good people. I could not complete my work without them all."

"Your work?" inquired Wolfe.

"Yes. My work." Sam Wolfe, with his inquisitive countenance, signaled to Kellas Somervell to continue. "Yes. I believe this island one day will come to its senses, demand civilization, and need to be educated as to how to run a Jeffersonian democracy."

"What does that have to do with you?"

"My girls, whether I am alive or not, will be able to teach the entire island. Like Bradbury's scholars on the railroad tracks, my aides here will, like the phoenix, deliver a proverbial rebirth to civilization here on the island when the inhabitants of Guam are ready."

Sam Wolfe, faithfully not betraying his own personal intent, smiled and questioned, "Can I assist?"

CHAPTER 4

"Elijah was afraid and fled for his life. He went a day's journey into the wilderness, until he came to a solitary broom tree and sat beneath it. He prayed for death: 'Enough Lord! Take my life, for I am no better than my ancestors.' He lay down and fell asleep under the solitary broom tree, but suddenly a messenger touched him and said, 'Get up and eat.'"
1 Kings 19: 3-5

Kellas Somervell continued his inquisition of Sam Wolfe as he gave the young exile a tour of his underground bunker, which proved much more than a barren room under the remnants of a methodically kept library. For starters, the light shafts feeding the mysterious tubs of water proved to be reconstructed gutters from the street above. Of Kellas Somervell's ingenious design, these gutters channeled rainwater to be utilized for drinking, cooking, bathing, and brewing. The tunnels led off to various underground rooms containing various forms of industry, which continued to stupefy Sam Wolfe for its elaborate construction. From a foundry to a brewery to a hydroponics farm growing the vegetarian diet, which sustained Somervell and his "aides" as he called them. After a light meal and conversation, Somervell dispatched his gaggle of girls to their various occupations.

"Well, my friend," Kellas Somervell inquired when the two were alone, "how did a smart guy like yourself end up on the island?"

"Stupidity," returned Sam Wolfe as he pulled up his shirt displaying the mélange of tattoos which formed a hodgepodge of pictures and expressions extending across his shoulders and down both arms.

"Surely, America has not become so draconian in their laws that they are condemning citizens to permanent banishment on an island over an over-exuberant bodily tattoo display?"

"No, not quite like that, but the tattoos started it all."

"By all means, explain," Kellas Somervell seemed incredulous.

"Well, my two friends in high school, Yorio and Boomer, wanted to be body artists after high school, or so they thought." Wolfe looked at the floor in mild opprobrium. "I let them experiment on me, because I wanted tattoos and lacked the funds to pay for them."

"I always thought tattoos reflected a lack of intelligence," interrupted Kellas Somervell. "Don't take offence my friend, but most of the people I have seen possessing multifarious art decorating their bodies were people of an inferior intellect unable to express their feelings, convey their ideas, manifest their desires, and ultimately, establish their identity." Kellas Somervell read the word "Always" written in script on Sam Wolfe's neck, chuckled internally, then continued, "Tragically, many confused young people attempting to find their way in the world fall into any one of those categories, if not all. Judging by your conviction to the art process, you probably fell into all four categories—not to mention unrequited love based upon your 'Always' there on your neck."

"You are perceptive. Lost sheep would have accurately described me."

"Not lost today, eh?" Kellas Somervell guffawed, the sound reverberating throughout the tunnels and chambers. "I would speculate that a life on L.O.F.I. would constitute being lost."

"Well, I would agree."

"So, explain how those tattoos resulted in your banishment from the greatest country in the world."

"Not the tattoos," Sam Wolfe wryly smiled, "the infection." Wolfe gazed around the room. "My two friends in their exuberance for the art failed to focus on sterilization and other such necessities. Needless to say I had infections."

"How did that result in your landing here?" Kellas Somervell inquired.

"Well, I couldn't go to my parents. They would have killed me. So, my rebellious nature unfortunately led me to acquiring medicine via my own devices. I got some oxy from a couple of connections on the street and raided Boomer's and Yorio's medicine cabinets, along with my own, and found all of the antibiotics left over from people not finishing them. I nursed myself back from the infection but got hooked on the oxy."

"That doesn't explain your exile to this hell-hole."

"The oxy led to me needing to make money to support my habit. Again, my rebellious nature, led me to selling, and my selling landed me in court with a felony and drug rehab to boot." Sam Wolfe dejectedly looked at the floor. "Problem occurred when I got out of the drug treatment center; I had a relapse."

"Oh, yeah. I know all about the difficulty in kicking the drug habit. I too got myself shipped here due to drugs." Kellas Somervell began to recount his tale, which led to his L.O.F.I. odyssey. "I used to be a welding engineer. An Ohio State graduate. I hurt my back and got myself hooked on the oxy also. Too easy to get drugs in the welding world. Welders consume a smorgasbord of every form of pharmaceutical a man can swallow."

"How did that land you here? You say I am intelligent; you have created this underground city."

"Well, I got popped for possession. Strike one. Strike two came when I got arrested for driving under the influence, which promptly got me fired and blacklisted from the welding world. In a drunken, impetuous rage, I broke into the warehouse from where I had been sacked, and stole some much-needed welding equipment in order to work under-the-table. Police were waiting outside. Strike three. I have been here ever since." Kellas Somervell looked resolute. "Well, that occurred over forty years ago. Got no regrets though. Fate landed me here; faith keeps me going."

"Faith in what?" Sam Wolfe incredulously inquired.

"God firstly; the rebuilding of civilization secondly." Somervell responded enthusiastically. "Don't you have a faith, son?"

"No. My parents didn't raise me with any."

"Tragic. Bloody tragic."

"I did meet a priest in the detention center prior to expulsion onto this island." Wolfe paused and dreamily gazed upwards. "I feel I have searched, but I have not found faith."

"You need to be on the lookout for a sign, son."

"I doubt I will receive any sign here."

"You would be surprised." Somervell shifted his stance. "Judging by your character so far, not to mention we seem to be kindred spirits separated by nearly sixty years, I may let you stay for a while, if you can behave yourself. And remember, the Lord manifests himself in strange ways to those He calls. Be on the look for a sign, my son." Somervell studied Sam Wolfe hoping his mien would betray his feelings concerning his statement of faith. "Well, son, you explained the first two strikes. What about the third?"

"The third happens to be as ignorant as the first." Sam Wolfe's posture slunk, "I went back to school to prove something to a couple of teachers. My intentions were sound; my execution proved irrational. Stupid."

"Explain."

"Two teachers visited me in rehab. A Mr. Moore and Mr. Wilde. My parents didn't, my friends didn't, my relatives didn't. They left me alone. These two teachers came, left me real paper books, gave me inspiration, demonstrated faith in me; they provided me with the will to soldier on, to overcome my addiction, to rehabilitate and come back to school."

"What did you do?"

"Well, like I said. My intentions were sound; my execution proved fatally irrational." Eyes downcast, Sam Wolfe continued the story of his fall. "I went to school to visit and show Mr. Moore and Mr. Wilde that I indeed kicked the habit. I had on me a bag of various pills. Nothing dangerous or special, but illegal pharmaceuticals nonetheless. I wanted to talk to them after school. Show them the drugs and together flush them. It would have been perfect. I wanted to pull their legs a bit. They were a couple of wisecrackers. I thought I would make them think I got hooked again. Then flush the dope, tell them I am coming back to school, and finish my recovery as a decent human being and productive citizen. They believed in me. I wanted to prove to them that I had not turned into an incorrigible and doomed person."

"What happened?"

"Well, my excitement to impress my two favorite teachers clouded my judgment. First, I should have never carried narcotics with two strikes. I didn't think I would get busted. I had them on me only for an hour. Second, I forgot about the 'eye in the sky.' Being a two-strike felon, the 'Thought Police' as Mr. Moore always called them watched and tracked. Having a felony required me to be tagged with a tracker. The law knew I had picked up the drugs and followed me to catch me selling. You know, a criminal two-for-one? They hoped to bust the buyer also. When I entered school grounds in the parking lot to get into the building, the police moved in. The law will not tolerate any shenanigans on school grounds. When they accosted me in the parking lot, knowing I had strike three in my pants, I bolted. Should have known I would never get away, but like I said, clouded judgment and impetuous execution. Just plain stupid on my part." Sam Wolfe sullenly gazed at the floor.

"Okay, then. You are here. What are your plans? You seem to have your wits about you. You were intelligent enough to come to the island with a plan. You made it here without getting killed. I am sure you thought about it. What will be next for young Sam Wolfe?"

"I plan on escaping. I am going over the wall!"

"Why?"

"Because. I am going over the wall, since the man who tossed me into this abyss of anarchy happened to be none other than Mr. Murray Mallory Moore."

———

Kellas Somervell, a man who over forty years of eking out an existence on an island of murderers, rapists, gang members, extortionists, and every other form of human offal, could rarely be shocked. Here, at this particular moment, that aplomb had been shaken momentarily. Incredulous at first, then contemplative, he spoke, "Why would your teacher expel you over the wall?"

"What do you mean?"

"Just that. Why would a teacher toss you off the wall?"

"After forty years here, you can't answer that?" Sam Wolfe inquired dubiously.

"My friend, I have survived by not interacting with the convicts. I have witnessed from a safe distance the ceremony of tossing inmates off of Hadrian's Wall, but I have never discussed it with anyone. Most of the inmates come in through the flood gate located on the other side of the island at the naval base."

"Well, apparently a special little ceremony occurs on Hadrian's Wall. Teachers becoming principals toss their former, fallen students into L.O.F. I. as their final initiation process." Kellas Somervell pensively mused. Contemplating the implications of a ceremony long and drawn out, which he had witnessed from a distance, trying to discern the necessity, he began, through deductive reasoning, to piece the enigma together.

"I do believe it makes sense, but I am having some difficulty piecing it all together," offered Kellas.

"Yeah. Apparently, teachers who are going to be principals must throw one of their former students in. One who has violated the three strikes policy. I guess they keep convicts around for the occasion."

"Do you realize what that means?" Kellas Somervell exclaimed, suddenly comprehending the gravity of the scheme and ceremony.

"A bit. Apparently, the principals are of some exalted status in the schools." Wolfe returned.

"Yes, but the principals! Exactly! That makes complete and logical sense. The principals serve as the O'Briens of society. Big brother. The Mustapha Monds. The Captain Beattys. Do you realize how beautiful of a system that represents?"

"No, why?"

"The teachers are the eyes and ears and gatekeepers of society. Think about it. In a school, you are under video surveillance incessantly. They can monitor, listen, and observe your actions along with your facial responses. You are watched persistently for seven hours a day, five days a week, forty weeks of the year." Somervell glowed, for in his long internment upon the island, he had not lost his fervor for learning, deducting, nor reasoning.

"Well, I gathered that the principals of the school represent a secret society. My two favorite teachers were on the wall. Mr. Moore and Mr. Wilde had to toss a former student over. Also, the crowd present to watch had been principals who had just completed their inaugural year of their principalship." Sam Wolfe paused in his story. "The military man made a big announcement about how they were full-fledged administrators now and must protect America from its domestic enemies or some other claptrap like that."

"Well, I did not know that." Somervell looked into the distant past over Sam Wolfe's shoulder. "I came in through the Guam Naval Base in 2035. I worked for a while during the years after the Great Compromise. Once I got into trouble with the drugs and pain pills and got fired, my welding career ostensibly over, I began to become resentful. Replacements were easy to locate. My third strike landed me on a C-130 with 89 others."

"How were those days?"

"Bloody. Incessant war, especially based upon race. Being white, not racist, and a pacifist, I hid until I found the library. I ate MREs that I found on dead bodies in the street. I hid in sewers by day or latrines or whatever other form of hellish nastiness which I thought would deter any deranged murderer from coming after me."

"How or why did the library become an oasis?"

"Not sure." Kellas Somervell smiled at this. "It had been weeks and months of perpetual blood bath on the streets. The putrefying bodies ubiquitous on the streets, the smell of burning buildings and flesh, the complete and total disregard for human life which exhibited itself in those times broke me. Every night hiding in human excrement, or under rotting corpses, or in open graves as bodies were tossed and heaped upon me, only to crawl out at night prior to burning and burying, all wore on me. Finally, after hell, months of this carnage, I lost my mind. I quit."

"What caused you to flip?" Sam Wolfe inquired when Kellas Somervell paused and began to smile queerly.

"I spent the night caught right here in this neighborhood, right out on this very street. I awoke to the sound of violence. I had dropped off to sleep accidentally in the middle of the afternoon in some back yard. I peered through a fence. I witnessed a group of a dozen or so white guys get cornered in this narrow, blocked street by a horde of black males. I heard the black men state without raising their voices they were going to pay those guys back for lynching part of their gang the night or two prior. The fight filled with blood curdling screams and howls nauseated me. I puked several times, but no one heard me over the din. The whites being surrounded fought to the last man, but never had a chance. Outnumbered three or four to one, it only being a matter of time, they were slaughtered."

"What makes that different from the other carnage?" Sam Wolfe nervously asked as Kellas Somervell howled with laughter.

"After the black gang had struck them down and killed them, they collectively bashed the heads of these white guys in until their skulls were mashed flat. Then, they stripped them of their clothes, taking them for themselves for some reason, and finally decided to castrate them all posthumously. So there lay in the street a dozen or so naked, murdered, quasi-decapitated, castrated human beings, while I hid." Kellas Somervell looked up at Sam Wolfe and gazed into his the eyes, "That represents only the tip of this horrific experience."

"How can that be possible?" Sam Wolfe asked horrified.

"After the black gang left, I walked out amongst the corpses. I don't know why. Morbid curiosity I suppose. I just looked at the carnage of human waste and thought to myself the horror of it all. At the very moment, I contemplated weeping for these souls and the souls of the men they had murdered the night prior. Then, I heard the chaos of a street fight coming from what seemed all around me. I panicked." Kellas Somervell dejectedly looked at his feet.

"What happened?"

"I stripped off my clothes, flung it over a fence, and crawled under a few bodies heaped together carefully covering my head with blood, brains, and limbs. I had to lie in a sea of human waste: carnage, gore, excrement, genitalia, brain, and blood. I hid to survive. This represented the nadir of my despair. I couldn't help but think of Joseph Conrad's *Heart of Darkness*. I muttered 'the horror, the horror' to myself. While I lay there thinking about British literature, I watched that same group of black men run past me trying to fight off and escape a Hispanic gang chasing them to God knows where. As I lay there, through the human gore, I saw the same library, which you entered. I said to myself that I had tired of living. For if this were to be the gist of my existence, there seemed no point in surviving."

"You abandoned all hope?"

"Yes, yes, and then I entered here." Somervell smiled. "I stood up, wiped off the carnage as best as I could, and I waltzed into that library stark naked. I walked right into the fiction section and scanned looking for the novel that I wish to read as these roving bastards found me and cut me down. I had come to an inner peace and would willingly die. It seemed fitting that instead of finding Conrad, I found *A Clockwork Orange*." Somervell smiled. "I sat down—cold bare bum on that wooden chair—and I read Burgess. I decided to read until they found and killed me. I read and slept, slept and read constantly until I had finished that book. The gangs never came in. I found Franz Kafka's *Metamorphosis*. I sat naked and read then slept, read then slept. Though fighting occurred around me perpetually, the gangs never entered the library. As if a force field of intellect prevented them from entering this edifice, the Viking hordes of L.O.F.I. never invaded the sanctity of the library. In forty years, I have never left. I have lived here. I have thrived here. I will rebuild society from here."

CHAPTER 5

"I am not what you call a civilized man! I have done with society entirely, for reasons which I alone have the right of appreciating. I do not, therefore, obey its laws, and I desire you never to allude to them before me again!"- Captain Nemo
Twenty Thousand Leagues Under the Sea – Jules Verne

Following the horrific history presented by Kellas Somervell, the pair, clearly developing the budding intricacies of a master and apprentice relationship, Sam Wolfe allowed himself to be guided through the labyrinth on a tour of forty years of isolated living. For twenty years or so, Somervell existed solely as a hermit until the ironically fateful day, much like Silas Marner, when he found his tranquility of isolation shattered by the discombobulating nature of a child. Working through his regular routine of checking the perimeter of his redoubt against chaos, he found a young female child playing outside the door of the library. Tepidly assessing the situation and making sure the street remained clear, he waited to see if anyone would come for the child. As hours passed and the child continued to play, sometimes cry, and once even nap, Somervell actually found the courage to emerge from the library and retrieve the child after an excursion from the room allowed him to see the remnants of murderous carnage up the road a bit, which could only be the mother of the child. Judging by the state of the mother's condition, she fought off multiple attackers for her body had been battered and stripped; he could only imagine the Viking violence that had been perpetrated upon her. As he snatched the child quickly into the library, barring the door behind him, Kellas Somervell conjectured that the mother, aware of her pursuers, hid the child and faced her end alone. The three or four year old child, which he originally named Sarah then renamed Hamilton for her incessant politicking in his humble citadel, grew up to be the loquacious and garrulous bundle of energy who diligently handled and maintained all the mundane affairs of running this oasis against barbarity, this sliver of civilization, the bastion of female freedom.

———

Kellas Somervell led Sam Wolfe on a tour, but insisted upon Hamilton to provide him with an explanation of the day-to-day affairs of what Somervell told him had been named Masada. At first, Sam Wolfe believed the catacomb to be a hurricane bunker of some sort or abandoned sub-basement of a previous edifice or of the public library, which had been linked with a few clandestine tunnels. However, upon the tour, Wolfe quickly realized that Masada contained more than had yet been revealed. Hamilton, along with two other girls, sentries he supposed, joined them in the cavernous opening where they had surrounded him originally for the beginning of their excursion.

"Hamilton," Kellas Somervell instructed, "let us give Mr. Wolfe the full tour."

"The full tour?" Hamilton responded disbelievingly.

"Yes, the full tour."

"Wait! What about him seeing the," she trailed off.

"Don't worry Hamilton. I believe this young man will be our Messiah." Somervell responded.

"Like the Bible Messiah?"

"No. I don't mean that sacrilegiously. He represents our long awaited something. I have been here forty years, you over twenty. You and I have seen the coming of many young girls, raised them, taught them, planned with them for the rebirth of society—a day when this island would adopt civilization and throw off the chains of anarchy, chaos and murder; a day when these men would sicken of the murderous blood bath of oppressive violence and adopt a world of culture, art, science, and hopefully, religion. Then, we could help them develop a sense of morality; teach them values; instill in them the principals of logos, pathos, and ethos. We could make this the modern day Australia." Kellas Somervell became energized in his delivery. Sam Wolfe became intrigued. Hamilton knew of Australia for Somervell taught her of the fabled rise to civilization as a child when he explained why she could not go outside to play. As she grew and matured, becoming more inquisitive, she began to read every history and novel he could find for her. A voracious reader, in her mid-twenties, she had amassed a reading repertoire that of a young college professor. She knew and understood Australia; furthermore, she comprehended the name of Masada and why they must defend this redoubt against the forces of evil until a leader emerged or a sign manifested itself, which called them to go forth beyond the ramparts of their citadel in an attempt to put into motion the plan Kellas Somervell had devised and utilized to give him purpose for the last forty years.

"Well Mr. Wolfe, let the tour begin." Hamilton began to traverse the cavernous room and move toward the far side—passed the tunnel which Wolfe had entered—and up to an offshoot just beyond. Moving down the passage which happened to be dark, Hamilton hit a switch on the wall and a faint illumination on the ceiling provided them with a soft glow leading them into a small chamber lined with shelving stretched for thirty or forty feet.

"Whoa! Wait a minute!" Sam Wolfe interrupted. "You have lights? I learned in school that all power, water, sanitation, everything, had been shut off, and the infrastructure left to rot. Mr. Moore constantly taught us the morality of abandoning the convicts to a paradisaical perdition. I remember his big lesson on the word 'juxtaposition.' God, he loved that word. Everything could be held in juxtaposition. Anyway, he explained that 'Guam served to demonstrate a sick, ironic, juxtaposition. A world where heaven and hell amalgamate into L.O.F.I.' So, how do you have electricity?"

"Ah, Mr. Wolfe. Firstly, you would do well to remember the teachings of your instructor from high school; his intellectualism you have divulged has proven itself to be worthy. Secondly, please be it remembered that Guam use to be a wonderfully civilized island with a naval and air force base. You are correct; the infrastructure suffered due to the abandonment by civilization and the subsequent release of the criminality. However, you forget, with a degree from Ohio State in engineering, talents of welding, and a promising career prior to my civic demise, I had developed into a renaissance man of intellectualism. If not for the drugs, I may have amounted to something in the states. But forget all that. My fate may be of a divine purpose. Like John Henry Newton, I came to this island at best an agnostic, more likely an atheist. My studies had been of Enlightenment thinkers and Romantic philosophers such as DeCartes, Shelley and Nietzsche; like yourself, I had no foundation. Consequently, after my night under the corpses and my abandonment of all hope, that I have already recounted when I discovered the library, that had been the first step in my rebirth, my personal renaissance—my amazing grace. However, that first step which served as my blast of literary light happened to be quickly followed by a spiritual light. For like Saul on the road to Damascus, the corpses served as my knocking down by God, but my solitude in the cave proved to be seven times the three days of Apostle Paul. Later on this grand tour of Masada, you will find my cave, my holy sanctuary, where I spent time studying and learning all that I feel God wanted me to learn. Twenty-one years of solitude until young Hamilton came to my door. I went forth, and for the last couple of decades, I have been raising young ladies to serve as my apostles. My twelve! We have been waiting for a cause to move. A sign; a Messiah. You, Mr. Sam Wolfe, are that sign!" A beaded sweat had developed upon the furrowed brow of Kellas Somervell; Sam Wolfe began to listen to the signs of redemption. The signs of faith, the need to believe. For when he had been expelled onto this island by his schoolmaster, Mr. Moore, he had vowed to return to confront his teacher; all he needed amounted to some form of assistance. Sam Wolfe began to believe that he too may have been led to Kellas Somervell by something far greater than his own intuition. Faith, Wolfe felt he had been blind, now he could begin to see.

———

After leaving the storage area where Kellas Somervell had pontificated upon the divine guidance which seemed to be manifesting itself all throughout their respective lives, Hamilton led them back from the storage chamber and into the cavernous hall again. He had been astounded as to how the shelving which surrounded the walls, which extended nearly thirty feet in length, had been filled to the hilt with found and recovered military issued MREs that were all organized to perfection. Handwritten labels served as demarcations of each style of food substance and the date of discovery had been listed which clearly demonstrated the "aides" incessant rotation of the stock.

"Nicole constantly takes the retrieved meals and charts, organizes, and rotates them utilizing the date stamp the military places upon them," Hamilton explained. "The military still sends in convicts with a few days' supply; consequently, since most men don't live a few days, and the barbarians are often far too busy trying to survive, they fail to capitalize upon this cherished commodity. We pilfer them."

"How? I didn't think you ladies left this place," inquired Wolfe.

"Well, we don't. Mike and Sally, the couple who have brought us all here over the years, they drop them off."

"Yes," interrupted Somervell, "Mike and Sally for years have found far more than they could possibly need. And since they move with great regularity, they only carry what they need. They always drop off extras through our various water shoots or with children they bring me."

"Yes, we do not believe in wasting any food for obvious reasons," Hamilton confirmed.

"Also," Wolfe continued as they left the corridor, and Nicole who had joined them turned out the illumination, "you never explained how you had lights."

"Simple, my good man," Somervell interjected, "as I stated my occupation and hobby from before; all of our electricity in Masada comes from solar power. While the released animals were raping, pillaging, and plundering the island, over the years I have purloined every useful item that I could procure. Needless to say, I have discovered a bountiful supply of solar panels all over this island. The military bases all had to be green-energy utilizing and self-sufficient by the middle of the century. I would periodically creep over to AB Won Pat, where the violence died down after the first couple of years, and simply remove a few panels and rewire them into the electricity in the library. Over the years, as Masada grew, along with my mouths to feed, I expanded as needed. Today we are a fully powered and self-sufficient society of twelve aides and myself. With panels located around the complex, along with some long lasting military-grade batteries for storage, Masada could be said to be on the grid."

"I am impressed Mr. Somervell. Brilliant." Sam Wolfe paused, looked back down the dark corridor toward the food storage, then continued, "You know what surprises me? You only eat MREs."

"Oh no, Mr. Wolfe," Hamilton burst in, "We have those in case our crops fail."

The Kellas Somervell tour of Masada continued to intrigue and captivate young Sam Wolfe who incredulously attempted to formulate in his mind how on an island of pure anarchy and mayhem, a man of so singular a purpose could exist with relative ease and sangfroid apparently in the quasi-lap of luxury. While the rest of the island wallowed in savagery and privation, barely maintaining to subsist austerely if they could avoid capture by the three main savage tribes that Wolfe knew existed on the island according to his pre-expulsion studies while in jail, Sam, remembering some of the history of L.O.F.I. from high school, also felt it obligatory in jail to research all he needed in hopes of a lifetime of survival on America's penal colony. For the convicts bound for L.O.F.I. who had been convicted of murder, rape and other violent acts, the penal colony served as their just reward for a life of transgressions. They thrived on the island much like a family at an amusement park. Consequently, the three-strike citizens of the United States, deemed unworthy of their respective citizenship, promptly had their rights revoked and felt the bitter neglect and solitude of abandonment upon the island where the "Jacks" ruled and the "Ralphs" were slaughtered. Sam Wolfe had reconciled his crimes; he accepted his guilt; would readily serve his penance. What broiled him though served to motivate him—Mr. Murray Mallory Moore's failure to listen to him prior to being hurled off of the wall into the abyss.

"This way please," Hamilton broke Sam Wolfe's reverie. "Down this tunnel we will see the foundry and blacksmith."

"Wait a minute! Mr. Somervell, I don't want to see the blacksmith! Well, maybe I do. Yes, I do." Wolfe stammered as his bewilderment grew for this center room seemed to be like that of a nautilus which spun out with corridors instead of chambers. "You said crops! What crops?"

"Ah, Mr. Wolfe, all in good time. The hydroponics rooms are located clear on the other side of Masada, a fair piece away." Kellas Somervell glowed with pride seeing the greatness in his work reflected by the amazement of his guest. "We must cross under Trinity to arrive on that side."

"Trinity?" Wolfe, gazing upon Somervell's inscrutable face, "Wait, you said hydroponics. You have a hydroponic lab? And Trinity? I am confused."

"Mr. Wolfe, patience my friend, patience." Somervell clasped his left hand on his right wrist behind his back in a most confident manner. "Please allow Hamilton to escort you and lead the tour of Masada; all will be revealed. We will show you the many wonders of our subterranean world."

As they descended into the chamber which held the foundry, the heat and smell of the fire proved palpable. Huddled over her work, a young wiry, small girl in her late teens, placed her task down, looked up from the ground, saw Sam Wolfe the newcomer, and quickly moved over to challenge them.

"A man! What brings him here!"

"Easy Lia, easy." Somervell opened his arms in an avuncular manner. "Relax."

"Everything alright?" Sam Wolfe inquired.

"Sure. Young Lia here has a strong loathing for men."

"Has she ever met one?"

"Well, no, not personally. However, she has been studying weaponry with me for the past five years in order to be the Keeper of the Foundry." Lia began to scan Sam Wolfe up and down scrutinizing every aspect of his clothing and his weaponry. "However, in her studies she has discovered through reading in the library, the brutality that man has inflicted upon one another with his endless pursuit of weapons. Winchester and Gatling have earned a rather nasty place on her list of reprobates. And by all means don't get her started on Sir Hiram Stevens Maxim and his machine gun."

"If she abhors weapons and men, why do you have her making arms down here?"

"Simple Mr. Wolfe, Lia understands the destruction and carnage caused throughout time by men and weapons, not to mention the bloodshed on the surface of this island. I don't wish Lia to be excited to make weapons; I want her to fear them; respect them. With a healthy respect, she can keep my aides down here equipped for defensive purposes. Nearly all of the weaponry you have seen today has been manufactured here by Lia, with help from me of course."

"Your name Isherwood or what?" Lia moved right up near Sam Wolfe invading his personal space bringing a certain level of discomfort to him like when a Chihuahua starts yapping at a German Sheppard.

"Isherwood?" Sam retorted.

"Ah, brilliant Lia," Somervell responded. "I see you have been reading the program of studies."

"Isherwood! Don't you read?" Lia's hospitality had yet to warm.

"Mr. Wolfe, Isherwood the literary character, he carried a hammer." He paused, turned to Hamilton, "Make sure when Mr. Wolfe beds down tonight, you leave him our copy of *Earth Abides*."

"Yes, Kellas."

"Wait! You want me to read a book?" Wolfe exploded. "For the love of Christ!"

"Do not blaspheme, Mr. Wolfe." Kellas interjected calmly. "I find your proverbial 'blinded' time in rehab and mine in this catacomb quite Biblical. In fact, as stated before, our similarities with Saul hardly seem coincidental." This comment startled Wolfe for he knew the early story of Christianity and understood the analogy. Given the improbability of all that he saw so far, Sam felt his resistance to Kellas's notion of a divine hand weakening.

"I realize that. But my God, I am overwhelmed! I have so many questions."

"Ask away." Kellas replied standing relaxed and akimbo.

"Where to start?" Wolfe initially forgot hydroponics, crops, foundry and all, then blurted out, "How do Mike and Sally escape death out there?"

"They operate at night and hide by day. We have food depots set up for them with MREs if they need anything. Usually, they leave more than they take."

"The crops!"

"I will reveal that later."

"The smoke in the foundry. How do you hide it?"

"I will reveal all." Kellas smiled.

"Why did you quit taking girls? That stopped a decade and a half ago. Surely, girls are still born on this island."

"Mr. Wolfe, Jesus himself limited his disciples to twelve."

"That works for you? Knowing more girls are suffering?"

"My dear Mr. Wolfe, my youngest aide has only reached fifteen. Not many survive birth, let alone early childhood. I know through Mike and Sally that there are young ladies out there. That should manifest to you a sense of urgency to get on with the Lord's work." Kellas maintained his composure.

"How about misnaming this fort?"

"Meaning?"

"Masada. It should be the catacombs if we are to burst forth with Christian civilization." Wolfe continued the inquisition. "Masada turned out to be a massive suicide pact."

"My dear boy, I named this place Masada while here alone. I resolved to die here. Though a Christian catacomb in many ways, if all goes wrong, we very well may meet, like the Jews, an untimely and savage death here too."

CHAPTER 6

"And Jesus said unto them, come ye after me, and I will make you to become fishers of men. And straightway they forsook their nets, and followed him."
Mark 1: 17-18

Kellas Somervell instructed Sam Wolfe to follow Hamilton down the main spiraled corridor leading off the main circular room where he had first met this eclectic collection of recluses. The small party had been quickly met by a few more young ladies who then began to proceed down a long dimly lit tunnel. Wolfe strolled with a relaxed air about him nearly forgetting that twenty feet or so above his head anarchy reigned supreme. Trying to fathom this underground world and grasp his good fortune to have been welcomed in such a hospitable group, Wolfe contemplated the verity of Somervell's story of being a spiritually-inspired genius.

"Well, Mr. Wolfe," Kellas turned and spoke, "since evening shall be coming fast, I had my aides prepare us a feast. I hope you will be pleased."

"Well, my teacher, Mr. Moore always said, 'Never turn down a meal; it could be your last.' That seems to be especially true here."

"Indeed, Mr. Wolfe. Indeed. This Mr. Moore sounds as if he represents the quintessential nature of teaching. Did he practice the monk lifestyle?"

"You know about the monks?"

"Indeed, again, Mr. Wolfe, I do." Kellas Somervell's charismatic equanimity effusively calmed Sam Wolfe, causing him to feel that he indeed walked in the presence of greatness. "Before my incarceration, I remember the monk lifestyle being introduced. Did he perform well at his craft?"

"Well, if being good at teaching means living in your classroom and spending every waking moment of your existence reading, studying, thinking, and investigating everything to bring some greater knowledge to your students all the while attending every school function where your students perform; well, if you call that performing the craft well, then Mr. Murray Mallory Moore proved to be the best." Sam Wolfe beamed at the discussion of his past instructor.

"How can a man teach if he fails to follow the formula you just put forth?" Kellas Somervell's prophetic statement carried him to the end of the corridor, which turned toward the left and off into the darkness. "Ah, dinner Mr. Wolfe. I do hope you are famished."

Hamilton stepped up to the bend in the tunnel, reached into her pocket, and retrieved a screwdriver length key of some sort. She stepped forward to the wall, felt around for an unseen crevice, then inserted the device and twisted. An audible, yet unseen, lock shot open and a crack appeared in the wall right near where the curve flattened out and led into the dark. She pushed the door open with the assistance of the omnipresent and reticent Kayla.

"Where does the hall lead?" Sam peered into the gloom.

"That Mr. Wolfe serves to deceive. A faux-passage, it leads down to a collapsed section of the tunnel. You see, the ruse ends here, for I can't have any intruder getting past this point. We call the door, Alamo."

"I thought Kayla guarded the place. I thought you stopped me at that first circular room for a fight. Don't you defend to the death there?" Sam Wolfe's head swam attempting to connect with the magnitude of it all.

"My dear Mr. Wolfe, do you think I would trust the safety of these young ladies to an open library door with the sole hope that the secret passage would not be found?" Again, the smiling Kellas Somervell stared long at Sam. "That door had to remain unlocked for you. As I said, we have been waiting for our savior. You sir, I believe, are it."

"We stopped you there to make sure. If we felt in danger, we would have retreated behind the Alamo." Hamilton clarified before pushing the door open completely, revealing an enormous banquet hall of a prodigious length. Six chairs extended down each side with a bigger chair at the head and foot of the dining hall. Behind the table, nine young ladies stood waiting; Kayla and Hamilton making eleven and twelve, as they were soon joined by a speedy Lia who scampered from the foundry.

"You see Mr. Wolfe, we have been awaiting your arrival for quite a while. I have built this facility, rescued and raised these ladies, and trained them to serve. We have been waiting for our Messiah to help us culture and civilize these Vikings all about this island."

———

Dinner proved to be a mesmerizing experience, not only due to the enormity of the victuals, but the bizarre and surreal setting of the elaborate dining hall set up like a seventeenth or eighteenth century Scottish mess hall. Though the ceiling did not stretch up toward the heavens, the low ceiling did possess the wooden, arched rafters, along with several ceiling fans, which operated at a pleasant speed. As the girls took their respective seats, Kellas Somervell indicated that the seat of honor at the head of the table had been reserved for him. The spread of food consisted of various fishes, along with a cornucopia of fruits and vegetables. The vegetables appeared to be steamed, the fish grilled, the fruits fresh.

"Well Mr. Sam Wolfe, what do you think of our little Masada now?" Kellas Somervell beamed with peacock pride at this palatial dinner and gentile setting. "Please eat from our bounty, a variety of fruits and vegetables, and nothing but fish for meat. We shall need our sustenance for we will all be fishers of men soon enough. Great work awaits us above!"

Sam Wolfe scanned the smorgasbord of endless food: peas, tomatoes, celery, broccoli, carrots, onions, potatoes, and squash surrounded by strawberries, blueberries, watermelon, and cantaloupe. All of Somervell's aides waited for him to pass his plate in order to be served. The steaming fish sat waiting to be dished. Sam Wolfe, in utter disbelief, sat stupefied as to how this enigmatic figure in front of him, all six foot four inches of girth and bluster could have produced an oasis of this magnitude on this island, which represented the ninth level of hell on earth. Sam Wolfe passed his plate nodding his head as the various young ladies placed food upon it. He conjectured that in their wildest dreams back in the halls of his high school last year that the great Mr. Moore and the incredible Mr. Wilde, for all of their knowledge of L.O.F.I. and the inhabitants thereof, would never have remotely fathomed this covert cultural center.

"Mr. Wolfe, please prepare to eat and enjoy!" Kellas Somervell bellowed with laughter. "Welcome to Masada! Ladies, bow your heads in prayer." Kellas scanned the table, then began, "Bless us oh Lord, for these thy gifts, which we are about to receive from thy bounty through Christ our Lord amen." With perfect unity the twelve young ladies recited their prayer.

"Eat! Ha-ha! I hope you enjoy either cardinalfish, surgeonfish, or damselfish. If you are a vegetarian, eat of the bounty of our harvest." Somervell burst with a pride similar to that of Ebenezer Scrooge on Christmas morning when he bought the prized turkey.

"Wait a minute! What? Where did all of this come from? The food, the hall, the wood for the paneling and rafters. I cannot process it all." Sam Wolfe's head swam attempting to swallow all that surrounded him literally and figuratively.

"Where should I start, Mr. Wolfe?"

"Okay, first the food. You said you do not leave. Where did you get these fruits and vegetables? How about the fish? Do these girls leave and go fishing?"

"The girls have never left Masada. I have for the past forty years, though less and less lately. Once my citadel finished being constructed, I have had little reason to leave. To where would I depart?" Somervell took on a serious tone, "What would you like to know?"

"Okay, the food."

"As I have stated, we have a hydroponics farm. We grow all of that food internally, with rainwater that we trap and store in collection containers that are natural and man-made. Hydroponics proved easy since I pilfered the universities years ago of their equipment, along with their books and seeds. Sarah here has been taught the finer points. She produces the food for the rest of us. We assist her whenever she needs our aide."

"Didn't the government take all of the valuables of the university before they opened up the penal colony?"

"Ha-ha, Mr. Wolfe. Never underestimate the foolish optimism of liberals my friend." Kellas grinned from ear to ear, "In order to placate the naysayers of the colony, the conservatives of the Great Compromise of 2025 agreed to leave all of the university equipment and great libraries intact. For you see, the pie-in-the-sky politicians believed the island wrong and that the inherent good nature of humanity would ferment into a revitalized society if only the means were left at their disposal. As you see, humanity lacks innate benevolence. They burned and looted all they could; they left alone all they failed to understand."

"What about the fish? Surely, you aren't playing Santiago down by the sea?"

"Again, my incredulous friend, we have constructed a fish farm. I have tanks constructed of hollowed out lava rock and lined with material procured from the universities. In my riskier days, I did fish. However, I didn't fish for the day, I fished for sustenance. I brought back my catch, bred them, nursed them, and fed them. Again, books purloined from the university provided me ample guidance." Somervell cut his fish, "Anymore questions my doubting Thomas?"

"Yes, myriad!" Sam Wolfe scanned the room. "Where did you get the wood for this vaulted ceiling? That type of wood doesn't grow here does it?"

"Illusion Mr. Wolfe. All an illusion." Somervell smiled his Cheshire cat smile, "Lauryn here has perfected the art of painting over her relatively short years." A long redheaded girl with a black eye smiled and waved, revealing small amounts of paint stained on her hands. "Ha-ha. Lauryn may be the best painter since Michelangelo; she most assuredly represents the best painter ever to take brush to canvas on this island; however, she tends to be a tad klutzy." Lauryn returned a faint smile, then dropped her fork. The rest of the girls snickered.

"What do you mean an illusion?"

"All painted with deception, deception, deception! Go up close. Touch the wall. MacNeil over there, our Keeper of Carpentry and second oldest behind Hamilton, constructed the scaffolding along the walls and ceiling to allow her to paint the hall. I had once been to such a hall in Edinburgh, Scotland in high school—always stuck with me."

"So you have a Keeper of Carpentry, a Keeper of Art, Keeper of Victuals, and a Keeper of the Foundry. Yeah, another question, where did you get coal on this island to burn for blacksmithing? How do you keep the smoke from alerting people to your presence? How does the government not know of this place?"

"Relax Mr. Wolfe. You will spoil your dinner. Our fuel comes from charcoal made from burnt wood. That art has been perfected for over two millenniums. Ductwork runs the smoke off and diffuses it into a couple of different subterranean sewers far from here. As for the government knowing about this place, can't say if they do or don't. As far as I am concerned, it matters not. If they know, I am sure we are being studied with great eagerness."

"Okay, so each of these young ladies represents the keeper of skills right? Lia, who I have met, keeps the knives, and…"

"Hey, get it right. I am Keeper of the Foundry. I am a blacksmith."

"Lia, steady." Kellas Somervell frowned and drew out the word. "You will have to excuse young Lia's tempestuous mood, Mr. Wolfe."

"How about the rest of these ladies?"

"Well, moving around the table. You have met Kayla. She keeps science. Nicole, who you have also met, keeps math. Becky keeps philosophy; Ashleigh here keeps history." Kellas continued to motion toward the variety of young apprentices. "Sarah you met who feeds us; along with Lauryn who dazzles us with art. Finally, we have Megan, the Keeper of Health and Hamilton, whom you have met, the Keeper of Literature. Bailey, the Keeper of Spirits, and lastly, this young cherubic faced lady, Mikayla would be, maybe the most vital for our well-being, the Keeper of Faith."

"Wow. You seem to have all of the bases covered."

"Mr. Wolfe, I assure you that forty years will prove to be ample time for any diligent, inquisitive man to prepare for Armageddon or the Rapture. I am hoping that when civilization reappears on this island, and the Viking-natured savages on the surface are ready to learn, we Morlocks, if you will excuse my literary allusion, will be able to instruct and rebuild society. My aides here are more than prepared to teach all the elements of a classical education along with the practicality of survival."

"What on earth does the Keeper of Spirit provide that would be different from the Keeper of Faith?"

"Bailey, please provide a palpable and palatable demonstration." Bailey, the androgynous female of the bunch, rose from her chair, walked down to Sam carrying three small snifters. "Mr. Wolfe, please indulge." Sam Wolfe attempted sips from all three vastly different tasting drinks, which all proved to be of an alcoholic nature. Not having yet reached twenty-one and only minimal clandestine experiences with booze, Sam Wolfe could not begin to surmise as to the types of wine he had just tried.

"Wow, they are strong."

"Yes Mr. Wolfe. Remember I said that Bailey happened to be the Keeper of Spirits, not spirit. At twenty-two, Bailey has grown into a master brewer of wine."

"Keep them to drink if you like," Bailey stated and returned to her seat.

"As I have said, Mr. Wolfe, Bailey keeps the spirits and Mikayla keeps the faith!" Again Kellas Somervell continued to guffaw, thoroughly enjoying his dinner. "Tomorrow, we will take you to the most magnificent structure of Masada! The cathedral, if you will, where Mikayla and Hamilton spend the majority of their time." With that Hamilton rose to her feet, approached Sam, and placed a book next to his dinner plate. Wolfe read the title, *Earth Abides* by George R. Stewart.

"Per request, Mr. Wolfe; for you reading this evening."

"Ah, correct. From our library." Somervell nodded toward the novel. "After dinner you will retire to your quarters. You will have a chance to relax and read, so you can begin to prepare the way."

"So, what do you have on the agenda for tomorrow?"

"Well Mr. Wolfe, tomorrow you see the crown jewel, our temple of Masada. Tomorrow we visit the library and the cathedral." Somervell continued to work on his fish.

"I saw the library. Or did I?" Sam Wolfe, after a day of endless extraordinary events, began to adjust to the incredible here with Kellas Somervell and his twelve young aides. It seemed improbable, supernatural, impossible. Wolfe entertained the idea of a higher power.

"Oh Mr. Wolfe, you saw our façade; the gateway into Masada. But as you witnessed in the entry hall, where we apprehended you, along with the subsequent chambers, all demonstrate a level of practicality, which could plausibly be found in any underground bunker. However, once you cross through Alamo you rest in the heart of Masada. This very banquet hall my dear friend represents more than a beautiful mead hall; we are currently eating in the undercroft of an abandoned church."

"You have another library? What about the one on the street?"

"That library upon closer inspection has been filled with items I would not classify as books. Rags. Pap. Propaganda. Or worse, love stories. Vampires, zombies, and all other forms of tommyrot. Books worth their salt were snatched, cherished, and stored in our main chamber. Our cathedral! Our library! Our Trinity."

"So tomorrow you are going to take me to your church or library?" Wolfe quizzed.

"Can you tell, Mr. Wolfe, the difference between the two?"

CHAPTER 7

"You shall not worship them or serve them; for I, the Lord your God, am a jealous God, visiting the iniquity of the fathers on the children, on the third and the fourth generations of those who hate me."
Exodus 20: 5

Sam Wolfe reclined in his bed located in a room off of the hallway leading from the church undercroft toward the hydroponics farm. Upon the completion of dinner, a couple of Kellas Somervell's aides, Bailey and Sarah, took him on a tour of the food production at Masada. The elaborate construction of artificial lighting, which Somervell clearly filched from universities and tanning salons, had been hooked up to his solar powered grid. PVC, which had been salvaged from the ruins of the razed housing, had creatively been utilized to channel off newly collected rainwater. The ingenuity of Somervell to rescue the scraps of destruction and resurrect it into a mechanism of functionality mesmerized the youthful mind of Sam Wolfe. Everything and more that had been served at the elaborate feast could be seen hanging from the ceiling and grown out of carefully fabricated PVC baskets. Racks constructed from destroyed playground sets, PVC tubing from a university hydroponics farm, along with every manner of raided piping from under sinks and toilets had been utilized to sustain the lives of twelve young women along with their ambitious leader. Nothing that could have been salvaged had been wasted. Wolfe thought of the thorough usage of the buffalo by the Plains Indian he learned about in school. Masterful from start to finish, and according to Kellas, the best would be presented tomorrow.

The room to which Wolfe had been assigned, comfortable enough, contained a bed, a nightstand, a small light powered by reserve batteries, all surrounded by plain walls. He had dropped off the book, his hammer and shank prior to heading down to the hydroponics farm, but upon his return found himself upset that his shank and hammer were missing. As he entered his room, Bailey and Sarah bid him good evening then exited toward their dorms.

"I trust you shall rest easy for the first night in many, Mr. Wolfe." Kellas Somervell consoled him prior to leaving.

"I suppose you will be locking me in this room for the evening?"

"Why on earth would I lock you in your room? Do I look like Captain Nemo? Count Dracula?"

"Well, you know…" Wolfe trailed off, embarrassed by his assumptions, and looked down at the tattoos, which extended all the way to his wrists.

"Are you referring to my aides?" Kellas Somervell guffawed again. "My dear Mr. Wolfe, my twelve young ladies sleep in a dormitory together, and besides you today, have never been in the presence of a man. I assure you if I felt you a threat you would have been put down like a dog when we surrounded you this morning."

"Well, I didn't mean anything. I just." Wolfe paused and held his tongue.

"You have seen too many movies. If you ventured near that dormitory, you would have to fear the wrath of those girls long before mine. A few are vicious." Somervell smiled again. "Besides, Mr. Wolfe, I built Masada and raised these girls from abandonment all with the faith that God would send me a savior for these poor souls, provide me a meaning in life, and a chance to redeem my sins by converting the Viking horde on the surface. Why would the good Lord betray me and send me a disreputable cad?"

"Not all saviors live up to their hype, Mr. Somervell."

"Oh ye of little faith, Mr. Wolfe, trust in the grand plan of the Almighty."

———

Sam Wolfe awoke with a start; he panicked, surveyed his surroundings, remembered Masada, then relaxed. Nothing in the room seemed out of place as he scanned the austere setting. On the side table, *Earth Abides* rested where he had left it last night after a couple of chapters. On the lone shelf occupying the wall still rested the Bible, Koran, and Torah. Wolfe had previously dabbled in all three but wondered why each had been placed there. He comprehended the Bible's placement but not the other two. Now, he chuckled to himself forgetting the religious texts, remembering the character of Isherwood who did indeed carry a blacksmith hammer like his own that he fortuitously discovered on his first day into his adventure. Sam's mind raced as to his next action. Kellas Somervell proclaimed Sam the savior—the long awaited someone. Wolfe existed for one purpose and one purpose only: to get onto The Great Wall and confront the man who tossed him into L.O.F.I. However, upon further contemplation, Sam Wolfe gathered, quite accurately, that his best chance of fulfilling his destiny lay with the man who not only survived in this Dante-esque inferno but flourished in it. He still felt uncertain about the Messiah talk along with all of the religious proclamations; however, he did find them intriguing. Either way, their two separate paths of fate would have to be amalgamated into one. Sam Wolfe would have to establish an inexorable bond with Kellas Somervell, which he feared, in the end, he may have to be shatter.

As Wolfe rose from the bed, a glint of light reflected in his peripheral vision; he turned and spotted the very item which may have been the source of his disruption from sleep. Placed on the floor, right inside the door, lay his missing hammer and clawed shank from the night before. He crossed to pick them up and smiled. He chuckled as he balanced the hammer in his hand, which clearly had been modified. The head of the hammer remained the same; however, the blunted point on the backside of the head had been chiseled to a point for a penetrating blow. The rudimentary clawed shank forged from a broken gardening implement had had its claw adapted from a hook to a softer curve to deliver a far more vicious stab into its victim. The broken handle had been modified and a grip attached, turning the crude implement into a treacherous skewer. Wolfe smiled; Lia, whom he felt sure would have been his Morlock, had crafted two tremendous weapons. The Isherwood hammer would prove deadly and his shank resembled a Velociraptor claw with a handle. Any close combat with Sam Wolfe could prove deadly for the assailant.

———

After a brilliant breakfast in the presence of all twelve aides and Somervell, the group escorted Sam out of the church undercroft up into what Kellas called his Shangri-La. The group, consisting of Somervell, Wolfe, Hamilton, Mikayla, and Becky, moved up the spiral steps onto the floor of the old Barrigada Catholic Church. When Sam Wolfe emerged onto the nave floor of the church, he stood in awe. The incredible solemnity of the structure transformed into not only a church but a library of such elephantine dimensions that Sam Wolfe's light-headedness manifested itself to the rest of the group.

"Ha-ha! You are right to be impressed, Mr. Wolfe!" Somervell once again nearly burst effusively with pride.

"How? When?" Sam Wolfe stammered looking at the mammoth bookshelves climbing the walls from the floor to the ceiling to where the roof joists and arches touched down onto the pillars. Sam Wolfe, thunderstruck, recalled a moment in class when his literature instructor, Mr. Moore, demonstrated to the class what all libraries should embrace as he displayed a picture of Trinity College Library. He jokingly—or so the class thought for they knew with Mr. Moore anything could have been possible—claimed that he had visited the library and wept due to the beauty of intelligentsia. The shelves, which soared thirty to forty feet into the air, boxed in the stained-glass windows, which also stretched toward the vaulted ceiling of the cathedral. The only light came in through the stained glass depicting countless Biblical saints. The myriad colors cast onto the open white marbled floor shone with utter magnificence throughout the cathedral.

"Well, Mr. Wolfe, as I have stated innumerable times since you arrived yesterday, I have been busy." Sam reconnoitered the enormity and majesty of the cathedral and library. The books extended ad infinitum up, across, and out. Every other pew had be re-carpentered into a bookshelf which attached to the church pew giving a bountiful amount of room for books and ample space for worship—especially the current twelve. "What do you think, sir?"

"I am flabbergasted! The books. The enormity. How has this survived?" Wolfe incredulous, again inquired.

"I can answer most, not the last. The hordes of savages on this island have never so much as laid a hand on the churches or the library in this section of Guam. I can only conjecture as to the rationale. But I ask you this Mr. Wolfe, why did the Vikings burn the books of antiquity when all they really wished to possess happened to be the wine, the women, and the monetary booty?"

"I cannot say."

"Ha-ha, Mr. Wolfe." Kellas Somervell peered into Sam Wolfe's eyes, "I too, cannot answer. Maybe some superstition, maybe a plan for the future, or maybe, Mr. Wolfe, God's will."

"You think God has protected this church for forty years so you could construct this Masada, this Shangri-La to raise the lost, wretched female souls of this island brought to you by some married couple who creep around the island saving little Jane Does?"

"The Lord works in mysterious ways, Mr. Wolfe."

"Yes, Mr. Wolfe," interjected the until now taciturn Mikayla, "as Keeper of Faith, I have studied the three major holy texts, along with the Book of Mormon, and I can assure you the Lord does move and work in mysterious ways."

"Well, I don't know about the Lord, but I do know that I am stunned Somervell. How could you pull this off?"

"As I told you my friend, after my epiphany, I resolved myself to do the Lord's work until the savior, in this case you, came to Masada." Kellas Somervell screwed on a more sober countenance, "Mr. Wolfe, I understand your lack of faith, but please allow me to finish my work of preparing for you the way."

"Mr. Wolfe?"

"Please. Mikayla, right?" Sam addressed the Keeper of Faith at first unsure of her name, "We are the same age. For God's sake; I mean goodness sake; call me Sam."

"Alright then, Sam." Mikayla furtively gazed at Somervell for a look of approbation. Receiving the nod, she continued, "I have been studying the three major religions for as long as I can remember; we have been waiting for you to help us deliver the heathen back into civilization and faith."

"Hey, America gave up on this lot. No angel of the Lord will be able to come in and clean up this mess. All this island needs would be a steady diet of fire and brimstone." Mikayla appeared dejected; Sam dumbfounded by their obsequious faith.

"Mr. Wolfe, let us climb the tower."

———

High above the Barrigada Catholic Church, a bell tower reached for the sky and Sam Wolfe and Kellas Somervell, following the rigorous ascension into the heavens and each donning a white monk cloak and hood to blend in with the building's color, stepped out to peruse the environs from a highly enlightened position in order to witness the cruel and horrific ways of the world.

"Mr. Wolfe, I find it lamentable that you could be of so little faith. However, for my plan to work and bring civilization to the island, you do not necessarily need to become the zealous follower of God. But I do believe in divine intervention; I do believe I have spent forty years on this island without any need to take another man's life for a supreme purpose. I do not believe that, as you so belligerently phrased it, my survival, my building, my raising, and my constructing of Masada and all who inhabit it, a mere whimsy of fate no more than I believe the moon, the stars, the sun, and the planets through the idiosyncrasy of gravity and the caprice of gases formed the earth and all on it by happenstance." A piercing scream proved audible in the distance. Somervell continued.

"In my time here, Mr. Wolfe, I have witnessed or come upon the remnants of countless murders, suicides, rapes, and even war. Senseless violence on an apocalyptic scale and untold horrors; I believe the Almighty has allowed me to exist, survive, and build to help save this world from destruction."

"What on earth makes you think I am the savior? Why aren't you the savior? You are the one with running water and solar power on this Godforsaken rock. You seem to be the savior to me!" A crash in the distance occurred with what could only be described as a "rebel yell."

"Mr. Wolfe, you have never studied the Old Testament have you?"

"Regrettably, no I haven't. Apparently, I should have since I am to be the Messiah." Wolfe added with a cynical sneer.

"Moses, Saul, Joseph, Noah, none felt ready to lead, but they did." Somervell placed a fatherly hand upon the shoulder of Wolfe. "And in the Bible, the prophets prepare the way. I am your John the Baptist. The Abraham to you, my Isaac. I have lived much as a hermit monk lived in Medieval Europe. I have studied, codified, organized, and experimented. The monks lifted the Western World from the ashes of the fallen Roman Empire. I will bring righteousness back to this island."

"What righteousness? This ignoble hellhole has been sanctioned by the Congress, minus the fourteenth amendment. These savages, or Vikings as you call them, are nothing more than Orwellian unpersons. They are pariahs! Persona non grata!" Sam had his fury distracted by the sight of a man running through a nearby street being pursued by three attackers. He fatefully and tragically cut into a figurative and literal dead end; the three mauled him to death with what appeared to be broken ax handles.

"Mr. Wolfe, not everyone on this island deserves to be on this island." With a short pause after his retort, both men watched as the three drug the dead man into a yard and down into a collapsed house basement. "That man very well may have been innocent."

"Why would they take the body?"

"Cannibalism, Mr. Wolfe. Cannibalism. Not all eat regularly here."

"Why not? You do. They could grow crops, plant orchards, fish the seas."

"They haven't the opportunity. Without law and order or at least a set of rules, no sensible life can exist here. As I have stated Mr. Wolfe, you don't have to accept God's plan, but I need you to complete God's work."

"Why are you so convinced?"

"Mr. Wolfe, you have spent an entire day with me and my twelve aides. Do you think they are the only twelve children born onto this island unfairly, fated to die a wretched death without the chance or opportunity to choose faith versus this folly?"

"I don't know what to think any more." Wolfe's head spun in circles trying to grasp the words of Somervell with the backdrop of L.O.F.I.

"Are you telling me that those girls deserve to be set loose upon this island of savagery?"

"Again, I don't know what to think any more. I am so overwhelmed."

"Do you believe they should suffer the sins of their fathers?"

"Doesn't the Bible say something like that?" Sam probed.

"Yes, but it also has a young Moses being rescued to lead his innocent people out of the fetters of bondage." Kellas smiled. "You Mr. Wolfe could be our Moses, I your Aaron."

CHAPTER 8

"The word of the Lord came to Solomon: As to this house you are building—if you walk in my statutes, carry out my ordinances, and observe all my commands, walking in them, I will fulfill toward you my word which I spoke to David your father. I will dwell in the midst of the Israelites and will not forsake my people Israel."
1 Kings 6: 11-13

The tête-à-tête continued in the bell tower; the philosophical and moral battle raged on as savage anarchy reigned below in the shattered streets of Barrigada, Guam. The two men, face to face, sat while Kellas attempted to persuade Sam as he failed to dissuade Somervell. As mid-morning gave way to the heat of the day, the two men witnessed street battles, rape, infanticide, murder, and cannibalism. Sam Wolfe once during the conversation even paused, choked down vomit, then held his composure to continue.

"Mr. Wolfe, how can you continue to maintain such a cavalier attitude toward this bloodletting when we have the apparatus here to enact some benevolence upon this island?"

"What could I possibly do that you haven't? You are a veritable magician with the detritus of a crushed civilization. What can I do that you thirteen couldn't get done?"

"My dear Mr. Wolfe, we haven't tried; we have been awaiting your arrival." The carnage continued on the streets. A scream became audible in the distance.

"Okay, Somervell. Just for a minute, let us pretend I will go along with you and be your savior, your Messiah. What next?"

"When you are ready, I believe the Lord will deliver into our hands the sign we need to proceed."

"You believe that? Really?" Incessant incredulity gripped Wolfe.

"Mr. Wolfe, why would the scoundrels over the years destroy every building in this town with the exception of the church and the library? Why would generation after bloody generation push old dilapidated, burned out cars up to the doors to block access but never touch the windows? Mr. Wolfe, if any man were to look into the stained-glass windows of this church they would see all the civilization and decorum with their very own eyes, but they do not dare! The savage, the Viking, fears the wrath of God. They fear the unknown. I believe the Lord has blessed and sanctified this consecrated ground that repulses evil."

"Now you believe God sent me, and I am going to bring civilization to this hell."

"Yes. Yes I do, Mr. Wolfe," Kellas Somervell's unequivocal reply nettled Sam Wolfe. The latter looked over the corpses strew upon the street to the ruins of AB Won Pat Airport, remembering the lessons learned in the classes of Mr. Moore and Mr. Wilde, how the savages had constructed a giant eight in Roman numerals with a question mark to call attention to the world they hoped would be watching about the injustice of the savagery perpetrated upon America's convicts. Mr. Wilde would talk about the moral ambiguity the United States had entered when it allowed this cruel and unusual punishment to be loosed upon humanity. Mr. Moore laughed, for at his very core he adored Lord of the Flies Island. He believed all here were guilty; he embodied the belief of kill them all and let God sort them out. Sam remembered how the two teachers would interrupt each other's classes arguing with one another in order to instruct their students—they truly did put forth a monk effort in raising awareness with their pupils. Sam regrettably felt his feelings stir due to his own failings and shortcomings, which landed him on L.O.F.I. and disappointed the only two adults who took interest in his life. Mr. Moore loved the revocation of the 14th amendment and had been thrilled by the adoption of the

29th amendment, which allowed Americans to be stripped of their citizenship and banished for a life of terror and despair.

"Mr. Somervell."

"Yes."

"May I change the subject for a moment?"

"Certainly."

"How did you acquire the books?" Sam allowed the idea of his being a Messiah percolate in his mind. He ruminated, paused, then continued, "God didn't put those there, right?"

"Ha-ha, Mr. Wolfe, no he did not. He protected me, so that I could put them in the church."

"Explain, please." Sam, whose life rarely experienced anything spiritual, had to acknowledge that this man and island manifested a mysticism new to his life experiences. Somewhere in Sam Wolfe's confused soul, he wanted to have faith. He felt he needed a sign.

"Well, in the early days, after I discovered the tunnel over to the church, my epiphany long established, I began to formulate a plan. In order to rebuild civilization, I would need knowledge. And knowledge, in this disconnected world, must be had through books." Somervell looked off in the distance, obliterating the now only periodic violence below and tranquilly gazed off as if reminiscing about his first love at a county fair. "I quickly learned of the various libraries around the island. So for a number of years, while alone, I moved at night from here to Mangilao, to Hagatna, to Yona, to Merizo, to Agat and all points in between, locating the public libraries and schools, scouring the premises for books. I left plenty to attempt to go unnoticed but took all of the books I needed to sustain life and teach the next generation." He paused.

"For nearly fifteen years, I labored alone hording books and transporting them to Masada. When I needed the space, I constructed the bookshelves in the cathedral. If I found MREs along the way, I picked them up. I taught myself hydroponics, blacksmithing, child rearing, carpentry, distillery, and rudimentary medicine."

"Weren't you lonely? How did you not go insane?"

"Oh, my dear Mr. Wolfe, when you have the compendium of world's knowledge in books, an intelligent man could never be lonely. Between the literature, the biographies, and the science, I found I had to force myself into a regimented timetable like that I discovered in *Poor Richard's Almanac*. Never underestimate the power of the thinkers from the Age of Enlightenment."

"When did the girls arrive?"

"Ah yes, my aides. I first met Mike and Sally in the middle of the night hauling books. I stumbled across them much the same way you did. We startled each other, realized we meant neither any harm. They asked me what I happened to be undertaking. I told them God's work. They confided to me their plan to save the children and voilà! From that moment on, they scoured the island in hopes of finding lost souls. It didn't start only as girls, they dropped off a couple of boys, but they died. After the third death, I decided that the Lord's plan called for me to save the lost females from the doom that awaited them upon puberty."

"Surely, there are more than twelve."

"Indubitably Mr. Wolfe, indubitably. But we take what the Lord delivers." Sam could not help but be moved by the tale.

"So you raised the girls and taught them the knowledge you acquired. How do I come into this plan?"

"Quite easily. I knew from the time I received Hamilton that it would take years for them to grow, mature, and develop. When I received the girls in a steady stream up until my twelfth, I knew another sign had been bestowed upon me." Somervell smiled at Wolfe, "You see, it needn't be complicated. Trust in the Lord. You too are part of the great plan for the delivering of the children born here paying for the sins of their fathers which I might add, though a reality, does not have to be thus."

"So you learned how to ferment wine, channel water, grow food, blacksmith weapons, and build a library, so why don't you lead the ladies forth and to the Promised Land?"

"Mr. Wolfe, I am of impure heart. I, like Moses, can't enter the Promised Land. You must be my Joshua. I have sat idle as hordes have been killed. Just over on AB Won Pat Airport, I have witnessed myriad executions; I have seen the carnage on these streets and have been too paralyzed to do anything."

"What about Masada? That definitely represents work!"

"A coward's work. Anyone can push a pencil or build comforts, but a true, courageous, and brave heart will be required to complete the final phase in this endeavor." Again, Somervell paused. Wolfe viscerally began to accept that he may indeed be part of some greater force at work. So many amazing sights in so little time bewildered him. "Only a coward will sleep during the day in a tunnel and at night scour the island, raid houses and pilfer the left over copper pipes, filch the scraps of material from the hardware stores, and purloin the PVC piping from houses, swimming pools, and schools. I confronted no one. I assembled. I constructed. I prepared the way for you, Mr. Wolfe."

"Well, Somervell, I don't know what to say. I think you have the wrong guy. After all, you believe you shouldn't be on this island since you are a non-violent criminal." Though Wolfe said it, he began to question his skepticism.

"On the contrary, Mr. Wolfe, I most assuredly believe in my exile. I committed my sins. Sure, they were not of a nefarious or mendacious nature; I didn't physically or mentally harm anyone, but I transgressed the law, and the law has been set down by our peers dating back to Moses and the Pentateuch. It represents the collective will of the land and ultimately God. The country believes in it, right?"

"I don't know about the country, Somervell, but my teachers from high school did. They incessantly praised the beauty of shipping America's murderers, rapists, and three-strike felons out of the country forever in order to import hardworking immigrants. Those two guys embodied the mentality that if a citizen refused to honor and respect his or her civic duty by being educated, trained, and dutifully participating in the running of the country, then he or she didn't deserve citizenship. Mr. Moore would always say, 'with free school, free health care, societal equality, and unparalleled freedom, if you can't remain civilized, then you deserve to rot on L.O.F.I.' I suppose if my teachers believed that, and the state mandates the curriculum, then they are representative of the values of America."

"So you, like I, believe that we should inhabit this island for the remainder of our lives?"

"Well, Somervell, society has been quite clear with the expectations. Work, drink, and be merry." Wolfe had long tired of the citywide bloodshed and had turned and sat, leaning his back up against wall. Wolfe felt nauseated by the carnage below. Streets strewn with rubble, periodic screams heard.

"Well Mr. Wolfe, I too felt culpable in my placement here. I have regrets, but no animosity to the state for banishing me; I had my chance."

"So, I suppose if you believe in your deportation for three nonviolent felonies you surely believe the rest are reaping what they have sown."

"Yes Mr. Wolfe, they are receiving the just punishments for their wickedness; however, judge not lest ye be judged! Sure, I belong here but what about those children born here who have never known another world? A lost generation of nonviolent citizens who never had a chance to be free." Somervell's eyes longingly appealed for empathy.

"Let us say for the sake of argument I agree to go along with your plan." Sam Wolfe felt Kellas Somervell represented his best chance of fulfilling his goal. "I will only do it if I get a crack at my teacher, Mr. Moore."

"Ha-ha. That will be no problem, Mr. Wolfe."

"I need to confront him. You must remember, I went to school to see them when I got popped by the police. Certainly, I felt assured that I would never see them again. They didn't come see me prior to my expulsion from society. I didn't expect them too." Wolfe appeared crestfallen. "The most bizarre situation occurred when I found myself walking the plank from the Great Wall of Guam to Hadrian's Wall. We learned about the expulsion process, that special criminals were ritualistically cast into the oblivion; the teachers explained that special circumstances allowed people to fly, under their own expense, to Guam and actually shove their perpetrator into the abyss."

"Yes, I came in through general population, and since I have never met any other convict, I cannot speak with authority on the manner." Somervell recounted.

"Well, when I came out onto the wall, I couldn't figure out why I happened to be getting the 'special treatment.' Well, after the authorities made the announcement that former teachers being initiated into the principalship had one final task to perform, I knew something strange would be happening. However, I did not know what the teachers and principals had to do with my being tossed into the abyss, but I didn't care for I felt I had only minutes to live after being thrown from the wall. Once I saw Mr. Moore, I realized I needed him to understand why I came to school that day with narcotics. I didn't want the final phase of my banishment for life to be a disappointment to the only people I respected. The man I admired, whom I felt would always be beyond my ability to contact once I received my third conviction, had ironically appeared for my expulsion."

"Ha-ha Mr. Wolfe, you believe that your teacher and you meeting again reflected no creator's planning and vision? All just a cosmic accident of gravity and timing."

"I don't know about all of that Somervell. I trust in what I can see, what I can touch, and who I can speak with. I never grew up religious." Again, his stern and rigid comments proved a façade, for deep down, Sam Wolfe felt a terrible beauty being born inside, faith. All of the evidence Kellas pointed out as planning by a higher authority kept manifesting itself to Sam.

"Well Mr. Wolfe, we believed in your arrival. I believe that your story and advent are cause for celebration. I believe fate landed you here over something silly; all beginning with items as innocuous as tattoos. You are pure in spirit, not mendacious or pernicious. You are nearly as innocent as my twelve aides. Besides, most great saints were sinners in the beginning! Redemption, Mr. Wolfe. Redemption! The Lord brought you here to complete his works! Furthermore, I believe that by helping you, we will redeem this island to civilization."

"Well, I don't know about your plan, only mine. I need to speak to Mr. Moore. He needs to know and understand who I am. I need to climb up that wall and prove I am no animal. He will return next year."

"What if I assist you in reaching him next year?"

"I would be indebted!"

"Did you ever think your being pushed by the teacher didn't serve as a sign from God?"

"I did not look at it in that manner. Like I said, I never grew up religious."

"Many of the great saints began as non-believers, Sam." Kellas became patient. "You must remember Mr. Wolfe, you are young and have much to learn."

"Well, I can't at the moment worry about God, mysteries of the universe, and all of that." Sam sat trying to wrap his mind about all that had happened. "All I know revolves around this; I need to get to Mr. Moore."

"What do you need from me, Mr. Wolfe?"

"I need help climbing up that wall."

"Why climb the wall?" Somervell answered congenially.

"How else would I reach Mr. Moore?"

Somervell smiled, "Because Mr. Wolfe, I can go under it."

CHAPTER 9

"Your brother's blood cries out to me from the ground! Now you are banned from the ground that opened its mouth to receive your brother's blood from your hand. If you till the ground, it shall no longer give you its produce. You shall become a constant wanderer on the earth. Cain said to the Lord: My punishment will be too great to bear. Look, you have now banished me from the ground. I must avoid you and be a constant wanderer on the earth. Anyone may kill me at sight."
Genesis 4: 10-14

Sam Wolfe, continually amazed at the seemingly infinite resourcefulness of Kellas Somervell, began to relent in his resistance to the grand plan; for in Kellas, Wolfe faced a man of seemingly unshakable piety who believed that God had delivered him unto this island at this particular time. Though back in the States, Wolfe had never been reared in a religious setting, and since America, despite being the last bastion of developed-world Christianity, had begun to shed its reverence for any form of deity, Sam Wolfe had had little exposure to any form of faith. To continue with the irony of the entire situation, though Somervell would call it God's plan, the only teacher he ever knew that practiced any form of faith happened to be Mr. Moore. He knew what Kellas would state if he divulged that information but that potential solidification of God's plan would have to wait, for at that moment, Sam Wolfe wanted nothing more than to discover how Somervell could get him under the wall.

"Ha-ha, Mr. Wolfe, I can't encourage you enough to read, read, and read! What a wonderful world we trod when we enlighten our mind and edify our intellect."

"You are telling me Masada stretches all the way up to Andersen Air Force Base in an underground tunnel?" Wolfe's incredulity began to waver and fade. Internally, Sam had cleared the façade of doubt already concerning the inscrutable Kellas Somervell. Now, his resistance to religiosity continued to erode.

"Not quite a direct shot, but a manageable distance and a tad circuitous. Still, I could put you on the other side of the two great security walls without much trouble." Kellas smiled. "During the Japanese occupation of this island in the 1940s, the Imperial forces constructed numerous tunnels to ward off the impending American onslaught. You came down a tunnel entry hole in the restrooms of the library. However, all around here the tunnels connect over into Barrigada Heights where the Marines broke the Imperial Japanese Army over 130 years ago."

"How far do the tunnels extend?"

"Many extend in a vast network that had been largely closed off or destroyed by Allied forces after the war. However, after finding some interesting military documentation in various places around the island over the years, along with a history of Shoichi Yokoi, I quickly discovered not only the maps of tunnels and entry points, but tactics for opening previously blocked paths."

"Shoichi Yokoi?"

"Read, my friend. Read." Kellas Somervell extended his hand and placed it on his shoulder again with a fatherly gesture. "Yes, Yokoi lived in the caves and tunnels from 1945 to 1972 still fighting the war. They are vast, durable, and a direct pathway to the north side of the defensive walls."

"How do you know they extend under the wall into Andersen Air Force Base?"

"Because Mr. Sam Wolfe, I have been to Andersen Air Force Base."

———

Andersen Air Force Base had a long and storied history throughout the twentieth and twenty-first centuries, but nothing as notorious as the day the United States of America declared that the island of Guam would become the new penal colony in its correctional system; a system which transformed from rehabilitative to punitive. This switch, followed by the great political compromise of 2025, shattered many of the broken traditions of American democracy and forged an alliance led by a radically moderate group of senators who believed in compromise before compunction. By revoking all citizenship for murderers, rapists, and three-strike felons, America deported its criminality to reduce the waste of correctional spending, and shifted it toward the healthcare of its obedient civilian population. Though the public initially had been troubled by the rumble of C-130s taking the criminality to a far off tropical island where life proved to be cheap and short, the citizenry could not help but see and feel the benefits of the, initially deemed, 'radical approach.' As the economy continued to soar, former prisons shifted to school and vocational training centers, and with health care and other societal benefits for all, the general populace, devoid of an over-powering moralistic outcry, could relax as the undesirables of their world were hauled out much like the trash in previous generations.

"You have been on the other side? Why not escape?" Sam Wolfe gazed off the tower far to the north of the island.

"Ahhh, Mr. Wolfe, you know the foolishness of the second question. Firstly, leaving the island would prove an impossibility. Secondly, I have been. The tunnel empties into two places. One, an abandoned sewer which takes you right into, with a few moves and secret passages, a waste water processing plant. The second into a sub-basement of a storage facility."

"How long ago since you traveled there?"

"Why, Mr. Wolfe, I traveled there not three days ago."

"What! You were just on the other side of those walls three days ago?"

"Yes. Actually, Mr. Wolfe, I saw the C-130 land that brought you and the other poor souls to be tossed from the wall."

"Are you telling me you just discovered this pathway in the last week?"

"Oh, no Mr. Wolfe; I have known of that access for decades. After the building of Masada, the establishment of our system of living, the raising of the girls to an age where they could be left, I began to seek out passages to the other side of the walls to assist you on your arrival."

"You are kidding me. You have had the pathway to escape for decades, and you have just been waiting here," he paused, "for forty years."

"Yes," Kellas Somervell replied, "like the days of Lent, or the journey of Noah, or the years of exile for Moses, I have been waiting, be it forty days or forty years, for you, Mr. Wolfe."

"What made you go to Andersen? Why not try and get into the Guam Naval Base on the other side of the island?"

"Simple, Sam." Somervell began to take on the air of an instructor or teacher, "I have watched this island. The Guam Naval Base has since its inception just dumped hordes of convicts onto the plains of Guam. Over outside of Agat sits a boarded up Mormon temple with a view looking right at the Brandenburg Gate, so they call it over there. I came through that gate. Countless times I have spent a day or two in the temple watching the C-130s land on that strip in the naval base. I watched the armed tanks and soldiers escort the convicts over to the gate and open it. I can tell you that once they shut the Brandenburg Gate, anything can happen." Somervell paused.

"What do you mean?"

"I have seen it all. Usually slaughter."

"Give me an example."

"Easy, once when the island had become dangerously over-populated from the influx of prisoners, I watched the three major tribes on the island call for a truce at the AB Won Pat Airport. In the subsequent entries of prisoners over the next three months, the tribes took turns attacking the ninety exiles as soon as the gate closed. They would charge out of the jungle, which had begun to engulf the remnants of the city, and butcher them right in front of the armed guards perched upon the defensive barrier. They would then drag the corpses into the jungle and city for a final resting place in a mass grave. Food being scarce, often times, cannibalism occurred; furthermore, if a woman would be seen in the carnage, she would be carted off for the pleasure of the men. Sam, women do not belong here."

"Awful." Unsure of how to respond, Sam remained taciturn.

"I witnessed that scene so many times that I actually kept a tally for a two month period when the classes were heavy. I gave the numbers to Nicole and Ashleigh to calculate the carnage and record it for posterity's sake."

"Grim."

"Not all of it." Kellas Somervell smiled. "I remember this one period after the fighting had been particularly fierce, the numbers had dwindled. All sides feared for their safety. Another truce, followed by a month of schoolyard picks. Small contingents of each tribe showed up and chose members to strengthen their numbers. This never would have happened in the early years when everyone coming off of the planes happened to be black, white, or Hispanic. Back then, the fighting proved terrible; however, in the last twenty years or so, as America's demographics rapidly began to morph into a steady brown, the schoolyard picks became more equitable. Pure luck of the draw for those coming in on the plane. Judging by their faces when the murderous hordes emerge from the jungle and dilapidated structures, the brutal nature of arrival on the island must not be public knowledge."

"What do you mean?" Sam asked quizzically.

"Did you not learn of the slaughters in school?"

"We were taught about Guam's history and race war."

"Not about the perpetual slaughter of incoming convicts?" Now, Kellas Somervell seemed incredulous.

"I guess not. We know that life has no value here, and that the population has stabilized."

"Sanitized and whitewashed I see. Typical." Somervell seemed agitated.

"Well, when did you last witness this type of carnage?"

"Been a while. I have been focusing on the other wall. Waiting for your arrival. I had been puzzled by the manner in which people were hurled into the fray one at a time on that side of the island. Perplexing, but you have shed light on this event."

"You hadn't figured that out?" Somervell for the first time did not seem to have the answer.

"Not being able to talk to them, never intercepting them, many of them not living long, all prevented me from solving that enigma."

"Yes, there were three on my drop. A brown one immediately got snagged by a black group, and the white guy met his maker. I ran for it. I knew enough from school that the first day on this island usually represented your only."

"I am completely fascinated. So the teachers and principals have something to do with the steady maintenance of society." Somervell rubbed his chin pensively.

"What do you mean?" Sam Wolfe asked.

"Ha-ha, my friend, your youth restricts your deductive reasoning. I hope to assist in that." Somervell grinned. "All things occur on this island for a governmental reason. The mass exodus of the criminality to be slaughtered on the western shores of this island manifest the indifference that America has for the convicts of the country. However, the elaborate walls and bizarre ceremony, which I have witnessed countless times, all had to be for a reason. The personal touch of sending one in at a time could not be based on pure whimsy. I have long concluded an initiation of some sort—a governmental or military rite of passage. But teachers," Somervell paused, "extraordinary!"

"Why extraordinary?"

"Mr. Wolfe, don't you get it? By having the teachers as the eyes and ears on the citizenry of the next generation, the principals must serve as gatekeepers between those in the inner circles of the government and those who are not." Kellas clapped his hands loudly together, "All things come to light sooner or later Mr. Wolfe. It appears that your Mr. Moore will be moving into the ranks of a secret society sworn to protect America from the likes of us or worse."

A cry of agony went out below as another victim fell to the shank, or club, or bludgeoning device of the island.

———

With a tear in his eye, Sam Wolfe stood shoulder to shoulder with Kellas Somervell on the altar of the Barrigada Catholic Church. Behind them the stained glass allowed the colorful light to illuminate the nave and highlight the multitudinous volume of books, which like the works of the Irish monks of the first millennium, had been rescued from the destruction of barbarians. Wolfe's emotions were wrought from his soul as he gazed at the artwork which climbed the wall, up the back of the altar, and stopped at the foot of a statue of Jesus. The images, copied from the frescos of the Sistine Chapel, had been recreated with dazzling accuracy.

"Ha-ha Mr. Wolfe, you are overcome with beauty." The pair had just returned from the top of the church.

"Maybe." Sam Wolfe reflected back on his days in Mayfield High School when he sat in Mr. Moore's classroom paying attention. Most of the day he had spent ignoring the instructors in a fit of rebellion. Once his pill habit reached full-tilt, he missed a tremendous amount of school and soon dropped out. However, he remembered Mr. Moore's first day when he took his class through the hallway, which extended from his room past the other eight classrooms, down to the restrooms and the Wall of Shame. The whole first day of class, Mr. Moore pointed out the names of former students, all dead or banished to L.O.F.I., whose names had been painted upon the wall above the urinals and leading into the toilet. The schools made it clear to the students: learn to work or risk the inevitable. So they, the teachers, believed the philosophy also. However, just before the restrooms, sat the Language Arts hallway upon which had been painted with the likenesses of literary characters and scenes from floor to ceiling and even upon the ceiling itself. Possessing a faithless childhood, Sam Wolfe failed to recognize the swelling of a budding epiphany mistaking it for simply a reason for being. Being here with Kellas Somervell offered him purpose; Wolfe still could not yet grasp the purpose came from the Almighty.

"Mr. Somervell."

"Yes, Sam."

"In my school back in Ohio, Mr. Moore and all of the department heads prior to him going back a hundred years had the hallway redesigned and stripped, then painted. Every inch of wall. Every spot on the ceiling. They even painted the classroom walls."

"Ah, Mr. Wolfe, art allows the soul to soar!"

"Not just that. Your art here, this mimics the Sistine Chapel, right? I recognize the hand of God here, along with Adam and Eve over there."

"Ah yes, Mr. Wolfe, when we rebuild civilization Sam, these poor souls will need all of the inspiration that we can assemble."

"Do you know what Mr. Moore called that hallway, Mr. Somervell?" Sam Wolfe felt an effusive rush of emotions well up from deep within his soul. An inundation of euphoria which he had never experienced. Faith began to bud.

"No, Sam, I do not."

"He called it the Sistine Chapel." Sam Wolfe's rush of emotion elated him, but he feared it would prove ephemeral.

"Ah well, Mr. Wolfe, still lacking faith my friend? Still believe in the great cosmic collision, which accidentally produced this earth, this climate, these lands, these people, our histories, man's tragedies, humanity's triumphs? Still believe this to be all an accident of gas and atoms, or does something deeper call to you now young Sam Wolfe? Could it be this represents your burning-bush, my young Moses? Could this be your epiphany to manifest to you the way, my young Paul?"

"I don't…." Sam Wolfe trailed off.

"My dear boy, please come with me." Kellas Somervell placed his arm around the shoulder of Sam Wolfe, turning him to walk down the center aisles of the church nave. Behind him the magnificent altar decorated with panels of the Sistine Chapel shown brilliantly. To his left and right, scores of book shelves rose to the ceiling as if God's hand had dropped them from the heavens to the earth. However, the destination now would prove to be a spot in this wondrous temple that Sam Wolfe did not at first realize. On the back wall of the nave where the door from the narthex emerged, a scaffold had been placed. Two aides, whom he recognized as Nicole and MacNeil from the dinners, diligently tightened the apparatus. Coming into view from the side, Lauryn held a palate of paint along with a brush as Becky followed, carrying the various accoutrements needed by the artist.

"Yes, yes, Mr. Wolfe, my young Lauryn, along with her team, has been quite busy for many years." All of the girls smiled, then turned to their work without a word. Sam Wolfe gazed in amazement, for the painting had been that of God pointing backwards with his left hand and forward with his right. Instead of the sun being at the tip of his right hand, an image of Guam had been painted. Under Guam and the right hand of God, Kellas Somervell had his image, while his twelve aides were all located, huddled together under his left arm. Finally, God's left hand pointed to an image of the United States, which in Rome would have been the moon. The other change wrought upon this work from the Sistine Chapel lay in where God had been pointing; instead of a figure with his back turned to the viewer, the cherub now pointed out with his front exposed. Every part of the painting had been finished, except the face of the mysterious cherub

"Am I to suppose?" Again, taciturn, Sam Wolfe trailed and could not finish.

"Ah yes, Mr. Wolfe, the adaption of Michelangelo's Creation of Sun, Moon, and Planets will be completed; today, Lauryn will paint your visage upon the wall."

CHAPTER 10

"On his journey, as he neared Damascus, a light from the sky suddenly flashed around him. He fell to the ground and heard a voice saying to him, 'Saul, Saul, why are you persecuting me?' He said, 'Who are you, sir?' The reply came, 'I am Jesus, whom you are persecuting. Now get up and go into the city and you will be told what you must do.'"
Acts 9: 3-6

Sam Wolfe diligently spent three months regimentally meeting with Kellas Somervell's aides, studying every facet of intellect that the enigmatic leader of Masada felt he needed in order to prove to be the Messiah and savior of Guam, thus bringing civilization to Lord of the Flies Island. Every day, Wolfe found himself tutored in the various arts of philosophy, science, mathematics, art, history, and literature; however, no day started without the first hour, prior to breakfast, being dedicated to religious studies with the Keeper of Faith, Mikayla. After his emotional epiphany in the Barrigada Church, Sam Wolfe allowed his skepticism to vanish, and he put his devotional faith into the hands of Somervell via the tutelage of Mikayla. She dedicated her guidance to that of Jesus; however, unbeknownst to Wolfe for whom piety proved a newly acquired understanding, Mikayla delivered an equal amount of study to that of Jewish prophets, reading from both the Torah and the Old Testament—especially Judges. Though he embraced the heroics and faith of Gideon and Samson, Sam Wolfe took a liking to the Judge, Ehud.

He spent a far less amount of time with Kayla and Nicole, for as keepers of math and science respectively, Sam quickly concluded that if his intended purpose on this island would be leadership, then the social sciences would prove more efficacious. Days would pass as he read on the floor of the church. Some days he would sit near the altar reading and admiring the museum-worthy art that spanned floor to ceiling. Other days he would sit in the back near the image of God and Kellas Somervell, his aides sending him forth to conquer and convert. When it came to the studies of literature and history, Hamilton and Ashleigh discussed and provided him with ample texts ranging from biographies of Lawrence of Arabia, to Ernest Shackleton, and back to George Washington; however, none found Sam Wolfe's favor like that of Machiavelli. Furthermore, to build his leadership abilities, a litany of speeches and arguments were also paraded in front of Sam, such from the likes of Churchill, Lincoln, King Jr., Gandhi, and Thoreau.

"With whom do you travel today, Sam Wolfe?" Kellas Somervell startled Sam as he meditated over a history, considering the options of leadership exhibited by various figures.

"Lawrence of Arabia."

"Ah, T.E. Lawrence, another who had greatness thrust upon him."

"Fascinating how he longed for a life of a celibate hermit; yet, he could not find peace."

"When the empire calls, one must go." Kellas again peered into that far off idyllic place he would travel when speaking of the imperial days of Britain, a country he had never visited. "The empire expected it."

"You love the British Empire."

"Scottish by ancestral blood, but an anglophile to the core, Sam Wolfe." Somervell smiled.

"Why? You were an American before the revocation of your citizenship and subsequent deportation."

"Yes, indeed, an American by birth. But, after all of the years of studying here, I have become quite fascinated by that industrious people on that rainy little island off the northwestern coast of Europe who in time controlled nearly one in four people on the planet all believing they were doing the Lord's work by bringing civilization, government, and bureaucracy to the masses of the world."

"We didn't study much about the British Empire in high school."

"Of course not, why would America teach about the empire which folded a hundred years prior? The United States' meteoric rise to the top during the 20th century, toppling the Brits, followed by one hundred years plus of economic, militaristic, and cultural dominance on the planet, would cause any nation to become narcissistic. The British behaved that way, as did the Romans and Greeks prior. The world followed the United States' every move before I landed here. By our conversations, not much has changed."

"No. In school, the teachers always taught us about the fifty years of growth in the economy, a perfected immigration policy, low crime, high standard of living, and social harmony."

"You have read George Orwell's *1984*; you have read propaganda at its finest. Tell me, how does America compare?"

"Well, Orwell paints up a book of lies. Rations are said to increase as the people go hungry and without. Not true growing up back in the States. My parents worked; we had everything we needed: government health care, money for vacations, nice cars, you name it. Some people had less than we did; some had more. The message in school reflected the life I knew. I just wish I appreciated it at the time."

"Well, I find it comforting to hear; for I lived during the early days after the Great Compromise of 2025. For ten years I witnessed the tumult of the cutting of government programs, the proverbial plucking of the nipple from the mouths of the lethargic. Thousands upon thousands of people killed around America in riots demanding government assistance."

"As violent as here?"

"Oh, no, my dear boy. L.O.F.I. represents carnal savagery on an unprecedented level. The riots were conducted by the refuse of society and, while violent, never turned savage. That being said, when the degenerates began to loot, the military moved in and gunned them down."

"Why?"

"Simple and brilliant, really. Nearly all of the people rioting and looting were not working anyway. They had had their government subsidies trimmed and cut. The idea to wean the herd worked for most; seeing the writing on the wall, many citizens took any job available. They quickly learned that with universal health care and a bit of hard work, they could survive on low income jobs. The government provided subsidies for low wage earners; however, the citizen had to work in order to receive anything."

"What about the rioters killed?"

"Oh, yes, yes. The shooting of the looters and rioters, much like the purge of the prisons, freed up American monetary assets. The public, either too callous to care or too apathetic to react, accepted the radical change because, as those who refused to work were gunned down and the murderers, drug dealers, and rapists were shipped here to die in a blood-bath, the economy expanded, immigration stabilized the population—only entering in numbers equal to that expelled from the country—and finally, the American debt began to decline, and the dollar's value increased."

"Just what we learned in school."

"At what price though?" Somervell pushed.

"Well, America seems to be running just fine now except I happened to be too ignorant to embrace it while there. We were taught that at one time in the 20th century, generations of family members lived off the governmental welfare programs. I can't image going to work every day knowing my neighbor leached off the system by the sweat of my brow."

"You are correct young Sam. The government of the 20th century, with its social welfare programs—benevolent in pathos, but flawed in logos—engendered a society which began to depend more and more on someone else to guide and provide for them. Once the percentage of people receiving some form of governmental assistance tipped over the fifty percent figure," Somervell paused, "well, game over as they say."

"Yes. Just what we learned in Mr. Moore's class. The masses began voting for bread and circuses. Whatever that means."

"Ha-ha my boy. You need to read up on the Romans!

"Well anyway, the teachers thought the American system fair, and I tend to agree. Follow the law and work. Period. I believe the system to be just."

"And do you think it just for those born here?"

"Well, no, but aren't we going to do something about that?" Wolfe inquired as he realized he just offered a sign of approbation for Somervell's plan, for he had begun to feel the tug of divinity.

"Yes."

"That may be the only flaw in the system."

"Well, Mr. Wolfe, I hope that through our endeavors, we can lead the people to a proper revolt, demand a sense of security and civility here, and possibly give the children of L.O.F.I. an opportunity to leave this island to go back to civilization."

———

At the end of Sam Wolfe's six months of monkish studies and intellectual conversations, Kellas Somervell called the twelve aides to construct a lavish feast to be held in the undercroft of the church. Though all meals were served in the commodious space, not all could be present due to the various duties performed by the girls. Besides guard and observation duties at various spots in Masada, chores and maintenance occupied the energies of many; Somervell ran the redoubt utilizing Franklin-esque precision, utilizing elaborate timetables matched to each aide's duties. Wolfe's edification allowed him to complete the Old Testament, dabble in the history of the Prophet Mohammed, explore the darkness of Joseph Conrad, read histories by H.G. Wells and Winston Churchill, and myriad inspirational leaders and orators. The feast, according to Somervell, would mark the change of direction in their mission to complete the Lord's work.

"Ha-ha," Kellas Somervell guffawed, "We are gathered here in a potential last supper, if you will. Today marks exactly six months since Mr. Wolfe joined us and six months until our mission must be complete." The spread, consisting of much more than bread and wine, contained a bounty grown in the hydroponics farm along with a plethora of fish. Bailey presented the wine; Sarah then rolled in the food as the rest assisted in the setting of the table.

"As we have always known, fate determined that we twelve only had twelve months in which to devise a plan to unify the island in the common cause of rebellion and revolt in order to demand a modicum of fundamental rights that all humans should receive to maintain a level of dignity—criminal or not." Kellas studied the table as all indulged while he spoke. "Through diligent studies and superb tutelage, Sam Wolfe has been rapidly schooled in all that, in faith, we hope he will need to complete his work. From this moment on, my loyal and devoted aides, you will no longer follow the instructions and orders of yours truly, but that of Sam Wolfe whom we believe has been sent to us by the good Lord to help fulfill his mission for me, and for us, on this island."

A general quiet descended upon the room as all ate and contemplated. Sam Wolfe had known that a twelve-month timetable represented all he had if he wanted to confront Mr. Murray Mallory Moore to explain that he indeed did not succumb to the temptation of drugs again, but that a foolish and impetuous stunt landed him on L.O.F.I. The epiphany delivered with Kellas Somervell, along with the religious instruction of Mikayla, only solidified the conviction that his journey to the penal colony at Guam had not occurred senselessly over an addiction of pain killers resulting from infection by shoddy tattoo body art. On the contrary, it occurred as a general plan by God to deliver unto this land, Guam, a Messiah to deliver this herd to their fate—after all Moses had a modest beginning and a murderous past. Sam had learned of myriad Catholic saints with far more humble beginnings or treacherous pasts. He had come to embody the notion of Kellas Somervell that he indeed may well be the Messiah to bring a final justice to the island.

"We now enter the next phase of our journey children." Somervell took on an avuncular tone. "Sam Wolfe, would you care to speak?"

"I admit that I am flabbergasted. Though I have studied, I have read, I have listened, and I have begun to pray, I do not know what the next step constitutes, and I shamefully do not have a plan."

"Ah, but you do have a plan Mr. Wolfe. You have always had a plan."

"I have?"

"The same plan you had when you arrived—to jump right in, improvise, and wait for a sign from the Almighty leading you down the path. After all, following that game plan led to your arrival here, allowing me and my aides to prepare the way for you."

"Well then, what next?"

"Why Mr. Wolfe, now, in order for you to fulfill your rendezvous with your former teacher for the summer expulsion, we must begin to gain support for the revolution. In order to do that, you, Mr. Wolfe will have to leave Masada."

"What do you mean Somervell?" Wolfe inquired with a degree of panic.

"You will have to go out, make contact with a group, try to curry their favor and begin the revolution."

"How will we make that happen?"

"My dear Mr. Wolfe, I suggest moving to the top of the bell tower to see what opportunities manifest themselves to you." Kellas smiled. "There, I believe, a sign or a burning bush by an angel of the Lord shall manifest itself to us all." Wolfe, who had begun to trust Somervell implicitly, faithfully agreed.

CHAPTER II

"A certain man went down from Jerusalem to Jericho, and fell among thieves, which stripped him of his raiment, and wounded him, and departed, leaving him half dead."
Luke 10: 30

Sam Wolfe and Kellas Somervell, while sitting and watching the sunset from atop the Barrigada Catholic Church bell tower, observed a black man running for his life on the streets below. Judging by the hobbled gait of the black man, he had been wounded; analyzing the panic in the turning of his head to and fro and the frantic swimming motion of his arms, his flight reflected that of a cornered animal in a life and death struggle. Spread out to the north of the church, the street below intersected with what would have been a main thoroughfare in the days of civilization. Beyond that stretch lay the ruins of AB Won Pat Airport, which, as Sam Wolfe had learned in school, had been designated as "execution alley," for the tribes used the area for truces, prisoner exchanges, and slayings. The convicts had also constructed a giant Roman numeral eight with a question mark, which could easily be seen from the air. Between the church and the airport lay a ruinous mess of broken, burnt, and bashed buildings left over from decades of wars, violence, and murder. The black man had scrambled through a couple of former yards, over a dilapidated fence, stumbled to the ground in agony, then slid into the ruins of a garage, which had more structure on the ground than standing erect. From their elevated position, Kellas and Sam viewed in pursuit a group of lighter brown men, possibly Hispanic, with crude weapons fanning out to find what appeared to be a former captive who had escaped.

"Tragic. Another wasted life." Kellas crouched a bit behind the parapet so as not to be seen in the dwindling light.

"Yes, he appears to be in a desperate way."

"I have seen so many ghastly and gruesome murders and pitched battles here; the deaths at times haunt my nights." Somervell reflected with regret.

"Yes. I can only imagine." Sam Wolfe observed the pursuers pause, confer, then spread out into a line and slowly march through the former neighborhood, keeping eye contact with one another so as not to allow the black man to escape.

"I have seen them frantically hide when pursued. Some seem shocked when they are pulled out of their spot, some resigned. Some have charged out in a banzai suicide attack. Others break and run. I have seen them beaten to death, raped, and eaten. I would say the man has only a few terrorized moments left on this earth, and then his problems will be no longer of this world." Kellas Somervell often became philosophical when he knew he lacked all powers to save a lost person.

"Well," Sam Wolfe screwed his faith to the sticking place, "that black man does have a difference which will set him apart from those of whom you speak."

"Yeah, what difference?"

"The difference? Simple. That black man will live." Sam espoused confidently.

"Really, what makes you so confident?" Somervell inquired.

"He will live because we are going to rescue him."

"What? Leave Masada? Bring in an outsider?" Somervell stammered— forty years of seclusion had neutered his willingness to engage boldly with outsiders.

"Yes." Sam Wolfe peered gravely into Somervell's eyes. "Besides, didn't you tell the aides that I am in charge now in order to fulfill our destiny of completing the Lord's work on this planet?" Wolfe's conviction and confidence in Somervell's faith soared at the sight of the black man.

"Indeed, I did, Mr. Wolfe." He paused, ruminating, then added, "Indeed, I did."

"Well then, Mr. Somervell, we are going out to rescue that black man."

"Sam, we have witnessed countless slaughter from this spot over the past six months. What makes this man so unique?"

"Well, Somervell, my first day on the island, after being tossed off the wall, and released into the wild, that black man had been present."

"Really? Intriguing."

"Well, Mr. Somervell, you brought me to the realization that more than fate allowed us to cross paths. You have preached to me for half a year that we are both caught up in the Lord's work starting with my unique path to the island, followed by my adventure that led me here to Masada. I have embraced the notion that I am an instrument of the Almighty who will bring justice to L.O.F.I. and its inhabitants."

"Why him?"

"When I dropped over the wall with two other inmates, that black man took one, allowed one to be killed, and let me go free. I believe destiny has brought us together a second time. God's ways are working again." Sam Wolfe smiled and looked at Kellas, "Besides, Mr. Somervell, a wounded dying man sits on the side of the road; the time has arrived for me to be the Good Samaritan."

———

The second three months of Sam Wolfe's sojourn in Masada saw him not only continue his intellectual edification but also include the study of combat which would surely play to his favor in this impending apocalyptic struggle over the proper judgment of the inhabitants of L.O.F.I. Kellas Somervell had Sam Wolfe study the attack plans of the Zulus, the tactics of the Irish Republican Army, the strategies of the Mujahedeen, the blitzing of the Navy Seals, the antics of the Green Mountain Boys, and the training of the Spartans. Somervell knew that any forays out into the wild would require a light and fast approach for it would be Wolfe and a small contingent of his aides. Sam chose Megan, Becky, and Kayla for their ability with the slingshot along with Lia, the black-smith, and MacNeil, the carpenter, for their handiness with implements. For his part, Wolfe practiced and learned how to throw a spear; however, his favor-ite proved to be the wielding of his hammer and the thrusting of his improved clawed shank. The possibility had been discussed for an assault team to repel any attack on Masada but more than likely a strike team to protect Sam Wolfe if his path of retribution led him to wander out into the jungles of the island. Furthermore, much discussion took place concerning the idea of Sam wander-ing off into the abyss on a solitary journey in order to strike entry into one of the tribes. In the end, Sam Wolfe and Kellas Somervell decided to put all of their faith in Providence to lead them to their respective duties.

Much time had been dedicated to how to approach the tribes, how to have them respond to Wolfe's requests, what plan of attack seemed the wisest. Whatever path lay before him, Sam Wolfe knew he would need to infiltrate one of the tribes, gain their confidence, get the tribe to call for a truce, and finally meet at "execution alley." Then he must devise the protest, riot, or attack best suited to draw attention to the outrage of their cruel and unusual punishment so that Wolfe could circumvent Hadrian's Wall and the Great Wall of Guam to attack from the rear and capture Murray Mallory Moore. Playing through the chess game of his future insurrection in his mind, Sam Wolfe could not image any scenario that did not require an armed team to assist him, especially dur-ing the thrust through the tunnels under the wall.

"You are certain that five aides comprise the extent of this strike team?" Kellas Somervell once inquired near the beginning of their training.

"Yes. I want a quick team who can hit from a distance but competent in close quarters." Wolfe had watched the aides train with pinpoint accuracy, nailing targets set up in the foundry with their slingshots. Lia not only combat trained herself but manufactured spears and worked with MacNeil and Wolfe on their finer points.

"You have matured into a young Gideon."

"Yes, with a trio of Davids."

"We will need a sign soon for it will take some time to gain the acceptance of a group and convince your potential flock." Somervell continued, "You sure you wish to attempt to raise an army from all three tribes? What about a solo mission on expulsion day and take your teacher hostage?"

"Mr. Somervell, justice and judgment must arrive on this island. If civilization can be established here, all ills must be expunged. You must have the foundations of a bureaucracy to keep the rule of law. We will rally the island around the abandonment of the Eighth Amendment's ban on cruel and unusual punishment; I will unite them under the common cause of liberty, explain to them the need for justice, and rally them in a show of force to demand action from the government." Wolfe paused, "I will bring retribution to this world."

———

Sam Wolfe decided on taking a team of five: Megan, Becky, and Kayla—due to their effectiveness at a distance—along with Lia and MacNeil. Armed with his clawed shank and hammer (which Sam took to calling Isherwood), the aides were armed with three slingshots, five knives, and two cutlasses. The object of the mission had to not only be the rescuing of the wounded black man, but also the taking out of his assailants as he watched in order to establish the ethos of their intentions. Prior to their leaving the safe confines of Masada and venturing out into the savagery and barbarity of the island, Kellas Somervell met them in the church undercroft with final instructions and information about movements made as the team assembled their weapons.

"Sam, I have left Hamilton on the tower. I will take you to the closest hatch, which emerges near the yard where the black man lies. An old Japanese tunnel runs near a well in a long-abandoned house. Pegs in the side of the well will allow you to move up and out quickly. The hatch you go through will have to be barred so your best bet will be to return through the library."

"Can we have aerial support from the rest of you?"

"Exactly. Hamilton will be in the tower. There are seven Hispanics searching the neighborhood for him. Two are closer to the giant thoroughfare called Purple Heart Highway, two more are just south past the library, and the other three are getting close. They seem to be fixated on the five ruined structures on the east side of the block."

"What will Hamilton be doing?"

"She will signal numbers of assailants first followed by a point of reference, followed then by their heading." Somervell stated this with axiomatic precision, figuring Wolfe would have no trouble interpreting, especially after all of the military studies.

"What does that mean?"

"Easy. For example, if you see three fingers followed by pointing up then a pointing down, you know that three Hispanics to the north of you are heading south." Somervell felt deflated for he felt Wolfe would have remembered these lessons with greater alacrity.

"I got it."

"Now, when you emerge from the well, you need to head up the walled section of the alley through the adjacent yard and housing structure. From there you will see some overgrown brush; in the overgrowth you will see the crushed garage with a wall in the back. The black man hid in that rubble, hoping that the hunters would pass it by, I assume." At this, Somervell's aide, Lauryn, came in with a small flask.

"As you requested, Kellas."

"Ha-ha, the bait to set the trap!" He took the flask. "Lauryn mixed some paint. Pour drops around; lay breadcrumbs if you can. Get them in the alley, then let them have it." Somervell looked strangely alive as if envious of the teams' task. While anguish at the thought of taking five teenage girls, who have never left the protective nirvana of their sheltered redoubt, into a street battle for the first time worried him, Sam Wolfe realized that he may indeed have to kill someone today. The dilemma of killing wracked his consciousness. When hurled into L.O.F.I., he resolved to make a break for it, to live a hermit, to try and survive. Though he killed the lunatic the first day on the island, the killing had been reactionary, instinctive. Now, he had time to ruminate upon the issue. Taking a life violated much of his recent religious teaching. The New Testament tended to frown upon the matter, but as he had spent much of his time reading the Old Testament, the rationale seemed to be made regularly. Sam Wolfe decided to allow fate and faith to run their course; if the Almighty had a plan, then God's will be done.

Upon emerging from the well, Sam Wolfe crouched down to his knees and hands. Not seeing or hearing anything near, Sam reconnoitered the overgrown yard, realizing that the back wall eliminated danger from that angle and the burnt structure with overgrown vegetation offered a decent view of the alleyway through which the assailants were likely to approach. He ducked into the bushes, pulling the clawed shank and Isherwood out of his belt as he awaited the aides to emerge from the protection of the Masada tunnels for the first time in their lives. Kayla popped her head up, looked hesitantly around, spotted Wolfe, then scrambled out of the well and over to the bushes with slingshot at the ready. Megan and Becky followed and Sam directed them to the far side of the yard so that the area could be covered in a crossfire if indeed they were happened upon by the black man's pursuers. Lastly came MacNeil and Lia, who quickly drew their cutlasses as they crouched on either side of the well. The plan, once they emerged, would be to have them skulk up the alleyway, quickly and quietly, to the entry of the overgrown pathway of the dilapidated barn.

Sam Wolfe led the team efficiently up the alley as he looked toward the tower to see the signal from Hamilton. Like Moses with his staff, she stood with arm raised and waved her hand flatly back and forth which indicated no movement, all clear. The team swiftly moved the thirty or forty yards up the alley, saw the path veer off to the west, and caught sight of the destroyed barn. The area offered the perfect hiding space for a covering crossfire. The pathways made a t-shape leading back to the ruined barn. Opposite of the collapsed barn, over the alley, the bushes provided cover for Kayla and Lia. On each side of the barn, clutter, trash, and overgrown vegetation provided cover for Megan and MacNeil on one side while Becky and Sam, who applied the faux blood in drips leading to the black man concealed inside, could hide on the other. Sam Wolfe conjectured the black man had to either be dead, unconscious, or laying in silence as he hoped that the party would move on. Minutes passed as Sam contemplated his attack. The girls, nearly overwhelmed with wondering eyes filled with excitement at this adventure out of their protective sphere, dutifully remained armed and ready. He had no idea what kind of fighters headed his way; nor did Sam have any idea how the young neophyte warriors would respond in combat.

Sam finally saw the raising of arms followed by the waving of Hamilton in the bell tower of the church. She flipped her hand, one, two, three, pointed up and then down. Three men headed from the north down the alley toward his location. In a moment or so, Sam Wolfe could detect the audible scrape, crunch, and snap of men walking. He hoped they would see the blood in the alley leading to the trap. As his heart raced, Sam scanned around looking at the girls offering them a calming look, hoping that his inner fear did not betray the look of equanimity he hoped to convey. Suddenly, a whispered voice, then a hush. The three, not at all careful in their approach, turned the corner into the minor alleyway leading back to the collapsed barn. The leader of the three pointed to the blood, tapped his club in his open left hand with an air of anticipation, then gesticulated with the club in his right for the other two to spread out on either side of him. The trio moved in toward the barn following the ruse that Wolfe laid to lead them into the ambuscade. The men moved without any sense of danger; Wolfe held his breath, envisioned his plan of attack, and uttered a small prayer as the first ball of steel from a sling shot smashed the lead pursuer in the face causing the battle to erupt.

CHAPTER 12

"When I blow with a trumpet, I and all that are with me, then blow ye the trumpets also on every side of all the camp, and say, the sword of the Lord, and of Gideon."
Judges 7: 18

Within seconds of the first musket ball slamming into the eye of the lead assailant, two more balls struck the other two men—one in the face and the other in the back of the head. As they all took their blows, Sam Wolfe, expelling that long held breath of anticipation, emerged from the bush like a trained killer from every age of human combat. In his charge from the bush, Wolfe quickly ascertained that the first man hit would be down longest—for being the initial target, it first allowed Sam to see him struggle with the steel in his eye socket. The man nearest to him had been hit in the back of the head by Kayla and the far man struck in the face. Quickly assessing the situation, Sam Wolfe raced past the lead man who bled profusely out of his shattered eye while screaming in agony and bolted toward the man nearest him who had been quickly regaining his faculties from the shot to the back of the head. With the swiftness of a hawk, Sam Wolfe lodged his clawed shank violently into the side of the man's neck, truculently tearing the flesh and severing his jugular vein. Letting go of his clawed shank, he ran at the far man, now rising to his knees and feeling for his club, and with the motion of a cricket bowler, Sam Wolfe extended his left hand out, hopped, skipped, and jumped bringing Isherwood down on the crown of the far assailant's skull.

The cranium did not hold the brain. The ferocious blow crushed the man's head, splitting bone allowing it to protrude out from the temples and oozing brain matter. Wolfe spun around and descended upon the first victim now on his feet, holding his bleeding eye socket with his left hand and waving for mercy with his right hand, blinded by trepidation. Wolfe offered no quarter. Running and swinging from the right gave no chance for the blinded man to see the blow headed toward his temple with the blunt, blacksmith hammer. The blow exploded into the man's temple killing him instantly. He collapsed like a felled tree. Wolfe then delivered a coup de grace to the top of the skull of the blinded man, ensuring his death. As Sam Wolfe stood erect in the triangle of destruction wrought by his hand, he observed Lia and MacNeil rushing toward the fight, which had ended as quickly as it began. The girls had cutlasses ready but never the opportunity to implement them. Kayla, Megan, and Becky emerged from the bushes with musket balls ready to fire again if needed. All five girls watched as Sam Wolfe reached down between the two men with crushed skulls and yanked the clawed shank out of the neck of the third who had finally bled out.

———

When Sam Wolfe began to tear at the downed planks of the collapsed barn, he found huddled under a tarpaulin, attempting to play dead, the black man he came to protect. When he ripped off the tarp, the black man attempted to scurry further back, murmuring something unintelligible to the team of six. Behind him, the five aides looked in awe at the sheer carnage that Sam Wolfe had unleashed in seconds upon the trinity of treachery. Even though he came to the island a questioning young man who had to be convinced for months of his role upon the island, Sam Wolfe surprisingly had unleashed a massacre in less than a minute. A massacre all in the name of God.

"Hey, come out of there."

"Don't kill me, please." The black man cried.

"We are not here to kill you." Wolfe scanned the area looking back at the girls. "Kayla, MacNeil, and Becky, secure that alley. Lia, keep an eye on Hamilton to see if the other four are heading our way."

"Who are you?"

"Well, today my friend, I am nothing less than your savior." Wolfe replied utilizing a bit of internal levity to diffuse the blood surging through his veins at a torrent pace for he had yet to regain his inner composure though he fought to maintain an external equanimity.

"Why you kill those men?" The black man paused, realizing the vacuous nature of the question. "You kill them to save me?"

"You were outnumbered seven to one. The odds seemed hardly fair." Wolfe stepped into the debris to offer the man a hand up. "Besides, I recognized you. I think you are important."

"You recognize me?"

"Yes, at my expulsion off the wall, you were there. You took a black man as the Hispanics killed a white man. You walked away, and the Hispanics chased me." Wolfe pulled the black man to his feet. "I guess I owed you one. You could have killed me, but you didn't."

"We had a truce. I got one; the Hispanics got one. Looks like you got away." Wolfe's belief that his being spared occurred due to his brown skinned became confirmed.

"What about the white guy?"

"They don't last long on the island. Not many come anymore. Not too many left from what I learned about the United States."

"You sound as if you have never been there."

"I haven't. Born and raised on L.O.F.I."

"Very interesting. Like I said before, I am conjecturing that you are important, no?"

"How so?"

"Well, you had the chutzpah to walk up to the wall with your armed escort and walk away with your new tribe member or victim, whatever you call them." Wolfe looked sternly into the black man's face.

"I have a small role yes. But, those men you killed, caught me and my troop, and killed them. They died allowing me to escape."

"I will help you get back to your people." Wolfe began to change the subject to reflect on his plan. He glanced over his shoulder. The girls in the alley indicated all clear, as did Lia via Hamilton in the tower.

"Why you do that?"

"Because I need you and your people to start a revolution." Though it sounded strange to utter such a statement, Wolfe decided that he enjoyed the feel of the bravado.

"Really, why'd we want to do that?"

"Because I plan on restoring order and civility to this island."

"That could be hard."

"With the Lord, all things are possible." Wolfe eased up in intensity, then reflected upon the words he uttered. Strange, not the type of language or beliefs he had heretofore possessed in life. Wolfe found it comforting and appealing. He understood a little better the conviction held by Somervell. Snapping out of his reverie, he glanced around. Lia waved. Hamilton had indicated that two men were moving in their direction from the south—the direction they needed to head for the open library. "You have a name?"

"Whatley."

"Well Whatley, you wanna stay alive? Stay with me." Wolfe turned and moved toward the alley, leaned over the first dead man and wiped the bloody clawed shank on his clothes. "Ladies, we need to move into positions at the bottom of this alley. Lia keep an eye on Hamilton in the tower. We stick to Somervell's plan. Megan, bag him."

"What the?" Whatley protested as Megan headed toward him with a sack of cloth.

"No time to explain Whatley. Our location needs to remain shrouded for the moment." Wolfe led his troops down the alley followed by Megan and Whatley. He calculated whether the best plan would be to avoid the two Hispanic males and avert further bloodshed or take the fight to them with a lightning strike. He knew they had to be coming north up the street past the library for an observer perched up in the church tower could not see behind the library's main structure onto the other street. He could slip down the lesser parallel road heading south and let the trackers head north slipping right past them. He looked up at Hamilton; she offered the same information—two heading north.

Upon further thought, Wolfe liked the idea of two fewer adversaries in his way, two fewer barriers to his mission to rally the island to revolt against the military authority of the United States of America which allowed this apocalyptic anarchy to reign down upon its former citizens. However, continuing that thought, he had to remember that today he took five young girls into combat who until that moment had never left the safe abode of Masada. Moreover, today represented his first attempt at planned hostilities. With three murderers killed, one Samaritan rescued, and no neophytes injured, Sam Wolfe decided to do his best to ensure that the bloodshed ceased for the day. He moved his group down the side street, hid, and watched as the two Hispanic males slipped by and out of view. When Hamilton gave the all clear, the team moved up to the back of the library where Kellas Somervell awaited their arrival armed with his gladius.

———

That evening, gathered beneath the undercroft of Barrigada Catholic Church, the twelve aides sat down for a victory dinner with Kellas Somervell and Sam Wolfe. Whatley had been safely locked in a room and fed, not to mention given the comforting speech that all would be well by Sam who would return for him after dinner. Wolfe felt exhilarated after the battle and rescue, recounting all of the heroic light combat much like he had read about over the past six months by the likes of the Green Mountain Boys, the Mujahedeen, and Seal Team Six. The studies of faith likewise strengthened his resolve; the exploits of Moses, Joshua, and the Israelites in the Book of Judges assured him that might in this sense made right. With dinner being passed around the table, Wolfe felt confident of his plan. His brief discussion with Whatley engendered within him an idea on how to move forward. Being born on the island, Whatley had no formal education and unfortunately proved illiterate. However, after a bit of teaching from the aides, in a few months' time, he could be proficient enough to assist Sam Wolfe in his endeavors.

"Ha-ha, well done ladies! Sam!" Kellas Somervell held up a glass. "A toast of Bailey's finest for a job well done, all."

"Huzzah!" Bailey exclaimed as she quaffed a dram of her best wine.

"The guests of Cana would be impressed young lady." Kellas looked proudly about his aides. "What next Sam?" Sam smiled, broke off a piece of bread and handed the rest to Lia.

"We have six months." Wolfe scanned his followers for now they were indeed his followers. Kellas Somervell had kept to his word when he turned the direction of Masada over to him—a supreme act of faith for a man forty years into the building of this oasis. "We have six months; that gives us three months to train and teach Whatley, so he understands our plan. After much thought and prayer, I have seen the light and the way." A spiritual resolution flowed through Sam.

"Please, divulge sir." Kellas maintained civil formality as usual.

"I believe that in three months we can give Whatley a crash course on the America he has missed by being born on this God forsaken rock; further-more, we can help him understand the injustices of allowing L.O.F.I. to exist. Moreover, that time will allow us to instruct him on the ways of civil liberty and civic duty. The ideas of life, liberty and pursuit of happiness all denied on this island." Wolfe smiled as the girls dutifully ate. "We can teach him a crash course on civics and American principals."

"A rather daunting task, Mr. Wolfe."

"Poppycock, Mr. Somervell. An easy task compared to leading a penal colony of murderers, rapists, and gangsters in a unified insurrection to de-mand that the infrastructure of civility be placed on this island of anarchy. Teaching Whatley will prove much simpler."

"Ha-ha! Touché, Mr. Wolfe. Touché, sir!" Somervell took a slab of bread as he downed a glass of Bailey's wine.

"It can be done. It will be done. Whatley represents our finest hope for setting forth on the very path that will lead us to the Promised Land." Wolfe stood for his finale. "Kellas, an epiphany led you to the library. Faith led you to building Masada. Providence provided you with aides, twelve I stress, to assist you in constructing a monastery here to rival some of Medieval Europe. The Lord brought me to the island via non-violent circumstances. The Holy Spirit brought me into the library full of the faithful waiting for my advent. Finally, God revealed unto me the importance of Whatley and delivered him to our door much like the wounded traveler rescued by the Good Samaritan. Whatley will prove the means by which we will bring retribution and civilization to the island." A hush smothered the room.

"Sam?"

"Yes, Kellas."

"Why do you believe Whatley will be the key to our work?"

"Because, he revealed to me that his father happens to be the king of the black tribe."

"Ha-ha, Mr. Wolfe! The Lord has delivered to us the light, the truth and the way for our plan to come to fruition."

"Indeed, Kellas. And in three months, I plan on leaving Masada with Whatley and traveling to Agat, the camp of his tribe. With his help, we shall recruit our legion and complete the mission the Lord has called upon us to undertake." Sam Wolfe sat and continued to partake in his bread and wine. He opined upon his recent conversion from agnostic to faithful. Though sudden, he felt sure of its validity. The explanations of Kellas seemed apparent. Everything, his inexplicable urge to go to school with drugs to prove a point to Mr. Moore; his safe arrival at Masada, the delivery of Whatley to his very doorstep; the improbable history and life of Kellas Somervell, all solidified the seeds of his faith and caused his passion for his newfound religiosity to grow. After all he thought, the Bible brims with similar examples of newly acquired faith and saintly heroics. Why should Sam Wolfe be any different?

"Well done, Mr. Wolfe." Kellas Somervell stood and clasped his hands. "Now may we say a belated grace and give thanks for that which we have already received."

CHAPTER 13

"But the Lord said: I have witnessed the affliction of my people in Egypt and have heard their cry against their taskmasters, so I know well what they are suffering. Therefore I have come down to rescue them from the power of the Egyptians and lead them up from that land into a good and spacious land flowing with milk and honey."
Exodus 3: 7-8

Sam Wolfe and Kellas Somervell sat in the nave of the church library as the books soared toward the ceiling. On the back wall, the painting of God sending forth Sam Wolfe with his right hand as his left hand held back Somervell and the aides had begun to undergo a new modification. Lauryn began painting in Whatley on the mural next to Sam; for in recent weeks it had become apparent that the two would go forth and spread the word, incite the rising, and inspire the revolution. Whatley, every day prior to lessons, moved about the church in abject wonderment. In his twenty or so years of life, all on L.O.F.I., he had never set foot in a structure as beautiful, kempt, and organized. His tribe, the most powerful on the island, mimicked the very sobriquet, which it had been given generations prior. The three tribes of the island indeed lived no better than Jack and Ralph in *Lord of the Flies*. The tragic reality though stemmed from the fact that American convicts had been on the island for nearly fifty years, and in all of that time, the former citizens of the United States had lived up to their predicted fate. As described by the politicians when they clarified their rational for the revocation of a convict's citizenship and then subsequent deportation to the penal colony—they were bloody savages. Due to the animalism in vogue on the island, Americans felt that the punishment fit the crime.

During the first weeks of Whatley's sojourn at Masada, Kellas kept him locked in his room with limited access to the subterranean area through which Wolfe first had entered the lair and found that he had been surrounded by Somervell and his aides. Slowly, however, Whatley earned the trust of his hosts during which time Kellas learned of the young black man's history as well as the nature and power structure of his tribe. Whatley, having been born on the island to a female inmate and fathered by the "king" of the tribe, obtained a reasonably important position. The Black tribe in recent years had seen a growth in their power under the leadership of a man named Chenoweth, but an undercurrent of disillusion had been brewing, for the "king" proved to be a ruthless dictator, wielding terrible power and exerting a heinous bloodlust.

Somervell had asked Whatley for more information on Chenoweth, the so-called king.

"Chenoweth like to do bad things to people." Whatley, still hesitant in the early days of Masada, looked imploringly at Kellas and Sam—also in the room.

"What do you mean?" Kellas pressed.

"Well, he has people killed all the time in front of him." Whatley, though affable, proved a bit reticent and uneducated.

"Why does he have them killed?"

"Sometimes cause they make him mad. Sometimes cause he jus' bored." Hamilton, also present at the powwow, winced at the broken sentence structure and ill grammar.

"What does he do to them?" Sam chimed in.

"He cut off heads. He open bellies and spill guts. Once he hanged a man from a tree with another man's guts."

"A regular modern day Kurtz." Somervell alluded to the Joseph Conrad classic he had required Sam Wolfe to read. "Continue please, Whatley."

"He drink out of a cup made from a skull." Kellas, an anglophile to the core, had spent innumerable hours in the past reading copious accounts of British explorers and their encounters with the inhabitants of the uncivilized parts of the world. None of this seemed to bother him, nor Whatley for that matter, who possessed none of the sensibilities of a young man reared in a society steeped in logos, pathos, and ethos.

"Why would he do that?" Hamilton interjected from the back. She had been annotating the conversation to keep track of vital information.

"He look at my mom." Whatley offered the curt reply.

"He favors your mother?" Somervell asked.

"Mom the favorite of all his wifes." Whatley smiled. "She most pretty of all women in our tribe."

"Well Sam, we have a veritable Lombard on our hands."

"Lombard?"

"Sorry. A barbaric tribe, which helped envelope the collapsed Roman Empire. They conquered with others like the Goths, Vandals, Saxons, and Jutes."

"Those I recognize from our studies. But not the Lombards."

"They are not as commonly known. Much like the Frisians in England who came with the Angles, Saxons, and Jutes; the Lombards are often forgotten."

"As barbaric as the Vikings?"

"Ah yes. Bloody ruthless." Kellas looked at Whatley. "What else can you tell me about your tribe?"

"Mother hate Chenoweth. Like to kill him."

"Really, why doesn't she?" Hamilton inquired quickly.

"She tell me Chenoweth keep me safe. She afraid he hurt me."

"How many people do you have in your tribe? Do you keep count?"

"Many, many people. They stretch down to the sea. When we all gather, like blades of grass in the field." Kellas felt disappointed with that nebulous and futile response.

"Can you tell me anything else unique about the tribe?"

"Much fun at feasts. Singing and dancing and eating meat." Whatley seemed to smile at the thought.

"Singing and dancing? Explain."

"Chenoweth have a singer and dancer on a chain around the neck. When he want to laugh, he pull their chain. One sing, the other dance."

"Interesting." Kellas looked at Sam and Hamilton, "A court jester and minstrel."

"Chenoweth like Quisno more than Topher though."

"What do you mean?" Hamilton interjected.

"Quisno sing real pretty. Have all his fingers. Topher not always dance good enough for Chenoweth. Chop, chop on fingers sometime." Whatley seemed dejected over the thought.

"Anything else about your tribe, Whatley?" Kellas requested.

"Yes. When you take me back to camp," he looked at Sam Wolfe, "you kill Chenoweth and free the people."

This conversation put the machinery of implementation into motion. Kellas, devout beyond reproach, had faithfully trusted in the delivery of Sam Wolfe to his doorstep; likewise, through the epiphany in the church nave, Wolfe took the reins of piety and trusted that the Almighty would manifest to them the path to freedom. With Whatley's early revelation that the most powerful tribe on Guam lay not only ripe for a revolution, but that the seeds of a coup d'état had been sown, the religiosity and faith of Somervell and Wolfe only blossomed to the full.

———

Lauryn continued on her mural, which incorporated the stately, yet simple-minded Whatley. Though at length his intellectual prowess had been conjectured upon and deliberated, Kellas and Sam concluded that the basic nature of his thoughts, mannerisms, and comments only solidified the path, inspired by a divine hand, that lay ahead. Masada's Somervell had much to risk in this venture; forty years of pleasant living and hard work could be discovered by the tribes. Any exposure to the mass of lunatics and hordes of murderers would place the twelve cherubic aides in mortal peril for the hordes of men would surely inflict upon them all of the indignities which have been wrought upon women through the course of human history. Kellas Somervell resolved in his mind a mercy killing of his twelve ladies followed by a fight to the last before he would allow them to be caught up, abused, tortured, and tormented all the rest of their lives. These thoughts, kept to himself, would prove more and more difficult to quell as the plan for the implementation of the social, civic, and religious revolution came together.

"Well, Sam, your thoughts now that you have monitored the tutoring of young Whatley these nearly three months?" Whatley continued to marvel at Lauryn's paintings on the walls of the church. Kellas Somervell continued, "I have some of the aides coming to discuss this; with spring upon us, we have but three more months to realize the revolution so that we may make our voices heard and provide you the opportunity to circumvent the two walls protecting Andersen Air Force Base."

"I think the time has come. His village believes him dead, but now, like Christ, he will rise after three months and present himself back into their midst." Sam smiled at Whatley, who now sat looking at an atlas. Having only recently learned of the enormity of the planet and all that he had missed in being born on L.O.F.I., it had only increased his curiosity and pushed his will to learn.

"Ah, ladies, please come in and sit." Mikayla, Hamilton, Nicole, and Ashleigh came through the undercroft stair and sat at the large table near the back of the church nave, which served as an intimate school desk for student and teacher. "Well, Mikayla, please," he paused, "provide us with an indication of Whatley's religious growth."

"Well Mr. Somervell, it has proven difficult to explain the complexities of religion to an illiterate, nearly feral young man who for all intents and purposes could be classified as a savage. His tribe seems to be purely atheistic. If his tribe has any religion, primitive or otherwise, he hasn't conveyed it to me. So, with no place to really begin, I found that he became most curious upon viewing the paintings upon the wall. So, I started there."

"Ha-ha! Brilliant, Mikayla. Brilliant indeed. The Keeper of Faith proves herself again."

"I believe the serenity of this church and the beauty of the paintings juxtaposed with the horrors of his life made him realize that no matter what we taught in here, it would prove worth trusting compared to the proverbial hell which he has endured so far in life."

"Well done! Splendid." Somervell looked like a proud father of not only teacher, but also student. "Where does he stand? For the time has come, Mikayla. The clock ticks. We must leave Masada to complete God's holy work."

"I dare say he understands the nature of God. I left out Jesus, the Holy Trinity, Mohammed, Mormonism, and the like for lack of time and risk of confusion. He understands the concept of heaven and hell because he has lived on L.O.F.I., and I have shown him pictures of civilization and all its wonders."

"A very wise approach, indeed. You are correct; the concept of Christ would clutter his mind."

"Finally, he understands that God sent Sam and you to lead his innocent people to the Promised Land. I have read to him the Book of Exodus. He knows Moses. He thinks of Sam as Moses and you, Mr. Somervell, as his eloquent brother Aaron."

"Well done, Mikayla. After we restore order to the island and present education to the people, we will teach young Whatley how to read and all of the joys of intellectual edification which follow." Somervell appeared pleased. Looking toward Hamilton, he asked, "What studies have you provided?"

"Well, Somervell, you left me the impossible! I have been charged with teaching him fiction! You know how many books that I have read! Where should I have started?" Hamilton appeared frantic much like a turtle precariously upon its back.

"Easy Hamilton. I pray that you have improvised like Mikayla."

"Of course I did. But I can't help thinking of the books that I didn't teach him."

"All in good time. You will have your life to teach. All of you will, and you will find the life of teaching pleasurable and gratifying." Somervell in his fatherly tone continued, "Now, Hamilton, review your lessons please."

"Well, I worked hand in hand with Ashleigh since she represents the Keeper of History, and we combined our time to educate him on what we thought most important to help spawn this revolution."

"Good. What did you cover?"

"Knowing we would soon set out to spark a revolt based upon the principals of life, liberty, and the pursuit of happiness, we chose speeches on the subject of freedom." Hamilton explained exuberantly. "We read early revolutionary speeches, and discussed the lives of Lincoln, Washington, King Jr., and Patrick Henry." Ashleigh now interjected.

"We figured in that short amount of time, the best thing to do would be to provide him the fundamentals of the United States, its Constitution, Bill of Rights, and Declaration of Independence. We taught him of the wars against tyrants like his father. Also, we taught him about the Great Compromise of 2025, which opened this island and banished America's felons here for a lifetime of depravity."

"We thought," Hamilton cut back in, "that Whatley should see the world in which he would live if he happened to be born on the mainland. In order for this to happen we paraphrased much of the founding documents into language he could understand."

"Yes, it has proven a tragic flaw by the government shipping the women also to Guam, for the American public in their callousness for the criminality refused to consider any potential children born upon this island who are unjustly punished for the sins of their fathers." Somervell commented. Wolfe looked troubled in his seat.

"Well," Sam added, "I think when the revolution begins, and it could be dangerous, we should sequester those born on the island in a safe place. Or as many as we can find. I hope this will be possible, though I am not sure how to identify them all. Whatever the case, let the guilty fight for the civility they need. If the revolt turns violent, I don't want these innocents possibly slain. You don't want to risk the girls do you Somervell?"

"Well Sam, we are here to complete the Lord's work. His will, through your planning, be done."

"Anything else Hamilton? Ashleigh?" Sam inquired.

"I read to him *Lord of the Flies* by William Golding." Hamilton offered matter-of-factly. "With all of the other history and speeches, I didn't have time to read any other."

"I take it, Somervell, that you had the aides withhold math and science?"

"Yes. With the success of the revolution complete, order installed, civilization born, and schools opened, we can begin the full regiment of education."

"Okay then, now would seem fitting to discuss the final phase of our endeavors." Sam Wolfe changed the subject. "How do we take young Whatley back to his camp?"

"I will send you with the same team which helped you nab Whatley to begin with. They proved more than adequate for the job." Somervell seemed rather confident.

"I don't think that plan appropriate."

"Why not?" Somervell's voice possessed a palpable incredulity.

"Because they are girls, Kellas." Wolfe seemed indignant.

"I dare say that after a century and a half of women's liberation in the United States, and my aides' aplomb during that battle with Whatley's attackers, that gender be deemed completely superfluous."

"Kellas, we are not traveling to America or in America, and if anything goes wrong, we won't be dealing with the protective laws of America."

"Ah, ye of little faith, Sam Wolfe; has not all that has happened solidified your belief in the Lord's plan for this island?"

"Kellas, you know the level of my faith. I have transformed from Saul to Paul; however, I am not willing to walk these chaste young ladies into a den of pirates and barbarians and leave their well-being in the hands of my abilities and my faith in the Lord Almighty."

"Surely, you do not think you will travel alone. You and Whatley if caught would be vulnerable." Kellas had forgotten his promise to let Wolfe call all of the shots. "Besides, once you enter that camp, Masada will be compromised. Whatley will tell them. You will tell them. All will be at risk either way."

"True, but if everything goes wrong, you are resourceful Somervell; you can run and hide with the twelve aides. If I walk them in there, they have no chance. Sam Wolfe implored Somervell, "Do you have any tunnels which could help us get closer to Agat undetected?"

"I do have a bit of a protected way." Somervell smiled. "And Sam, have faith. Faith the size of a mustard seed can move mountains."

CHAPTER 14

"They took up such supplies as the soldiers had with them, as well as their horns, and Gideon sent the rest of the Israelites to their tents, but kept the three hundred men. Now the camp of Midian sat below him in the valley. That night the Lord said unto Gideon: Go, descend on the camp, for I have delivered it into your power."
Judges 7: 8-9

"The road to Agat will be arduous and perilous!" Kellas Somervell felt the pressure of the next phase of the mission to rehabilitate the island. The fifteen miles through No Man's Land to the edge of what had been the black camp would be difficult to navigate without being spotted or attacked. The black camp, established in the early days of the United States Penal Colony on Guam, had resulted when the early 21st century prisons, filled with Hispanic, whites, and blacks who formed into ferocious gangs, were let loose on the island unfettered as if in one big prison yard while the guards were on break. In the decades since 2025 when this post-Great Compromise initiative began, the Race War on the island horrified American politicians. Though the public received information about the carnage occurring on the island, the vast majority turned an apathetic head. In general, the nation felt that these men and women had had their chance, having been born into the greatest nation on earth, and they chose to commit heinous crimes, repeatedly in many cases; therefore, deportation and citizenship revocation remained the law of the land. As the decades slipped by and the American demographic picture morphed from black, white, and Hispanic into a mulattoed chocolate, the original tribes on the island began to have an identity crisis for nearly all of the new inmates were an amalgamation of the planet's genetic soup. Though the tribes were still referred to by their original nomenclature, they no longer represented the original meaning; the black tribe, white tribe, and Hispanic tribe were mostly brown in nature.

"I realize the fifteen miles will be tough, but do you have another idea?" Sam Wolfe also felt the strain of the task at hand. Trekking across this island with Whatley alone for two nights and heading into an extremely hostile camp would be a daunting and perilous task.

"Look, I know we have quarreled on this point, but you must have a contingent with you. Maybe an armed escort up to the edge of their territory, then they can slip back towards Masada." Kellas looked about the banquet table; all were seated and eating.

"Whatley," Wolfe broke in, "you told us that your group had been on a mission to the wall for another potential expulsion when your group had been attacked."

"Yeah."

"So you are well aware of checkpoints and places to cross into your territory right?"

"Yeah. You go west on Purple Heart Highway to the sea, then south on Marine Corp Drive. Once you get to naval base you hit first checkpoint with warriors." Whatley concisely pronounced.

"How dangerous would you say the journey will be?" Wolfe inquired.

"Here very dangerous. Much death. March to sea filled with zombies."

"Zombies?!" Wolfe spouted incredulously.

"Yes, zombies. They attack in packs and eat what they kill." Both Kellas and Sam had witnessed the cannibalism from the Barrigada Catholic Church tower. Whenever their attacks were witnessed, they ran in packs of three to five.

"Any other areas of imminent peril young Whatley?" Somervell continued.

"Yes. War Park. Two roads go around it. Vampires attack from the trees."

"What do you mean by vampires, Whatley?" Wolfe again.

"Like zombies; they eat the dead. They attack with blood smeared on face and lips though. They fight naked covered in blood."

"Bloody hell," Somervell sat back in his chair quaffing a dram of Bailey's wine. He looked around the table at his young innocent girls—young ladies he had contemplated sending out into this hostile environment. "We have a regular modern day group of Picts upon this island."

"Why do your people call them zombies and vampires?" Sam asked.

"Always call them zombies and vampires. No other word."

"Sam, don't trouble yourself with the words. Obviously, these represent an appellation bestowed upon lost souls by previous generations. They are cannibals. Nothing more." Somervell held up his glass. Bailey rose to bring him more wine. "Whatley my boy! Please, what other carnage awaits upon the road to Agat? Wizards? Warlocks?" His audible chuckle lightened the mood in the room.

"Don't know those. After War Park the naval base. No zombies or vampires. Road clear. Long way and quiet walk. Just south of naval base you come to Agat Bridge. Warriors guard crossing above the river. You safe there all the way to Agat."

"How many times have you traveled this route?"

"Many times. Too many to count. Always go to wall for new warriors."

"Well Sam," Kellas interrupted, "this presents a devastating conundrum."

"Yeah?"

"To walk that with only the two of you would seem suicide, day or night."

"So you want me to take the girls so they can be raped and cannibalized?" Sam scoffed. "I will go alone thank you."

"Hey!" Lia in her usual assertive manner blasted in. "I can handle myself. And Kayla, Megan, and Becky are deadly accurate with their slingshots."

"Somervell, have you taught these young cherubs about the proverbial birds and bees? Lia and the rest, more importantly, have you forgotten about the Vikings with their rape, pillage, and plunder, or the ruthless Saxon conquest of England, or the Japanese rape of Nanking?" Sam Wolfe appeared to be seething. "Come on Somervell, many innocent young Christians were trusting in God to protect them there. It didn't happen. If Whatley and I go, and they kill me, mission over, girls saved. If I take them with me and they are captured, well, I don't want to think about it."

"I think we leave it up to them." Somervell offered.

"Look, I am not afraid of anything." Lia responded. "Kayla, though she doesn't say much also doesn't care, I am sure." Kayla stoically sat without revealing her thoughts. "Besides, Megan who can shoot, also being the Keeper of Health, will be good with any medical attention we need."

"I don't know."

"You can't go alone Sam." Lia's voice wavered from tactical to emotional. A rare display of her feelings. All heard it. Lia, dejected, looked down at her food. "You can't go alone." She repeated much like a frightened dog who will offer a final perfunctory bark as it limps away.

"I will think it over tonight."

———

Sam Wolfe descended spiral stairs of the church into the undercroft. He had spent a morning in the library reviewing the leadership characteristics of Lawrence of Arabia, George Rogers Clark, and George Patton, looking for any insight that could assist him in his impending endeavor. Recent days had him frantically cramming for the mission but also contemplating whether to take the team. A din of noise emanated from the undercroft as Kellas Somervell in his karate gi worked through his kata. Standing at the ready with large mitts upon their hands, Becky and Megan had been allowing Kellas to continue the maintenance of his martial art skills. Even though an octogenarian, Somervell moved with the agility and speed of a healthy man half his years. As he finished his routine, Lia entered from the tunnel carrying his gladius and scutum with a Christian cross etched into the metal.

"Somervell, how on earth do you do it?"

"Do what young Sam Wolfe?" Kellas inquired as he bowed to his aides for their assistance in his combat training.

"Constantly move, learn, train, build!" Wolfe further enraptured with incredulity continued, "You have a Roman shield and sword. I mean, you never cease!"

"Ha-ha, Sam Wolfe, explain our purpose on this earth if not to incessantly edify ourselves, mind and body, for our individual mission."

"I don't know. Normal people don't live this intensely. Have you ever rested here?"

"On an island without the Lord's influence, Sunday does not exist. Therefore, no rest until the Almighty's plan for me achieves completion."

"Uncanny, the only word that comes to mind."

"I can assure you, Mr. Wolfe, that my days are numbered, and then, and only then, will I rest." Somervell wiped the sweat from his furrowed brow with a towel.

"I mean, the other day, I come in here and you are doing pushups while Hamilton reads the Bible to you." Sam's voice intensified. "Last week, while bathing in shorts, mind you, you had Kayla reading to you the bullet points of the Zulu attack formations, along with the mistakes you deciphered from the Battle of Isandlwana."

"Ah, Mr. Wolfe, I stole that approach to learning by two extremely influential figures in the history of the western world—Sir Winston Churchill and Benjamin Franklin. Their philosophy: maximize every waking minute of your life to accomplish your tasks."

"I think in school we read one excerpt of Franklin about a kite, and I don't think anything by the Churchill person."

"Tragic. I see the American public schools haven't improved too much since the Great Compromise of 2025." Kellas walked over toward Lia who stood holding out the weapons. "I suggest, Mr. Wolfe, that you read Poor Richard's Almanac along with the biography of Sir Winston. You will learn what you can accomplish with bull-dogged determination."

"I sharpened your gladius and strengthened the strap on your shield, Mr. Somervell."

"Excellent, Lia." Somervell offered her a countenance of approbation. "Combat ready. Nice." Somervell wielded the gladius in successive tenacious swipes followed by two intense step-and-thrust movements.

"I also assembled pouches of steel artillery for the three slingshots; furthermore, all knives have been sharpened and cutlasses honed."

"Well done, Lia."

"What gives, Somervell? You planning on going somewhere?" Sam Wolfe possessed an air of suspicion.

"Well Mr. Wolfe, you are going to need a team to cross the highways and make the journey down to Agat. I will let you chose, but the challenges remain clear. You and Whatley cannot safely make that journey alone."

"I thought you determined months ago that I called the shots on this spiritual journey and revolutionary mission?"

"I did and I have, but you must face reality, Sam. I understand your reservations about taking the aides; however, all of our work will be for naught if you are killed on the journey over."

"I thought your piety assured you of the success of the mission, that God would see me through to the end. I don't understand."

"Apply a bit of logos, Sam. The good Lord delivered me unto Masada; he kept the barbarian hordes out of the redoubt. Furthermore, the Lord placed into my care, much like Moses with the Pharaoh's daughter, these twelve aides. In these forty years, I have used everything at my disposal to make way the path for you, the savior."

"And you have, but now I go alone."

"Young Sam, all has been provided to take you on this journey. Like the Lord needing to arrive in Jerusalem, you must be delivered unto Agat. After you enter that city, as you stated, you must work alone." Somervell paused, then continued, "I respect your plan to enter the city alone with Whatley; however, you must respect my plan of escorting you to the safe confines of the naval base with the armed team you already utilized in battle once before."

"You can't go, Mr. Somervell," Lia beat Wolfe to the protestation.

"I can; I will."

"What happens if you get killed? You must lead Masada."

"If it be my time to die, then let it come as the Almighty sees fit." Somervell smiled. "Into his hands, I commend my spirit."

———

After an evening of prayer led at the altar by Mikayla and a procession similar to the Stations of the Cross in Catholicism, reflectively moving from pious mural to pious mural in the nave, the disciples of Masada feasted on a late dinner, all retired to bed with the exception of Somervell, Wolfe, and a bottle of Bailey's finest wine. The plan had been set, the team chosen, and the mission understood. Sam Wolfe would lead Whatley home to the black tribe in Agat past the naval base. Kellas Somervell would lead an escort team of five—Lia, Kayla, Megan, Becky, and MacNeil—to assist the pair of missionaries through the ruins inhabited by roving bands and cannabilistic "zombies" as well as overgrown War Park, occupied by the Pictish "vampires." The path would be arduous and perilous, but Sam Wolfe, with Kellas Somervell's insistence, acquiesced. Into the jungle they would go. Upon leading them to the safety of the road parallel to the naval base, the escort team would head back to Masada and relieve Hamilton who would be left in charge to "carry on the Lord's work" should the team never return. The plan, timed to go through the ruined section with cannibals at night while emerging, at best estimate, at the War Park at dawn, Kellas and Sam hoped to avoid contact with any group daring to confront the party. Somervell then planned camping a day, followed by heading back with the same time table to Masada. From that moment on, Wolfe and Whatley would be completely at the mercy of the natives, the wits of Sam, and the will of God.

CHAPTER 15

"But the righteous one, though he die early, shall be at rest. For the age possessing honor comes not with the passing of time, nor can it be measured in terms of years. Rather, understanding passes for gray hair, and an unsullied life represents the attainment of old age."
Wisdom 4: 7-9

The Barrigada Catholic Church connected to a tunnel, which led under several dangerous streets to a subterranean basement in an old, abandoned elementary school, which had collapsed in on its foundation but still protected, miraculously, the connection from one tunnel to another. Kellas Somervell had pilfered all of the library books prior to the school's total destruction in a raid and fire in another brief race war decades ago. From one tunnel into another, the team of missionaries made it several more blocks up to the Church of Jesus Christ of Latter-day Saints. Emerging from a rat-infested subbasement in this dilapidated but relatively unmolested building, Hamilton would turn loose the pilgrims about to embark upon their journey, and head back to Masada with Ashleigh and Nicole who had accompanied her on the dank journey. With two or three miles of treacherous journey behind them, Kellas, Sam, and Whatley, along with Kayla, MacNeil, Lia, Becky, and Megan, emerged hesitantly into the darkness out onto the overgrown Purple Heart Highway which, due to the formerly four lanes of concrete, though overrun with moss and grass and trees upon the sides, had maintained itself as a well-worn thoroughfare though dangerous at every step.

"Alright ladies," Kellas hissed his instructions, "As we practiced, Kayla on the point, slingshot at the ready. Lia follow her with Cutlass. Megan, MacNeil, and Becky at the rear. The cargo will remain in the middle. In the event of an ambush, push forward. Usually the purpose of a few assailants will be to ensnare you in a worse predicament in the jungle. Got it?"

All understood. Whatley had been relatively quiet in the recent days. Though enraptured to return to his home and mother, an apprehensive melancholy overtook him for the thought of seeing Chenoweth the King worried him. From the perverse abuses of women, to the detestable murders of tribesmen, to the villainous abuses of his jester and minstrel, this King Chenoweth had proven himself a sociopath of the first order. Sam Wolfe knew from the moment he stepped out onto the street from the Church of Latter-day Saints that within a fortnight either Chenoweth or himself would be dead, for the island could not let them both live and have Somervell's plan for civilization come to fruition. As they marched by moonlight, as Kellas had insisted, Sam tromped down the road with his sleekly modified clawed shank in his left hand, Isherwood in his right, and a Lia-special dagger in his belt.

After traveling without incident and only seeing sporadic campfires, which they avoided for fear of a large group due to their brazen burning, the group took a reprieve in a small park, which jutted out into the sea. Fanning out in order to search for any potential threats, the team found the park empty with the exception of a statue on a pedestal gazing out to the sea. Following Kellas to the edge of the park where the sea wrestled the coast with its surf, the party noticed that the diminutive statue, the size of a woman, bore the familiar shape of the Statue of Liberty.

"Since we made safe passage through the first part of our journey, I expect we have time for a brief sojourn prior to dawn."

"This looks like a mini Statue of Liberty." Sam Wolfe squinted as he strode closer.

"Indeed, Sam, indeed." Somervell kept scanning the moonlit surroundings.

"Where on earth did it come from? How come it hasn't been destroyed?"

"Well, Sam, that second question hits me quite profoundly also." Somervell drifted into a reverie, "I think the statue survives unmolested for the same principals which have allowed the library and church of Masada to remain inviolate. Sure, the island, inhabited to the core with the degenerate of America, would seem a ripe place for all forms of civilization to be destroyed, but I have a hypothesis."

"We are all listening." Wolfe bestowed a look of disbelief upon Somervell.

"The institutions and ideals of freedom, liberty, equality, and fraternity are inherent in all humanity. Even the murderers and rapists know this; furthermore, my dear Mr. Wolfe, these lost souls unconsciously long for a higher calling. This lack of faith, lack of piety, lack of civility serves as a siren song to all on this island. This, in my mind, explains why churches, libraries, and this statue have managed to survive without desecration."

The group looked at the six foot tall statue as the moon shone down upon lady liberty's visage and allowed the words of Kellas Somervell to sink into their collective consciousness. Finally, after a moment of serenity, Sam Wolfe broke the silence, "Well stated, Somervell. However, I think it may be time to push on; dawn has broken." Wolfe pointed to the east as a hint of light began to illuminate the horizon. "And may your theory, with God's help, prove correct."

———

As the sun rose behind the marching missionaries, the tops of the trees in War Park began to light up. With Kayla and Lia on the point, Sam Wolfe followed about ten yards behind. With dawn breaking, he decided to hang his clawed shank around his neck inside his loose fitting jacket. Behind him walked Whatley and Somervell, who in his karate gi with Roman gladius and scutum, seemed an oxymoronic anachronism. In the rear Becky, MacNeil, and Megan scanned the trees as they began to close in on the verdant park, which over the decades had morphed into an overgrown jungle. With two former roads, also overgrown, encircling the park, the traveling party opted for the shorter road closer to the ocean to provide them with a more direct route. The group moved swiftly and silently unmolested past a ruined section of a former town with the remnants of a Harley Davidson motorcycle showroom near the path. The jungle began to move in closer to the road thus knocking back some of dawn's early light. The mood of a glorious morning began to transform into a gloomy pitch.

The jungle to the east of the road began to evolve from a welcoming haven of vegetation to a sinister nest of malevolence. Immediately the group set on edge as a palpably eerie feeling began to envelope the traveling troupe. Sam Wolfe noticed the perceptive unease that had overcome Kayla and Lia on the point—they kept turning back toward Kellas and Sam for a sense of comfort. Sam felt sure that he heard the rustle of slight movements in the bush and wanted to attribute them to wildlife but felt a visceral realization that something more nefarious had begun tracking them.

"Easy everyone," Kellas reassured the coterie in front and back. "Slings, be ready to fire. Lia and MacNeil, remember: defend the slings while reloading." The tangible trepidation effusively moved through the crew. More rustling in the bush began to confirm the inevitable truth that they were being stalked. Sam Wolfe peered into the bush, but nothing discernible manifested itself. Wolfe cautiously pulled his dagger from his belt. Up front, Kayla skulked with her sling ready to fire while Lia with her hand on Kayla's waistline marched right behind her. The intensity reeked in the group as it awaited the strike of some beast. A snap of a twig caused Wolfe to wince then turn just catching a glimpse of a naked human moving in the bush.

"Vampires!" Wolfe hissed toward the group.

"Easy. Easy. Remember the plan." Kellas with a discernible equanimity prepared for war. "When they attack, push forward."

"Right." Wolfe returned as Whatley gripped his knife in his hand.

"Megan! Becky! MacNeil! Move in front of me and prepare to shoot your way through." Kellas, walking in his karate gi stopped as the girls passed, sticking his shield in the turf along with his sword. Sam could see more than one faint visage in the bush; an attack proved imminent. Wolfe turned his head to see, as Megan, Becky, and MacNeil strode past him, that Kellas Somervell had disrobed. With his gi tossed to the side of the path and his gladius and scutum in hands, Kellas Somervell swaggered up the trail stark naked; Sam Wolfe then realized Somervell's inexorable plan.

The jungle exploded to life. A score of vampires—savage naked men covered in blood—erupted from the bush in front, behind, and on the east flank of the missionary group. Sam Wolfe observed the three slings raise their arms as they drew back to fire. Wolfe had no time to look forward or aft because instantly a vampire charged him from the bush; instinctively, he crouched as his martial arts had trained him and thrust the dagger high into the belly of the assailant with his left hand, then followed with a devastating blow with Isherwood down upon the crown of the head which caused the ears to explode with brain matter.

"Fire!" Sam Wolfe bellowed to the aides in the vanguard as he yanked back his blade allowing the naked vampire to fall dead to the ground. "Fire and move!" In the road two naked, club-toting lunatics began to charge the aides on the point, who immediately let fly. Both assailants doubled over as a metal ball struck one in the throat, the other the forehead. At that moment, Lia and MacNeil charged forward delivering the coup de grace. Another two emerged from the bush on the flank only to be met by a volley from the slings followed by Sam Wolfe utilizing his hammer and Whatley with his dagger.

"Move!" Sam Wolfe hurled forward watching Lia and MacNeil run out in front followed by the slings at a less brisk pace, holding their weapons at the ready. Wolfe pushed Whatley forward with another assertive, "Move!" The mad scrambling panic seemed to be successful when Sam turned to make sure that Kellas indeed managed to keep on his heels. At this visual of Somervell, Sam Wolfe knew that the plans devised back at Masada had been inevitably modified. Kellas Somervell stood his ground, naked as a Celtic warrior, with nothing on his person but the Roman gladius and scutum ready for mortal combat. His defiant stance, his manifest preparedness, his palpable willingness to sacrifice himself all struck Wolfe viscerally for he realized that Somervell's training had been all for this such inevitability.

"Run aides! Run Wolfe!" Kellas Somervell banged his sword upon his shield as six naked vampires began to encircle him clearly giving up on the group, for one victim would feed their tribe for days. Kellas thrust his shield out for protection as he raised his gladius, perching himself onto the balls of his feet, he began to turn with a cocksure aplomb that would strike fear into his assailants.

"Kellas!" Lia frantically screamed.

"Run. I got them!" With death imminent, followed by mutilation and cannibalization, Kellas Somervell never wavered. Outnumbered and surrounded, Somervell would try to the last. Before his body, he threw his warlike shield with the proverbial 'lay on' for the vampires. His last words as the survivors moved swiftly south on the road, "Come on you bastards! If you take me, may you choke on my gristled flesh!"

———

Sam Wolfe with great insistence ushered forward the aides who were clearly struck with tangible horror at the loss of their leader, role model, teacher and for all intents and purposes, their father. Whatley moved much more readily, for his parents and safety lay ahead. For Whatley, with the unknown behind— as experienced by his narrow escape of death, his feared incarceration in his cell, his surprise education at Masada, and newfound sense of belonging—he exhibited all of the energy of a young man whose adventures proved bountiful, but nonetheless wished to return to the land of his birth. As Wolfe pushed them at a steady trot to safety out of War Park and into the open expanse of the road paralleling the sea and the naval base, the team, no longer in danger, began to slow and let emotion set in. The tears and sobs began to effusively flow from all but Lia.

"Are we safe, Sam?"

"As near as I can tell, yes." Wolfe looked around at the setting. To the west, the enormous wall of the naval base loomed above, patrolled by guards looking down with the anticipation of children at a show or sporting event awaiting the action to begin. To the east lay an expanse of desolate, flat ground, which extended for hundreds of yards, requiring any enemy coming their way to expose themselves to harm. To the south lay the anticipated safety of the black tribe's checkpoint, which should welcome in their lost son, and to the north the immense quiet of the foreboding jungle from which they just escaped but where Kellas Somervell remained. "Yeah, I think we can rest and eat. Then we must move on."

"I am going back then; I am going after Kellas." Lia adamantly proclaimed.

"No way Lia." Wolfe proclaimed as the other aides muffled their sobs of loss for their life-long role model.

"Watch me! You try and stop me, and you will have to fight me!"

"Lia, you can do nothing." He grabbed her as she attempted to pass him. "If you find him, you will witness something worse than your last memory. He went out nobly. Hemingway couldn't have devised a better end. Let it go."

"No! He may still be fighting."

"And if so, you will join him on the plate of those animals."

"I would rather do that than sit here like a coward!"

"We are not cowards. It takes great courage to do what we are doing. Greater courage to sacrifice yourself like Somervell did." Wolfe let Lia loose for he felt her intensity slacken in his arms. "Besides, I will need your feistiness and skills for the rest of this journey. I can't afford to lose you."

"Yes, Lia. We need you." Becky offered.

"Lia, we will need to devise a plan." Wolfe looked around at the group. "Let's sit here and eat. Megan, pull out the MREs. All, keep your eyes peeled on the horizon. We keep the wall to our backs. Lia, we need to discuss how you will lead the aides back through that vampire and zombie hellhole to Masada after we make contact with the black tribe. I need you to lead."

CHAPTER 16

"Ill-gotten treasures profit nothing, but justice saves from death. The Lord does not let the just go hungry, but the craving of the wicked he thwarts." Proverbs 10: 2-3

"If we die, you must carry on!"

"How would that be possible without you or Kellas?" Lia inquired with an air of sassiness.

"Look, I have faith that the Lord will lead me into the black tribe and back to Masada. However, if that proves to not be the will of God, you must carry on." Sam paused in speech; for internally, he reflected how far he had transformed spiritually since he had been banished to the island. Besides, in this empty world, he figured it represented his only hope. "You must carry the torch the best you can."

"What next then? Let me hear your plan!"

"Well, judging from the lack of traffic on this road, it should be a straight shot to the checkpoint." Sam Wolfe paused, then glanced at Whatley for affirmation.

"Yeah. Checkpoint at bridge down road." Whatley spoke as he longingly stared south toward home.

"Look, now seems a good time to head back through the War Park."

"Why? Tell me why!" Lia contemplated his suggestion, only to be overcome with revulsion. "Because they are probably eating Somervell! That why?"

"Lia, forget that. We are talking about survival. Now would be a good time. Period." Like any wild animal after a kill and feast, the pattern of sleep usually ensues. Lia had deduced his thinking quickly and correctly. Though horrid in thought, it would seem rational.

"You want me and the others here to forget about the man who raised us! Taught us! Made us!"

"Don't make it any more difficult. Move up through the park. Find a place in the ruins to rest for the evening. Then at dawn break for Masada." Sam Wolfe had begun to get frustrated with Lia who possessed feistiness which grew wearisome after a while.

"Fine. Then what about you?"

"Whatley and I will proceed to the checkpoint. I will trust in the Lord from there." Again, Sam ruminated upon his words of faith at times. Though he periodically questioned his new found devotion, based upon all he had seen since his arrival, Sam felt what he perceived as a calling. It had to be a calling from God. "If I am not back in a week or so, don't expect me. Otherwise, I will return with a contingent. Have Hamilton keep watch from the tower. I will build a fire by the Mormon temple, or signal you in some other manner so that you aides can emerge from the tunnel there. If things go wrong, maybe, just maybe, Masada won't be compromised."

"Fine. We will finish eating and begin moving north."

"And Lia," Wolfe appealed to her, "be a leader not a ranter. A time comes in life where we must transition. The other aides will need leadership."

———

Wolfe and Whatley boldly gamboled down the southbound road heading into Agat. Whatley armed with a knife similar to Wolfe, who also had Isherwood in his hand and his clawed shank hidden—tied by a slip knot around his neck dangling under his oversize, loose shirt. They both approached, bold as brass, for Whatley's standing in the tribe nearly assured him a warm welcome. Sam Wolfe looked down at his feet as he walked, reflecting on what felt like an absurdity waltzing into the black tribe stronghold. He had to assure himself that his brown skin would be one advantage, while returning Whatley home a most important second. He chuckled to himself as he spied a couple of tattoos on his arm due to their contradictory nature. His left arm had an anarchy symbol while his right had not only a Christian cross on one part, but a shamrock on the other. He laughed to himself at the absurdity of the contradiction but also realized how lost he had been just a few years ago—the mistake he made in trying to prove himself to his teacher which landed him here, all in contrast to the metamorphosis he had undergone since his tutelage from Kellas Somervell. It all seemed ludicrous to him as he ambled toward this hostile camp. While trying to impress his high school instructor, Mr. Moore, he had landed himself on an island with a greater teacher, Kellas Somervell, who bestowed the burden of God's plan of justice and retribution on him for this island. Yet, he accepted it all. As they approached the bridge, Wolfe could spot some frantic movement as the men prepared to greet, challenge, or kill the on-coming travelers. Judging by the less than smooth movements by the guards, Sam surmised that they did not receive many visitors.

"Long live Chenoweth!" Whatley blasted at full volume.

"State your business!"

"I am Whatley! I am home!" Sam Wolfe carefully scrutinized the men as they surveyed the situation. Still about fifty yards away as the men on the bridge remained hidden behind a protective barrier. "Who now stands on guard duty?"

"Huffer and Sawyer!"

"Good, it Whatley. I want to go home."

"Whatley has been missing for months! Come closer so we can see you."

"I know I am missing for months. I am home now, fool. Take me to Chenoweth and Charla!" Whatley began to grow in confidence as he got closer to the checkpoint.

"By God, wow. Whatley you are home!"

"Huffer, good to see you."

"Man, I will get relief." Now Whatley and Wolfe had closed in on the bridge and barricade. "I will walk you home." Wolfe scanned the area. The road running north-south parallel to the western coast of Guam crossed a river or a cut channel extending into the interior of the island. The black tribe closed off the bridge, guarding it with an overturned car and other flotsam and jetsam of the island. Next to this improvised barricade sat a hut that housed some of the tribe's warriors.

"My mother okay?"

"Man, Charla has been crushed since your party didn't return. We sent out warriors to find you and only found a couple of your bodyguards' bodies."

"Well, I am home, and I come with a friend." By now some relief soldiers emerged from the hut about fifty yards down the road to take over guard duty on the bridge.

"Who are you?" Huffer inquired of Sam.

"I am Sam Wolfe."

"Well, Sam Wolfe, I must disarm you if you are going to meet Chenoweth and Charla."

"Understood." Wolfe handed over Isherwood and his dirk lodged in his belt leaving the clawed shank around his neck in hopes it would pass for a necklace—out of sight, out of mind.

"How tribe doing?" Whatley asked.

"A bit crazy man. We are glad you are back." Wolfe glanced at the reticent Sawyer who held his weapons. Huffer looked at the relief soldiers from the hut, "You guys man the post until I return or you are relieved." They nodded and the party of four continued south on the road.

"What you mean crazy?" Whatley asked once they were out of earshot of the other warriors.

"Chenoweth has been worse than normal." Huffer eyed up Wolfe, scrutinizing him in an attempt to ascertain if he could divulge tribal secrets.

"You can talk. Wolfe good. He saved me and taught me. I am taking him to Charla."

"Well, Chenoweth has been crazy—bloodier than ever." The group moved unimpeded down the road into the center of Agat. Sam Wolfe found Agat amazing, for houses were still standing, people moved in and out, down the streets, through yards. This lifestyle represented a far cry from the pure anarchy where Masada rested. A sense of normalcy pervaded the scene. In their many talks back at Masada, Whatley had expressed to Wolfe that the village of Agat did operate with a sense of habit. Crops were grown, people fished, houses were maintained as best as they could. Compared to No Man's Land, where Barrigada and other ruined towns laid, Agat appeared to be a functioning city. The village order though had been maintained through the fear of their self-proclaimed king, who, with his inner circle of soldiers, ruled with an iron fist. Sawyer shared one disturbing aspect of the tribe that stemmed from the treatment of women—the few that existed. Whatley had shared this story with Kellas and Sam at Masada; with a ratio of one hundred men to one female, women were not only at a premium to the men, but they were at the wretched mercy of the men's will. As they walked, Wolfe recalled the conversation back at Masada with Somervell.

"How does Chenoweth prevent another Pitcairn Island?" Somervell inquired oblivious to the fact that Whatley would have no knowledge of the mutiny on the Bounty and the subsequent anarchy and violence, which resulted from fighting over the women.

"I didn't teach him about that historical incident." Wolfe informed Somervell.

"Ha-ha, well that historical reference has been lost." Somervell guffawed. "Whatley, how does Chenoweth keep the men from killing each other over the women?"

"Chenoweth keep ten women for himself and his private guards. He keep one just for himself. That be Charla."

"His very own Praetorian Guard and private harem." Somervell rubbed his chin. "How about the rest?"

"When new women come to island, Chenoweth take them, and put old girls into house near old school where Chenoweth live. Men visit those girls when they want."

"A free brothel. That would keep the men happy."

"Chenoweth's guards keep peace at house so no trouble. Men come and go all day long. If they cause trouble, Chenoweth make it so they don't want to visit women." Whatley made a cutting motion.

"Ingenious Sam." Somervell chuckled, "Abuse the harlots and you become a gelding."

"What do you mean?" Sam asked.

"He castrates them."

"Does that word mean he cuts off their..." Whatley had been cut off.

"Exactly young sir. Ha-ha, exactly." Somervell smiled. "It would appear that Chenoweth exhibits excellent control, though barbaric. Women's lib movement would be horrified." Somervell grinned a disturbing grin.

"When new women come, Chenoweth have feast in park across from building he live in. The old school like his castle. He sit in big chair at home plate of baseball field and have feast. He keep Topher and Quisno on chain to warn the warriors to behave."

"Quisno? Topher?" Wolfe asked.

"Quisno and Topher made Chenoweth angry when they bad with women. He keep them now to sing and dance. Quisno have pretty voice."

Sam reflected upon the brutal torture inflicted upon the aforementioned men, and the most important of factors concerning his mission to Agat— Charla hated Chenoweth and wanted him dead. Chenoweth, a Kurtzian ruler who would survive in any tribe of British colonial Africa or Borneo, here had sown the seeds of his own demise by falling in love with a woman. His passions would cloud his ruthlessness and offer Wolfe the window needed to complete God's plan.

Sam Wolfe sat in an abandoned classroom in the former elementary school that the tribe referred to as "the palace." The run down school, being the largest surviving structure in Agat, served as a symbol of power. Wolfe awaited the next step in the process, hoping against hope for a sign from the Almighty in any form that reveal to him a strategy for freeing the tribe. The assassination of Chenoweth seemed apparent, but the timing would prove delicate. Wolfe hoped that meeting with Charla, the proverbial queen, would shed light onto his plan of action. A shuffle outside his door, followed by the turning of the lock let Sam Wolfe know that the time had come. Whatley entered first, followed by the man Huffer, who he had met earlier, followed by a rather dignified looking and radiantly beautiful woman who could only be the Charla who had been discussed as Chenoweth's siren. Back in the United States, this Charla would be hailed as gorgeous; however, on an island of savagery with warring factions, cannibalistic zombies, flesh-eating vampires, and roving bands of murderers and rapists all wallowing in dilapidated and ruined infrastructure of a by-gone area, it served only to magnify her radiant attractiveness.

"So, you the man who saved my boy." Charla bore a mien somewhere between aggravated and gracious. "I suppose you want something for that."

"Not sure what you mean." Sam Wolfe demurely responded.

"Every man always wants something when he does a woman a favor."

"I am not sure."

"Forget it! You obviously haven't been on this island long."

"Not really. About nine months."

"My boy tells me you on a mission from God. Well Mr. Wolfe, look around; there ain't no God here on this island." Charla's level of agitation rose. "If God existed, Mr. Wolfe, he'd be here cleaning up this mess. We got women held as sex slaves, people being tortured, poor souls eaten by those crazy vampire bastards up the road, and your scrawny ass came here on a mission from God." Charla cocked her head downward, curling her lip upward. "Shit. You gonna get us all killed!"

"Well, I would love to spend time discussing all of the elements of my faith, but I have a sense that we are strapped for time." Though Wolfe's level of belief seemed tenuous at times, as if a house built upon sand, Charla's complete lack of faith actually strengthened his and provided him with resolve.

"You damn straight we strapped for time. Chenoweth going to want to meet you; he will have you on a chain as a prize. I don't know how much time we have anyway. The last I saw him, he said he had to sleep off a night of hard drinking. Good thing for all of us he won't let nobody disturb his sleep."

"Why will he want to kill me? I returned his son."

"Man, he don't care about that boy. He care about me. If I left this place, he would feed Whatley to the vampires. I just happened to be the favorite of his harem, the disgusting bastard." Charla approached Sam closely and lowered her voice. "Whatley tell me you come to Agat to kill that son of a bitch."

"Yes ma'am. I do believe in order to fulfill my mission, the Lord's work, I will have to remove him from power."

"By yourself? Ha! You a crazy bastard; he'll kill you and be drinking his wine out your skull."

"The Lord always provides."

"I guess you want me to get my gigolos to help."

"Gigolos?"

"Yeah, gigolos. You know that word?"

"I do. But what do you mean?"

"I mean my young warriors who, shall we say, offer me some relief from that funky bastard. They in their twenties, they healthy and strong, like this one," she hooked a thumb toward Huffer, "he one."

"How many young gigolos do you have?"

"Ten at the moment."

"Will they help?"

"Sure, they want that bastard dead too. They just waitin' for me to give them the signal. I'm too afraid of Chenoweth's inner circle of guards. They ruthless."

"Well Charla, you see, the Lord provides." This scenario caused Sam to reflect upon his religious studies on the island. All of the prophets and judges, no matter the tale, always had the pieces of their destiny fall into place according to divine intervention. All of this fortuitous information served to strengthen his faith and resolve. "I need some help in pulling this off. I now have ten young warriors, you, Whatley, and myself. All we need now would be a feast. I am sure you will have a feast or celebration for the return of Whatley right?"

"Damn straight and more than likely tonight." Charla looked over Sam's shoulder and out of the window across the school grounds to the baseball diamond, park, and ocean. "That sick bastard really going to feast tonight, but ain't because my boy Whatley home. An it sure ain't you comin' here he celebrating."

"What then?"

"That bastard got a new catch! His boys on patrol brought back a prize. He and his men be out of their mind with lust tonight."

"Why?"

"They brought back five teenage girls from the forest. Don't know where the hell they came from, but their lives goin' be turned upside down tonight."

CHAPTER 17

"My son, you are here with me always; everything I have will be yours. But now we must celebrate and rejoice, because your brother who had been dead, has come to life again; he had been lost and now has been found."
Luke 15: 31-32

Sam Wolfe accepted his escort down from the palace across a ruined block to the Agat city park, which offered a vast, verdant space between an old baseball field and the sea. Accompanying him were guards in hooded cloaks, which made it impossible to see their faces. As they made their way to the park and baseball field, Sam Wolfe saw what must have been a couple of thousand revelers gathered in the park for the feast to celebrate the return of Whatley and the gift of the girls. He could not help but also notice the majestic sea illuminated by the moon. Though Chenoweth had not placed Sam formally in custody, he felt the palpable grip that his Praetorian Guard lorded over him. Music being pounded out on some form of drums, singing bellowing out amongst the inhabitants, and the cavorting of scores of savages, all rallied themselves up for the prize of the evening. Wolfe felt sick to his stomach, not that he might kill a man tonight, not that he may be killed himself, but that he may not be able to save Kellas' five aides from a fate far worse than death.

The guards and Wolfe, along with indiscriminate others, approached the field and park allowing the full view of a rigged stage which sat near home plate and looked out over the field toward the sea. Upon the stage sat a throne where Chenoweth perched himself much like a rooster upon this dung heap of a village. More of his guards stood upon the stage along with two sickly looking men in loin cloths and of course Charla, attired in all of the traditional garments expected of a south Pacific woman. Crossing the street into the park, Sam Wolfe could see Chenoweth sitting upon his throne, tearing meat off a bone and holding a cup in his hand that upon closer inspection proved to be a human skull. As the crowd mingled and celebrated, directly in front of the stage stood a few guards holding a chain. Bound by the chain were the five aides that Sam Wolfe left at the naval base wall where he had hoped they would safely make it back to Masada. As he approached the raised platform near the girls, Sam regretted that he did not have Isherwood or his dirk but felt comforted that his clawed shank hung undetected under his shirt. Tied with a slip-knot, it offered Sam some comfort in possessing a weapon. He began to fret, not knowing what direction to take but decided to say a quick, silent prayer for guidance, allowing piety to provide a path. For in this dark world, it seemed apparent that a reliance upon faith would prove his best resource.

Chenoweth seemed oblivious to Sam Wolfe being escorted up onto the large stage with him, for he seemed consumed by beverage and meat. On the arm of his throne sat a shell attached to a chain which rolled out, split, then extended around the neck of two males who sullenly sat near his feet. Near the throne, standing with regal elegance, Charla awaited Sam Wolfe's arrival and, most importantly, his plan of action. The stage seemed complete for the recognition of Whatley's return and, judging by the fervor in the crowd as they jeered at the five bound aides, some sinister sort of ceremony. Chenoweth tossed down the bone he had been gnawing upon, grabbed the conch, and slammed it into Topher's chest. Topher, whom Sam recognized by the three fingers on one hand and two upon the other, picked up the shell, drug himself and the chain toward the end of the stage, and began to blow through the shell the long, muffled droning bass of alert, which began to settle the crowd into an obedient attentiveness. After three robust, Roland-esque blasts, Chenoweth stepped forward to speak.

"Welcome, welcome." He paused to receive his diminutive and obligatory cheer. "We are here to celebrate a very welcomed surprise. We have found five young dames willing to join the ranks of our other ladies of the tribe whose sole job will be to make life on this hellhole tolerable." A roar from the testosterone filled audience. "They are young! I will share them with you tonight!" More cheers. "To celebrate, I will have Topher dance." He took the shell from his hand then smacked him lightly on the head.

Topher then began to dance out on the stage in some bizarre choreography that reflected a South Sea Islander touch without any proper instruction. Topher valiantly danced with the alacrity of a poor soul attempting to please; however, Chenoweth's patience when reached, yanked the chain around Topher's neck, flinging him to the ground. Chenoweth howled into the night, walked over, then kicked Topher in the abdomen, howling again. Sam Wolfe remembered the conversation he had had with Whatley about the treatment of Topher and Quisno. Chenoweth had a policy that after every poor performance, he cut off a finger and once all gone, he cut off the head of the poor soul. Topher's dancing days were numbered. He lay there on the ground, curled into a ball wishing he had a God to pray to for help and guidance.

"Alright. Alright." Chenoweth bellowed, and the crowd, already subdued by the abuse of the dancer, became quiet. "Before we all begin meeting our new female guests, I want to introduce you to the guest of honor, Sam Wolfe, who found, saved, and returned my son, Whatley, back home to his kingdom. For that, I will grant him one wish." The crowd roared; Chenoweth grinned, "But first, a song." Quisno quickly jumped to his feet. "Sing that rainbow song, and sing it good!" Quisno cleared his throat and started to his best ability, even under the strain, to sing "Somewhere over the Rainbow," a repulsively antediluvian and ironic song request for such a devilish leader. Chenoweth sang along in a diabolical undertone as he watched the young bard sing in the girlish voice of a castrato. As Quisno hit the crescendo of the nearly century and a half old song, Chenoweth crept up behind him and punched him in the kidney, dropping him to the floor in a crumpled heap. Chenoweth laughed his sinister laugh, and the crowd raucously huzzahed the senseless violence, for the quicker that their leader had his sadistic pleasures fulfilled, the sooner the five new instruments of entertainment could be passed around the herd.

"Now that the entertainment has completed its job," Chenoweth addressed the crowd as he held up the shell, "we must get on with some formalities.

Whatley has come home, and we have Sam Wolfe to thank." He held out the shell. "I give you the cornucopia."

"Thank you." Sam Wolfe held the conch shell thinking to himself that Chenoweth's ignorance must rival his brutality.

"I would like to offer you a wish, Sam Wolfe, for bringing back my boy Whatley." Sam Wolfe glanced around the stage. Chenoweth's two escorts stood near, Charla hung next to the throne, the minstrel and jester crawled toward the throne, and two hooded guards posted watch on each side of the stage. The girls, corralled in front of the stage, looked terrified and fearful of their own fate and equally melancholy over the fate of Sam Wolfe, for they knew what he had planned to request of the black tribe and judging by the crass brutality of its leader, no assistance would be forthcoming. "Tell me your wish!"

"Chenoweth, great king, as one who has studied the Constitution of the United States and has been recently schooled in the rights and freedoms that the institution of America should provide to its citizens, the state of living upon this island impels me to raise an army for a revolt. A revolt for better living conditions. A revolt for protections from anarchy. A revolt for the well-being of the incarcerated of this island." Chenoweth stared at him in disbelief; Charla bore a countenance of trepidation at the wrath to come. "I request that you, Chenoweth, with all of your power and your mighty warriors, raise your army and lead with me a revolution to exact better treatment from the government of the United States of America for the inhabitants of Guam." Chenoweth rose, snatched the shell from Wolfe, and held it up as he scoffed at Sam Wolfe. Sam anticipated the answer, but he felt he must exhaust all of his options.

"I laugh at your proposal." The crowd began to jeer Wolfe. "I laugh for I do not see any of the terrible things which you describe." He roared a hearty laugh. "We have food! We have drink!" He raised his skull mug into the air followed by a leg of some animal. The crowd cheered. "And, we have women!" At this last, as Chenoweth pointed toward the five aides hogtied awaiting their doom, the crowd erupted in such a tumult that several minutes passed, and Chenoweth had to blow a blast upon the conch to bring them back to order.

The king then walked toward Sam Wolfe, kicking Quisno and Topher who still lay prostrate on the ground, and brushed by him toward the edge of the stage.

"Now, I said that I would offer you a wish, but I never said that I would grant it." Chenoweth raised his arms like a deranged evangelist and swayed back and forth as if in a drunken stupor. "Guards!" The two hooded figures seized Sam Wolfe by the arms; the crowd roared. "I don't take too kindly to outsiders, especially those new to the island, coming to my camp, my tribe, and telling me what to do—especially when that idea possesses all the marks of insanity." Sam felt his faith strained. Surely, if Kellas' plan had God's blessing, all wouldn't unravel now. "Revolution indeed. You revolt when life has become unbearable! When you can't find any meaning in life. When you are abused and oppressed." Chenoweth turned and scanned the stage, viewing Sam Wolfe held between two hooded guards, along with two more standing akimbo on either side of his throne with his queen Charla in all her magnificence, and the poor minstrel and jester still huddled in pain. "Have him show some respect!" The right guard delivered a harsh blow to the kidney of Sam who proceeded to buckle and collapse to his knee, followed by a swift kick from the left guard knocking the wind out of Wolfe and convulsing his body with pain.

"Not looking so high and mighty now, my friend, eh? Coming in here with your highfalutin ideals. What shall we do with him?" Sam Wolfe bowed his head in dejection as he violently attempted to regain his breath so preciously lost. Flummoxed as to his next move, since he felt that not only had civility abandoned him, but also his ideals, faith, and cause. Before him he saw five innocent girls at the mercy of this tribe—a mercy they would not survive—an impossible situation for himself, all of his own manufacturing with neither a sign nor an idea for hope. Chenoweth, as he stepped to the front of the stage, once again thundered, "What shall we do with him?"

"Eviscerate him," the crowd responded.

Sam, facing the crowd upon his hands and knees, hung his head so low he could see the throne and guards, though the vision presented itself upside down. The crowd had erupted in some indiscernible chant that Sam Wolfe felt

sure offered him no satisfactory conclusion to his life. Wolfe, with end imma-
nent, closed his eyes and offered a prayer for the girls and begged forgiveness
for failing in his mission of retribution and civilization for the islanders. His
faith being galvanized and certain, he felt no remorse for the end of his life,
only in the failure of the Lord's work. At the conclusion of the intimate prayer,
Sam Wolfe opened his eyes still on his hands and knees, still lugubrious, still
feeling his clawed shank hang from his neck laying on his loose shirt. As he
continued to gaze backwards, listening to the crowd chant for his destruction as Chenoweth verbally encouraged them, Sam Wolfe witnessed a peculiar
and bizarre vision. The guard nearest to the throne stepped back out of the
peripheral vision of the other guard. He reached up, flipped off his hood,
then opened and dropped his robe. Standing upon the stage, absolutely naked
minus a pair of Roman sandals with a gladius and scutum knotted about his
neck like the Ancient Mariner's albatross, stood Kellas Somervell in all of his
resurrected glory. An explosion of adrenaline surged through his body; Sam
Wolfe prepared for action; for deliverance had manifested itself. The Lord's
will would be done.

Kellas Somervell, pulling the gladius and scutum from his neck, bolted,
naked as a Pict, in a gallop toward Sam Wolfe's position. The last statement
that Sam heard Chenoweth utter as he cocksuredly bellowed oblivious to the
tumult of destruction heading his way came in the form of an absurd question, "Should I give him the cornucopia and grant him a last request?" With
the stealth of a warrior, yet easily masked in the crowd's din, Kellas Somervell
charged, raised the gladius and hacked down hewing the guard's left arm
asunder. With lightning quickness, Kellas squatted in a karate stance and
thrust his gladius through the befuddled abdomen of the second guard. Chaos
ensued upon the stage as the first guard howled in terror; his brachial artery
had been severed and blood exploded from his wound as he rolled around in
the panicked throes of death. Kellas pulled the Roman short sword from the
recently smote guard who had put his hand to his wound and buckled to the
ground. As Somervell turned backwards to challenge the armed guard who
moments ago casually stood next to the throne, Sam Wolfe reached under his
shirt and yanked free his clawed shank, jumped from his crouched position

like a track athlete exploding from the blocks, and attacked Chenoweth who by now had turned with arms still spread like Christ upon the Cross from his glorious taunt of a moment ago to a now pathetically exposed position. Sam Wolfe plunged his clawed shank into the belly of Chenoweth and unseamed him from the nave to the chops. As Chenoweth plunged to his knees, the shock of his landing dislodged his viscera all over the stage as Sam Wolfe grabbed the shell out of his lowering and perplexed hands. Wolfe placed his hands up into the shell and utilized it as a naturally-constructed weapon. Driving the crushing coup de grace upon the side of Chenoweth's face grossly distorting the ovalness of the cranium. Kellas Somervell charged the approaching guard and blasted him in the chest with his scutum then drove his gladius to the hilt through his neck. Club-wielding guards who Wolfe recognized as the gigolos of Charla now charged the stage. Sam raised the conch to the heavens in the hopes of silencing the crowd. He blew into the conch and prayed. Prayed that this would not be the end.

CHAPTER 18

"We will have no truce or parley with you or your grisly gang. You do your worst, and we will do our best."
Sir Winston Churchill to Adolf Hitler - 1941

As the crowd began to push towards the stage in a frightened and furious flurry, Sam Wolfe, filled with trepidation, called to Charla and Whatley to calm the crowd. From all directions, armed men surged upon the stage and in front. Sam Wolfe stood terrified alongside the naked Kellas Somervell who, with perfect equanimity, prepared to accept his fate. Surely, the path the Almighty put before them wouldn't end here with an ignominious death at the hands of Chenoweth's lynch mob. Charla approached Sam, took the conch, held it up as the stage completed the course of its filling. All of the armed warriors stopped behind Wolfe and his contingent and continued to surround the approach to the stage shoulder to shoulder leaving only room for Kellas, Sam, Charla, and Whatley. All stood in or around the gore and offal of the eviscerated Chenoweth and his three deceased comrades. When the soldiers had completed filing in, Charla lowered the conch and spoke to the huddled and hushed masses.

"Fear not all! This man, Sam Wolfe, has traveled far and trained long to come here and rid us of Chenoweth." In the quick, but decisive coup, a score of men or so had been immediately struck down when attempting to come to the aide of Chenoweth. However, when the masses witnessed Chenoweth disemboweled and Charla upon the stage, the crowd had quickly become subdued—more from curiosity than conviction; for in this world, loyalty proved fleeting and fickle. Sam looked as a bit of shuffling took place and six men were pushed to the front and dropped to their knees. "These men before you are all that remains of Chenoweth's guards. Today starts a new chapter for this tribe." The crowd cheered. Charla whispered, "Say something to the crowd." Then she handed Sam the shell.

"Greetings!" He held up the conch. "I am Sam Wolfe. I mean this tribe no harm; I do not wish to rule, only to educate. Let this conch remain the symbol of civility, which it has represented for generations. I will lead if called upon and willingly serve if needed. My destiny need only be servitude and liberation." He handed the conch back to Charla who then passed it promptly to Whatley.

"You listen to Sam Wolfe. He good. He save me from zombies. He save me from vampires. He come from God. He make my dream come true. I dream that we get one day to live a nice life without all the killing. Sam Wolfe good for tribe." He handed the conch then to Charla who understood the cheapness of life on the island and the value of pleasure. The loathing for Chenoweth and desire for entertainment would easily distract the herd from the tumult of the fight. A fight which claimed lives once again in front of her people. A fight which clearly toppled the hierarchy of power in the tribe. A fight which now needed her people to have a vented, emotional release.

"Now, y'all can feast. Enjoy and behave."

———

In the palace, the former lunchroom of the school had been converted to a banquet hall. Charla had all of the members of the coup d'état gather for a dinner and powwow to discuss the next move for this impromptu govern-ing council. Kellas Somervell sat with his aides who needed comforting after the day's traumatizing ordeal. Sam Wolfe sat with Whatley when Charla and members of her gigolo troupe entered with her. The modest food and austere setting reminded Sam of Masada and offered him far more comfort than the exposed feeling of being in the park with the entire village. Nine men came in and sat around the table to prepare to eat; a tenth, a tall, fully black dignified looking man of about thirty with afro and glasses stood next to Charla. With an overpowering impression of gravitas, he moved to the head of the table.

"Hello. For our new guests, I am Keiondre. Mr. Wolfe and Mr. Somervell, I am glad you arrived when you did. Bravo for your exploits today. I am the leader of a small band of men who were bent upon revolution. Charla and I had been setting the stage and planting the seeds of insurrection. We sought only a catalyst. Thanks again gentlemen; you enabled my vision to come to fruition."

"I call them my panthers." Charla smiled. "I have been assembling them for years for this task."

"Indubitably." Keiondre maintained his stoic demeanor. "Charla approached me a couple of years ago and asked me to help her overthrow Chenoweth. My task lay in the realm of assembling enough," he paused and coughed, "healthy, strong, virile men whom she could trust and who would be loyal."

"Well, you can't have no revolution with weaklings."

"Indeed."

"Well, Keiondre got them all together. We have been plannin' the right time for a while now. We only stopped because Whatley got taken. I didn't care no more. Then you," she grinned at Sam Wolfe, "brought my boy home to me, and I jus' knew you would be the one to lead us to the Promised Land." Sam Wolfe, gratified at this news, knew that his mission to mobilize this tribe to action against the Great Wall of Guam and the Andersen Air Force Base would prove a bit easier than he anticipated for at his feet lay a tribe of lost sheep.

"Distinguished guests, I would like to introduce you to my coterie of revolutionaries." Keiondre began to walk around the table and tap the men as he circled and described them. Nine in all, not counting Keiondre, the following were introduced: Greco, Brennan, McCormick, Hoffart, Boitnott, Hoffman, and Sanders, along with Huffer and Sawyer who Sam Wolfe had already met.

The men had been secretly recruited by Keiondre's cunning and Charla's insatiable beauty.

"You guys were something else on that stage. You gave that pathetic fool Chenoweth what I been wantin' to do for years. The sick bastard."

"A most impressive plan, Mr. Wolfe. I must admit my level of enrapture at your coordination with Mr. Somervell in his brilliant disguise and emergence at the proper moment."

"I didn't." Sam did not finish.

"Ha-ha!" Somervell guffawed. "He never knew of my presence!"

"Correct. In fact, due to the helter-skelter nature of it all, I have yet had time to inquire as to how Kellas came back from the dead."

"Came back from the dead?" Charla inquired.

"Yes. The last I saw Kellas, he had a contingent of vampires surrounding him in the park. He told us to run as he prepared to meet his end." Sam still sat mesmerized by the emergence of this enigma from the eternal depths of death.

"Indeed. Well, all present here I feel are distinguished people; never underestimate the tenacity of an octogenarian with adequate martial arts skills, a Roman gladius and scutum, a will to fight to the last, and the Lord Almighty on his side."

"No doubt, Kellas, but how did you escape?" Wolfe continued to press.

"Well, I fought those scallywags for a while and inflicted considerable damage upon them. The pell-mell struggle continued through the woods and back towards the sea as I attempted to lead them away from you and put the ocean at my back for defensive purposes."

"How did you get away!" Charla blurted out.

"Well, before I could make it out of the woods, one of those Grendel-esque creatures leapt onto my back from a hovering limb and sunk his teeth into my shoulder." Somervell, dressed in the hooded robe of Chenoweth's guard he had apparently killed prior to taking the stage, pulled the shoulder over to reveal the bite marks and missing flesh. "Well, I panicked. Death no longer looked glorious. Ha-ha. I realized that I would be dinner if I stayed much longer, so after I sent my faux vampire off to meet St. Peter at the pearly gates, I dove into the sea. I guess those tree-hugging ghouls do not swim much. That or they learned I packed a punch, but either way, they let me go."

"How did my sword hold up?" Lia, along with the other aides, who had been terrorized and taciturn, spoke up.

"Brilliant, Lia. Absolutely brilliant."

"How did you end up on the stage then Kellas? How did you get into the camp?"

"Easily into the camp. I floated with current out at sea down towards the naval base. I can tell you dragging the weapons in the ocean proved a difficult task, but I made it. Now, I knew I could not swim around the base; I came ashore since I knew I had cleared the park. A bit of an awkward walk down past the naval base to the whistles of the soldiers patrolling the wall. Ha-ha. Not every day you see a naked man wielding a gladius and scutum." Somervell had now become fully enthralled by his story. "After I passed the naval base, I thought I would maintain the benevolence bestowed on me by the sea, so I waded out into the water and slowly drifted down the coast awaiting night fall."

"A well-devised plan, Mr. Somervell." Keiondre applauded.

"Well-devised my naked arse, sir! Ha-ha. I trusted the Lord would provide a pathway. And a pathway he did. While I floated gently up to my neck in the sea, I passed the bridge and noticed to my chagrin that your tribe, Mr. Keiondre, had my girls."

"My tribe, sir, but certainly not my men."

"Well, my mission seemed self-evident at that moment. Save my aides or die trying."

"How did you manage to position yourself up on the stage in a guard's robe?"

"Well I will tell, Mr. Keiondre, the last thing a man expects as he stands in the surf urinating into the sea would be a naked man running a sword through his bread basket before he can bring his hands up to fight." Kellas chuckled. "After taking the robe and pushing the body out to sea, I meandered and drifted into the crowd." Kellas, in his element detailing his saga, perused the crowd certifying that all still paid attention. "I quickly realized that I didn't just kill anyone, but some highly respected warrior. I had the hood on initially to cloak my identity, then realized the medieval monk look proved the norm. So I sashayed up toward the girls, then the stage when I realized what the night's events may be and that young Sam Wolfe may need my assistance. As to the rest, you all witnessed."

"An impressive odyssey, Mr. Somervell. I commend you for your cunning and thank you for your temerity."

"How are your weapons, Mr. Somervell?" Lia followed.

"They may need a sharpening and definitely a cleaning. They have hacked a tremendous amount of flesh this very day."

"Well, I must say," interjected Sam Wolfe, "I thought we were all dead when Keiondre and his men stormed the stage with the scores of men."

"All part of the plan," the guard Huffer offered. "We had been instructed to round up ten to fifteen trusted haters of Chenoweth."

"That proved easy," Sawyer continued.

"Yep. We were to wait and watch for a signal; the most obvious would be the killing of Chenoweth. While you did your work on the stage, me and the boys dispensed with a few of Chenoweth's finest men. That explains why the fight ended quickly." Huffer finalized. "Which reminds me, what on earth did you gut him like a pig with?"

"Well, when I began my journey, I thought my crude and rudimentary clawed shank had been modified and sharpened, but I feel that blacksmith may have greatly altered the weapon." At this comment he smiled toward Lia who sat proudly.

"If you call melting down that shoddy gardening tool and crafting you a hooked blade from stainless steel, fastening it to a spongy grip handle, and sharpening it on a whetstone to be as keen as a scalpel, then yes, I altered it." Smugly, Lia gloated.

"Like a scythe through wheat or knife through butter, it eviscerated Chenoweth like you were unzipping a jacket." Somervell offered as dinner continued.

"Well Mr. Somervell and Mr. Wolfe," Keiondre picked up the conversation after a brief pause, "what do you propose we do next?"

"Firstly, this tribe needs to have someone put in charge. A quasi-interim government to rule until after the revolution." Somervell offered.

"Revolution?" Keiondre asked.

"Yes. A revolution. Mr. Keiondre we plan to lead this island in a revolt, storm the Great Wall of Guam, and capture the air force base. From that moment, we can demand an establishment of civility on this island. If we are to be incarcerated for the remainder of our lives, we should be able to live in a modified society. Here, as the island stands, we live somewhere between anarchy and holocaust."

"Mr. Somervell, how do you plan to over-take an air force base and the wall's defense system which have stood impregnable for nearly fifty years?"

"Yeah, you crazy?" Charla exploded.

"Believe in Sam. Believe in Kellas." Whatley added.

"I promise to reveal all: plans, attacks, and methodology in due course. You have to trust us and in the Lord."

"Yes," Wolfe interrupted, "Like Somervell states, we have a plan, God's plan. However, you need an intelligent leader first." Wolfe placed the shell he had kept with him upon the center of the table. "People willfully follow and respect intellectualism. The weak succumb to ignorance. This conch shell represents law, order, and civility. Anyone who would call it a cornucopia represents the bottom of the intellectual barrel. This tribe had been ruled by a imbecilic madman."

"What do you think we should do?" Charla inquired.

"Put Keiondre in charge. He manifests all that a leader needs to be. Calm. Equanimous. Erudite." Wolfe finished. "He can lead the people in the revolution. With his leadership, we can rally this tribe, create a truce with the other two, then revolt."

"Though I am not uninterested in leading this tribe, for Charla and I have been planning our coup for a while, I am apprehensive about leading my people into a suicide mission against the military establishment of this island."

"Trust me Mr. Keiondre, the overwhelming force of the inhabitants of this island upon those walls will overcome any defensive system they have in place. The trick lies with unifying the masses."

"How do you plan on doing that?" Charla requested.

"We need to send a delegation to each tribe for a meeting." Somervell offered.

"We can call a truce and meeting at Execution Alley."

"Exactly, Mr. Keiondre. Exactly. Ha-ha."

"Bring in Erbskorn please, Boitnott." An awkwardly brown skinned yet blonde member of the dinner party leapt to his feet and moved out of the building at Keiondre's order. "I have all the reasoning for a gathering of the clans at Execution Alley." Boitnott quickly returned with a cloaked figure who had his hands knotted behind his back.

"What do we have here?" Kellas chimed in.

"Erbskorn. The leader of Chenoweth's private body guard." Keiondre explained. "We apprehended all six; you two killed the other four."

"Your plan?"

"We will take them to Execution Alley, so we can sever the remaining link to Chenoweth." Keiondre walked over to Erbskorn who stood cuffed and held by Boitnott who promptly spit upon Keiondre's shoes.

"You are no boy scout Erbskorn." Kellas offered.

"No sir, you aren't. Your years of sycophantic support of Chenoweth filled with murder and rape and abuse will be ending." Keiondre glanced around the room to emphasize the importance of his edict; then he continued, "Very soon you will have a first class journey followed by a first class execution."

CHAPTER 19

"But Saul, also known as Paul, filled with the holy Spirit, looked intently at him and said, 'You son of the devil, you enemy of all that be right, full of every sort of deceit and fraud. Will you not stop twisting the straight paths of the Lord?'"
Acts of the Apostles 13: 9-10

The feast had all but broken up. After Somervell's five loyal aides decided to turn in for the evening, the trusted ten of Keiondre and Charla lost interest in the conversation since the girls had departed and one by one, the young men drifted off to bed. As the coconut rum began to run down and inebriation took its toll upon the revelers, the evening ended with Charla holding out to speak to Somervell and Wolfe alone. The night's conversation established a plan to assemble the warriors and travel to Execution Alley to exact justice upon the remaining Praetorian Guard of the late Chenoweth. Also, Keiondre agreed to send a delegation to the other two tribes in order to meet at Execution Alley for a summit on the possibility of an armed insurrection against Andersen Air Force Base. Besides the logistics being discussed of the pilgrimage up to A.B. Won Pat Airport in order to dispense justice, the panel of Keiondre and Charla, at the urging of Somervell, agreed to scour the woods of War Park while heading north and exterminate all of the so-called vampires; for others, such as Chenoweth and previous leaders, utilized that horde of barbarians as a buffer between the zones of each tribe. Kellas urged that civility, order, rule, and law cannot be maintained with elements such as that running amuck.

Furthermore, the force of warriors, which needed to be sizeable to carry out the mission, must also flush out and exterminate the cannibals, or zombies— the sobriquet bestowed upon them by Guam's inhabitants.

"You must promise me one thing, Somervell," Charla spoke up as Keiondre left, drunk, and headed for his new bed, which until last night served the needs of Chenoweth. "You must take care of the innocents. Don't let them engage in the fightin'." Charla had her mind on her son, Whatley, born on this island, fathered by Chenoweth.

"Agreed."

"I mean, I deserve to be on this rock. I shot my husband to death in his sleep." Charla seemed to turn lugubrious at the reminiscence. "I just kept shootin'. I emptied the clip." She paused and looked at the floor.

"What on earth provoked that?" Somervell inquired.

"We did drugs." Charla came to life again. "We smoked and snorted. But then, he got me pregnant. I tried to clean myself up. We started fightin' and he like to put his hands on me. One night while drugged up, he beat me like he never done before. I lost the child."

"Damn." Sam inserted.

"My life had been a wreck. Dropped out of school, took a felony drug charge. Fell into snortin', shootin', and smokin', but I tell ya, when I got pregnant, I woke up. I realized I had a child growin' in me. I needed to be a mama."

"Many lost men and women found themselves and established their purpose in life with the advent of a child." Somervell coached in his fatherly manner.

"When I lost that baby, I took to the drugs again. One night while he lay passed out, I got to thinkin' what he done to me, what he took from me, so I got his gun and unloaded a clip into him. Another felony drug charge for possession along with murder, well, you know what happen, bound for this hellhole."

"Sorry to hear that tale. Must have been difficult upon your arrival."

"Yeah, but it didn't take long for that sick bastard Chenoweth to find me. Made me his queen he would say. I realized that if I wanted to eat and be safe, I had to be his wife or girl or whatever he wanted." Charla paused in her tale to wipe a tear away. "But I gotta tell ya; I deserve to be here. I did my crimes; I do my time. But Mr. Somervell, my boy don't deserve to be here. He ain't done nothing. He a victim of my crimes, doomed on this island. He ain't the only one neither. There children all over this island born here who did nothin'."

"Indeed, Charla, indeed. My aides are all suffering the same fate."

"You gotta promise me, Mr. Somervell, that when all the fightin' happens, you keep those innocents out of it. They shouldn't have to fight and possibly die for the sins of their mothers and fathers. You let the men and women fight. You make them restore order on this island. They owe their kids. I owe Whatley. That's why I did what I did to find Keiondre and all those other boys. I make them happy. They do what I want; they protect my boy."

"Charla, I believe I can do one better." Sam Wolfe interrupted. Charla looked at him with a countenance of hope. "I plan on trying to get the innocents off the island! Especially, the young ones who haven't been completely corrupted."

"Well, God bless you if you do, Mr. Wolfe. God bless you." Charla smiled and looked up toward the ceiling, but clearly looked beyond. "God." She paused again. "You know, I done gave up on the Lord once I came to this island. Figure no God would let this happen to people no matter how bad we are. I grew up a Southern Baptist. My mamma sung every Sunday with a right powerful voice. I fell away from the Lord with the drugs. I tried to find the Lord when I come here. He never answered my prayers." She stopped and smiled. "Then I realized Mr. Somervell, Mr. Wolfe, the good Lord did answer my prayers. He sent you to save my Whatley. He just done it on his own sweet time. Well, the Lord works in mysterious ways."

"Miss Charla, I am truly sorry for all of the trials and tribulations that you have suffered in your young life. And you are correct, the Lord certainly moves in a mysterious manner." Somervell concluded.

"Well God bless you both. And I sure would be thankful, Mr. Wolfe if you did get my Whatley off this island. He don't belong here. Neither do those girls you call your aides, Mr. Somervell. They deserve to go to America too!" Charla appeared drained. "I am going to bed." She quaffed the remaining dram of coconut rum and careened off toward the door leaving Somervell and Wolfe to finish the evening alone.

"Ha-ha, Mr. Wolfe," Kellas began with his usual chuckle after Charla had left the room, "the Lord's plan seems to be coming to fruition. Now, do explain to me your plan for removing the innocents from the island."

"Simple." Wolfe had been considering this option for as Charla had stated and he already knew the innocents should not have to fight for their liberty. They should not have to possibly die for a modicum of civility to be imposed upon this island; furthermore, they should not have to endure this island, for none committed a crime for which they were damned to this penal colony. Wolfe felt it a stern obligation to remove them. "The way I see it, we need four armies. Three to form the Zulu 'Horns of the Bull' to attack the wall. The horns can circumvent the walls by sea, the head can pound the wall straight on."

"The fourth army Mr. Wolfe?"

"I will take the fourth army underground and emerge on the blind side. From there, I will lead the innocents to safety, to liberty, to freedom. When I get onto the wall and take selected honorary guests hostage, then I will have the eyes and ears upon me and our cause. The innocents will remain protected. The aides go with me."

"Well devised, Mr. Wolfe."

"Indeed Kellas. I have been studying the various options. This seems best, to overwhelm and breech the wall system with the mass of the islands tribal inhabitants. The military cannot stop the rush of 100,000 to 200,000 or so charging inmates."

"Where did you get that number?"

"We learned that in school. The estimated number."

"Sam, there aren't that many people on this island. Apparently school has failed you."

"Really?"

"The black tribe has been the dominant power for a few years now, in skill, numbers, and brutality. You saw that gathering tonight. With most of the tribe present tonight, I would venture to estimate their numbers between 25,000 and 30,000. You will be lucky to amass 75,000 people for this raid. The holocaust on this island has been far greater than presented back in the states."

"With what the Lord provides, we shall proceed."

———

The following morning Keiondre commenced to dispatch Huffer with an armed escort to the Hispanic tribe and McCormick with an armed escort to the ironically named white tribe—which ceased to be a majority white decades ago and therefore which a traveler would be lucky to find a purely white man due to the demographic amalgamation of the United States. The meeting at Execution Alley which would occur seven days hence afforded the envoys time to travel to and fro and the tribes then to move in the direction of A.B. Won Pat Airport. Upon the return of Huffer and McCormick from their respective missions, they reported to Keiondre that indeed both tribes would not only send representatives to discuss the truce, but also would have justice of their own to dispense upon a few poor souls of their own villages.

"In the past, tribes generally only send a delegation of fifty or so men to Execution Alley." Keiondre spoke on the evening his envoys returned. "I propose sending one thousand."

"Why so many?" Charla asked as she looked about the banquet table, which contained all of the men and five young ladies that it had on the night of the coup d'état.

"Simple. In order to execute Somervell's plan of clearing out the vampires from War Park, we need a line to sweep through leaving no tree untouched or hole unearthed they could hide in missed."

"Brilliant, indeed Mr. Keiondre. We shall discover their true numbers, the barbarians."

"Exactly. A thousand warriors will sufficiently flush out and cover that park. Furthermore, in the days following the revolution, we can make strategic use of that jungle's resources instead of wasting it."

"Did you tell the other tribes you were bringing that many soldiers? Won't they feel threatened?" Wolfe inquired, extremely concerned. "This meeting will prove a delicate negotiation giving what we are asking—armed insurrection against the military."

"Precisely. They will feel threatened. I will share with them our deeds in clearing out the vampires and zombies, demonstrate our superior numbers, but in a display of benevolence, I will allow them to negotiate unmolested or influenced by our numbers."

"Ha-ha, Mr. Keiondre. You are, as I stated before, brilliant. What did you do in the real world?"

"I worked for the government. Low level, internationally." He paused to reflect. "Let us just say that I sold some military secrets of which I caught wind and thought that I could profit. It just so happened that the contact proved to be an agent, a sting. They got me on three felonies, thus three strikes."

"How do you plan on feeding the army on the march?" Wolfe inquired more concerned about the future and less about the past.

"Every man will start the journey with two MREs. Every time the new convicts are released through the naval base, if we chose like we did in the past to cut them down, we took their allotted food. Also, over the years, I guess religious groups back home in the States would get to the government and would send a relief shipment."

"I have witnessed those drops over the years."

"Yes, the Mormons and the Catholics loved to send Bibles, Books of Mormon, MREs, seeds, and farming manuals. You know what they never realized?" Keiondre did not wait for a response. "Every time they made that drop to save us, hundreds if not thousands of convicts would be mutilated and killed trying to fight and secure those essentials for life. They always dropped them at A.B. Won Pat Airport, right in the middle of all three tribes." Keiondre smiled. Sometimes they would drop conch shells, parliamentary procedures, and the book *Lord of the Flies*. I don't know if they were attempting to help guide us or patronize us. I confiscated both books and hid them in my possessions for a long time; a man with a book turns into a man with a bull's eye on his back on this Godforsaken island."

"Why?"

"No one likes the educated here—only the barbaric."

"Will two MREs be enough?"

"Probably not. What we will do after the army leaves will be crucial. I will have teams of people set up stations along the road and up beyond the naval base toward War Park. They will be porters moving food up from our farms and fish pens. We will keep them fed."

"Impressive! Indeed impressive, my dear boy. A veritable Sherpa service train. How apropos! As if we are conquering another Everest. Kellas and Somervell would be proud."

"Excuse me. Aren't you Kellas Somervell?" Charla blurted out. "You talk like you are two people."

"Ha-ha," Kellas's guffawing continued, "My mother didn't name me; I did. I took the name while on the island."

"You gave yourself a new name? Why?"

"Charla, the first few years here I fought depression. I saw awful sights. I bore and endured brutal hardships, then I found the Lord and he led me to Masada."

"Masada?"

"Yes. When we finish at Execution Alley, Keiondre, Charla, and the rest of this company will all journey with me to Masada; my redoubt against the malevolence of anarchy for these forty years."

"A re-what?"

"A fortress or citadel, Charla." Keiondre informed. "A castle if you will."

"Ah indeed Mr. Keiondre, indeed. There I have studied, have prayed, and have become a new man. I built a vast library, established the house of God, raised these five young ladies and seven others. I learned what great works can be wrought upon this island, this planet, if a man willingly puts forth a noble and glorious effort." He smiled at the audience for he generally enjoyed speaking to any gathering. "When I felt that indeed I had become a new man, I followed in the footsteps of my heroes George Orwell and St. Paul. I took a new name."

148

"Who are Somervell and Kellas then?" Keiondre asked as the table listened intently.

"Two great men who helped George Mallory ascend to the heights of Mount Everest. Two great Brits who endured untold hardship and misery in the World War I and then dedicated their lives, without fanfare, without notoriety, to help the English achieve the unthinkable in the 1920s, to set foot atop Mount Everest. How apropos that I am in a quest to help young Sam Wolfe lead a revolution in which he hopes to capture and confront the man who threw him onto L.O.F.I. A man named Murray Mallory Moore. What about fate and destiny now my comrades. Ha-ha!" Sam brooded upon the subject of faith as Kellas exalted the divine path he perceived as placed before him. Wolfe periodically wavered. However, when he would confide this in Kellas, Somervell would remind him of countless saints who deliberated over the same matter in every century. Sam, a religious neophyte, proved no match for Somervell's powerful persona.

Kellas Somervell raised his glass. "The Lord indeed, though he works in mysterious ways, provides bread crumbs to strengthen our faith along the way!" Somervell nearly exploded with pride and piety. That type of inner strength and gravitas had served him well lately as he fearlessly battled overwhelming odds at his advanced age. All of this dialogue only strengthened the faith and the mission in Sam Wolfe and rejuvenated a sense of religion in Charla.

"Mr. Somervell, like Orwell and St. Paul, I suppose you had a less than adventurous name."

"Indeed I did. Indeed I did." Somervell raised his glass. "Tough to do the Lord's work and bring civility and order to an island of anarchy, savagery, and cannibalism with a name like Don Lynn!"

CHAPTER 20

"After this the Lord appointed seventy-two others whom he sent ahead of him in pairs to every town and place he intended to visit. He said to them, 'The harvest will be abundant but the laborers are few; so ask the master of the harvest to send out laborers for his harvest. Go on your way; behold, I am sending you like lambs among wolves."
Luke 10: 1-3

Much to the surprise of some and chagrin of others, Kellas Somervell led the army of the black tribe, wearing nothing but his gladius and scutum, up former Highway One for the eleven mile jaunt to Hagatna before the turn eastward and the remaining four miles or so into Barrigada. The afternoon prior, the thousand-man march left Agat, paraded past Guam Naval Base and camped around the Guam Veteran Cemetery a few miles beyond. Setting up night watches and perimeter guards, the majority slept in comfort as the warm sea breeze fanned the army. Prior to dawn, the black tribe split the army into their pre-arranged platoons. Kellas convinced Keiondre to camp at the cemetery to make use of the intersection of Highway One and Highway Six—the two roads which enveloped War Park, the home of the vampires. Each of Charla's ten loyal men—Keiondre being substituted by Kellas Somervell—led a large platoon which stretched from one road to the other in order to move through the bush and jungle so that the vampires could be flushed out and exterminated. With Greco, Brennan, and McCormick taking their respective platoons up the right flank on Highway Six; Hoffart, Boitnott, and Hoffman moving up the left flank near Highway One; the remaining four—Sanders, Huffer, Sawyer, and Somervell—moved up the gut through the heart of the jungle and bush. With nearly sixty men per platoon, Keiondre's forces projected a powerful fan of six hundred men slowly moving in a line, pushing, walking, stalking, and killing anything in its path.

"We are prepared to move out!" Kellas Somervell bellowed as he stood atop a large stone wall surrounding the cemetery and addressed the command structure of the army. "Remember what I told you: keep contact with the line. Make sure your platoon when in the line keeps contact with their right and left flank. The line will be flat or straight when we begin. However, as we move, the line will begin to arc on the ends turning into the letter C and then into an O." Kellas paused, looked around, and feeling that all were not completely clear on the instructions, continued, "Greco!"

"Yes, sir!"

"Greco, you are the far left flank on Highway One."

"Exactly."

"You, I mean you personally, must be the man closest to the ocean. Your job will be to walk faster causing your platoon to begin to bend upwards. You will be able to move quicker than the center, for you don't have to contend with the bush or jungle."

"Roger that." Greco continued.

"Now, Boitnott!"

"Here!"

"Your platoon will be the far right flank heading up Highway Six. You, too, will personally be on the most eastern edge of the line moving quicker and pulling your line up the road."

"Right."

"Now, Brennan and McCormick on the left flank and Hoffman and Hoffart on the right, you will notice your platoon bending upward and getting ahead of the center of the line. No problem." Kellas hopped down and began drawing in the dirt wondering why he hadn't thought of it earlier. "After a couple of hours of a slow march up the road and all points in between, Greco, you and Boitnott should come face to face somewhere around the intersection of Six and One. At that point the enemy will be encircled—sitting ducks. Then we must only march inward, closing the circle, and killing everything in the middle. When we restore civilization on this island, these animals would be beyond hope having lived on human flesh. Jesus may have saved prostitutes, lepers, and tax collectors, but he surely didn't save cannibals."

"Brilliant plan, Kellas!" Keiondre applauded. "You were a military man back in the States I presume?"

"No. A welder forty years ago though."

"How do you know all of this military strategy?"

"I have been reading plenty, my friend. This type of move has been utilized by armies stretching from Alexander the Great to Genghis Khan to Napoleon and Patton. I am going off the books my friend." Somervell concluded, "Any questions?" None.

———

As Sam Wolfe marched behind Kellas Somervell's platoon accompanied by Keiondre—who wished to be part of the action—the men observed how in both directions the troops stretched through and out of the jungle in a bowed line of club-wielding warriors. From their angle, Wolfe and Keiondre observed how the bow began to develop and take on the shape of the circle as Somervell had instructed. The six hundred men cut a low swath through the bush and jungle, periodically flushing out vampires causing them to run north to escape the advancing army, completely oblivious to the devious encirclement being perpetrated upon them. As the men tramped through the bush, Kellas, without clothing again, dropped back to address Keiondre as they marched. If the men of the army had not rallied behind the octogenarian's leadership, or his combative prowess, then they certainly found humor and affability in his insistence on approaching combat like an ancient Celt.

"When the two ends meet at the intersection," Somervell addressed Keiondre, "your raw army will experience a complete and utter victory which will build their confidence in their ability and trust in your leadership."

"Unfortunately, I have contributed nothing to this campaign. I am solely relying upon your expertise in this field. How will that build trust with my tribe?"

"Indeed, Mr. Keiondre. A good leader knows how to field an army and chose a military leader; that constitutes leadership. With our inevitable victory today, your trust shall be established."

"I suppose you have a plan for attacking the wall?"

"All in good time, Mr. Keiondre, all in good time. One battle a day, sir!" At that, a stir came first down the left flank, followed by the right flank; the ends of the line, Greco and Boitnott, had met at the intersection. Following Kellas Somervell's instruction, when the two points connected, they were each to convey by word of mouth back down the line that contact, thus encirclement, had been complete. Within minutes the buzz of the completed circle reached the ears of Somervell, Wolfe, and Keiondre. Kellas excused himself then moved back through his line and turned to the now circle of men who were within earshot. "Pass the word to the left and right, time to close the noose." Kellas looked at his men who all seemed eager for combat. "On my mark, pass the word, pinch and kill."

A murmur went down the band of men in both directions; Kellas Somervell, in the vanguard like the Arc of the Covenant, walked out in front of the enveloping circle of men so as to ensure first contact. Wolfe and Keiondre maintained about a twenty-five yard gap with their armed guards between them and the fighting force. Within five minutes, both men could see vampires frantically running away from the surge of men; within ten minutes, both men could see vampires spasmodically running toward the surge of men. As the vampires began to swirl like foam collecting on a drain as the water runs down, Wolfe and Keiondre could begin to see the far arc of the circle as the men began to move closer from their original six-foot gap all the way down now shoulder to shoulder. All in all, about fifty or sixty vampires were corralled in this manner as the six hundred club-wielding warriors of the black tribe moved in for the kill. Kellas became the first to make contact when a vampire charged him in panic—maybe he recognized Somervell from the previous battle—and Kellas deflected him with a thrust of his scutum.

The vampire, knocked to the ground by the blow, felt the wrath of clubs rain down upon his skull putting him quickly out of his miserable existence. A moment later, another charged Kellas, who took a knee and lifted his scutum, thus fending off the rush, which exposed the vampire's underbelly, allowing Somervell to penetrate the abdomen with his gladius all the way to the hilt. After this kill, Kellas allowed the circle to pass him as they pinned the vampires like naked mole rats together, shoulder to shoulder, where they were promptly bludgeoned to death in the most ignominious and sanguine manner.

———

Evening fell upon the black army as they settled in and around Paseo De Susana Park where Kellas Somervell, Sam Wolfe and the aides stopped and saw the diminutive Statue of Liberty again as they had on the way to Agat many days ago. That night, per the orders of Charla and Keiondre, the troops were to dine upon an MRE with the promise of fresh food once they vanquished the zombies in the Barrigada area near A.B. Won Pat Airport and Execution Alley. Kellas and Sam had been careful to have the aides avoid the carnage wrought upon the vampire peoples of War Park. After the complete envelopment of the two flanks, the encirclement had clubbed about sixty human beings to death much like any ancient barbarian raid. In a celebratory mood, Keiondre ordered and had delivered—via the Sherpa system of logistics he had established—two measure of coconut rum for each soldier. A prodigious effort had to be undertaken to deliver this reward, but all members of the war council knew it would only serve to further vivify the ranks to complete their morning task of warfare. As the troops sang and danced off in the distance, cheering their new benevolent king and queen, the war council considered their options in the upcoming days.

"Tell me Somervell, how do you plan on getting the other tribes to commit to attack that system of walls guarding Andersen Air Force Base?" Keiondre inquired as the group, including: Kellas, Sam, Whatley, Charla, and the platoon leaders, enjoyed a meal.

"Ha-ha. Quite simply sir, through fear. If these other two tribes do not join the cause right away, I will be sure to mention the enormous cache of weapons you are bound to acquire upon your victory. With guns and ammunition, their two tribes would not last a week upon this island."

"Tell me then Somervell, since I am playing devil's advocate; let us say the other two tribes decide that this mission of yours, to overrun this base, amounts to nothing more than suicide. The other two tribes sit it out; we are massacred; now they have another third of the island out of the way in which to rule."

"Indeed Mr. Keiondre, indeed a stupendous inquiry. However, let me dispel any notions of doubt. With our subterranean access, like today, we shall envelop the enemy in a different manner. Their attention shall be diverted by the chaos of fighting the internal infiltration by our sapper group. Then, we will breech the wall with grappling hooks and rope ladders. These weapons can be constructed rather easily by my aides at Masada."

"Sapper group?"

"Forgive my jargon, Mr. Keiondre." Somervell smiled, then looked about the group. "Sappers specialize in tunnels and trenches for undermining an enemy position. I shall refrain from the overuse of military terms."

"No problem. Now, what if your sapper group cannot get through the tunnel?"

"Mr. Keiondre, prior to my leaving on this journey to visit your tribe and help engender this coup, I navigated those tunnels and emerged on the other side of the Great Wall of Guam and Hadrian's Wall, out into a series of buildings on Andersen Air Force Base. I assure you that the American government's complacency stems from believing their fortress impenetrable."

"Also, I am afraid that I need some more convincing as to why we wish to embark upon this insurrection which will surely result in the deaths of many even if we are victorious." Keiondre soberly inquired.

"A little late to ask this?" Wolfe interrupted.

"Well," Keiondre interjected, "I got caught up in the killing of Chenoweth. Everything seemed so simple. Since then, I have had time to think matters through. I am a tad skeptical at the moment."

"Indeed Mr. Keiondre, indeed."

"Plus, this Sam Wolfe character here, going through all of this to what, get to a former teacher? I am beginning to question all of this Somervell."

"Peace, Keiondre, peace." Kellas calmed. "May I dissect that concern?"

"Please do. You are talking about a Herculean effort here."

"Firstly, you cannot want to live on this island with its perpetual and incessant anarchy. Though the inhabitants here have all committed their crimes and deserve to be removed from society, we can all agree that we should not have to endure this cruel and unusual punishment inflicted upon us by a government engaging in policies which run counter to the founding principles of the United States." Somervell gathered in his audience with his pause and gaze. "Secondly, a leading force must be established to construct a society here on this island, which contains quasi-civility. You are that force. Thirdly, if we lay the foundation of a civilized society, maybe the island of Guam will one day manifest itself as a modern day Australia—a former penal colony turned good."

"Okay. I can accept all of that; for as Charla and I have discussed, along with my council of nine here tonight, we determined that living under a tyrant like Chenoweth unacceptable. However, we could establish rules and just occupy the southern part of the island. We don't need to attack that wall, especially for this Wolfe character to confront a former teacher. We could retreat within our proverbial shell down south and be left alone."

"Please, Mr. Keiondre. Surely you do not want to subsist here on Guam with the perpetual responsibility of slaughtering those getting off the C-130s and pushed through the naval wall, or hoping to find warriors in those people tossed off the wall ceremonially over on the other side of the island." Kellas looked gratified for he felt his retorts had resonated with the audience. "Besides, if you had not wanted a better island, you would not have just led troops through War Park exterminating a tribe of barbarians. You wish for better."

"Well, what about this ludicrous scheme of Wolfe getting to his teacher? Doesn't sound like the good of the whole."

"Simple, Mr. Keiondre. In order for the demands of civility and order to be met, we must make the government of the United States, a government that revoked our citizenship despite it being our birthright, see that their policy here manifests an injustice. We are not demanding to be repatriated; we only request measures that will allow us to maintain civilization, such as a military presence on the interior of the island. We want to be able to teach and learn and build. This human endeavor can be found in the American Constitution which has been denied the inhabitants of this island."

"You still didn't explain this harebrained scheme of Wolfe confronting his former teacher."

"My dear Mr. Keiondre, in order to take that air force base, I need a team to circumvent its protection, the walls, and eliminate the firepower upon said wall. Sam Wolfe's sole purpose upon this island from the moment of his expulsion has been to stand on that wall. In three months, his former instructor will be matriculated from his honeymoon period as a probationary principal into the hierarchy which maintains the American social order. As a full-fledged principal, his instructor will have clout. And Mr. Wolfe will be there to meet him."

"What?" Keiondre palpably appeared vexed.

"I do not wish to expound upon the megillah of the power structure in the modern world. Suffice to say, America's quisi-utopian world exists as a pedagocracy. The public schools exist as the manifestation of big brother government. With that said, just know that it represents Sam Wolfe's only rationale for living. I need to take that wall in order to restore this island to the living; Sam Wolfe needs to take that wall to restore himself to the living. Have faith in the higher order of things Mr. Keiondre." Somervell paused. "Trust in the works of the Almighty."

CHAPTER 21

"Be careful to observe all my statutes and all my decrees; otherwise the land where I am bringing you to dwell will vomit you out. Do not conform, therefore, to the customs of the nations whom I am driving out of your way, because all of these things that they have done have filled me with disgust for them."
Leviticus – 20: 22-23

As the sun rose in the morning sky, Keiondre—followed by his armed contingent of bodyguards, along with Kellas Somervell and Sam Wolfe—led the six doomed prisoners, which included the recalcitrant Erbskorn, to the blocks located on the tarmac of Execution Alley. The thousand black tribe warriors lined the runway of A.B. Won Pat Airport for a full view of the impending execution of the Praetorian Guard of the late and eviscerated Chenoweth. The white and Hispanic tribes had also begun gathering with their much smaller coterie of soldiers and leaders. Keiondre's inner-circle of bodyguards escorted Charla and Whatley out in as much of a regal parade as their modest tribe could provide. The night prior, the leaders all met out on Execution Alley to discuss the formalities to follow. Keiondre and Charla formally introduced theirselves to the leader of the white tribe, James, and the leader of the Hispanic tribe, Collins. Kellas chuckled again at the irony of the names for hardly anyone in the white tribe actually had white skin. Similar to the Hispanic and black tribes, nearly all present manifested a swarthy hue of chocolate; the names had remained generationally.

Collins, the leader of the Hispanic tribe, upon his presentation to Keiondre, proved to be a man of limited intelligence and still more limited vocabulary. In conversation, Collins rarely moved beyond monosyllabic diction when expressing himself, demonstrating to Kellas Somervell that the black tribe indeed now would have an advantage being guided by an educated soul such as Keiondre. On the contrary, James, clearly a convicted sexual deviant or pedophile from the United States, frequently asked Keiondre and Collins if they had come into contact with any young women, or boys, they would be interested in trading. Sam Wolfe internalized a sense of nausea in the presence of Collins and James for he felt clear that their rise to the leadership of their respective tribes reflected all that he had learned in school from his teacher, Murray Mallory Moore, who incessantly proclaimed that if all ignorant and uncivilized people of the world were stacked together, they would stretch to the moon and back several times. If Wolfe's dream and plan came to fruition, Collins and James would be dead before the end of summer.

"I wish to extend my gratitude for meeting me here on such short notice," Keiondre offered to Collins, James, and their respective entourages. "Though my vaulting to leadership of the black tribe proved grievously bloody, I assure you that I wish to engender a new direction upon this island. I hope to establish a culture of peace and civility."

"Yo man, then why'd you bring all those guys with sticks?" Collins offered up with as much eloquence as he could muster.

"In a diplomatic gesture, I had hoped to establish a vision of the proverbial peace through strength. My warriors assembled are to demonstrate a new initiative upon this island." Keiondre and Kellas had rehearsed prior to the assembly the modicum of decorum that he should attempt to maintain. Keiondre, recognizing that he would be dealing with intellectually inferior leaders, decided to take a diplomatically moral high road while discussing any political matters with them.

"You know you only 'spose to bring about fifty men."

"Again, as I stated before, I wished to demonstrate the strength of my tribe but also the benevolence. Furthermore, we conducted a military campaign on the way here eradicating the vampires living in War Park."

"Did you take any women hostages? Or young?" James, licking his lips, inquired. The palpable perversion of this portly pedophile pervaded the group.

"No. The mission, purely seek and destroy, proved efficacious as we exterminated the nest. We wish to establish civilization upon this island. Furthermore, we are here to formally request your participation in the military activities, which will occur this July when the expulsions at the wall commence."

"Why'd we do that?" Collins asked in his best attempt at interrogation.

"Our armed insurrection and revolution will be for the establishment of a military contingent to be placed inside the walls to help maintain order or train a local, inmate-run security force. We wish to have an orderly release of prisoners into the island from the naval base to eliminate the slaughter that occurs monthly, and we would like assistance in agriculture to allow us to subsist upon our own farming endeavors. We, as a unified voice, will demand those rights guaranteed under the protection of the United States Constitution, the protections so unjustly stolen from us upon the heinous revocation of our citizenship and banishment to this lawless, anarchy-filled penal colony." Keiondre, speaking in the manner of a true statesman, unfortunately wasted his words upon the dull minds of Collins and James who had no business leading people or attempting to contemplate complicated societal philosophy; however, since they reflected the unfortunate pied-pipers of their own respective legion of followers, Keiondre found himself forced to try and rationalize with the intellectually inferior.

"You crazy, man!" Collins responded.

"I assure you gentlemen, that indeed, we are serious. Tomorrow, after our political executions, I wish to meet with your contingents again to elaborate upon the training, timeline, and logistics of the mission." At that Keiondre, Charla, and the inner circle turned and marched back toward the camp. Only Kellas Somervell and Sam Wolfe remained to face down the two dunces, Collins and James.

"Hey man, you with this guy?" Collins asked. "He crazy!"

"Ha-ha, indeed sir, indeed, we are with Keiondre. We led the coup d'état."

"Coup de what?"

"The black tribe revolution. We killed Chenoweth." Wolfe clarified.

"Can I ask a question?" James, who had yet to cease in licking his lips, scanned the area to where Keiondre and his coterie headed. "Who own them five girls?"

"No one owns anyone, especially my five aides." Kellas Somervell indignantly replied to James's outrageous insinuation. He choked down his revulsion towards the sexual deviant in hopes of finalizing a plan of cooperative attack upon the wall.

"They your aides. I trade you for them." James looked past Somervell and Wolfe in a most indecorous manner. "You like boys? Little boys?" At this proposition and spotting Sam Wolfe's visceral snarl, Kellas Somervell attacked James.

"Well Mr. James, I must warn you, your comments reveal a terrible perversion. Between your twisted predilections and this mental midget you have partnered with here, I can only surmise that your eradication and conquest at the hands of Chenoweth's tribe only did not come to fruition due to that late psychopath's laziness."

"Man you crazy." Collins stated then spit. "My tribe ain't helpin' you."

"The white tribe won't either." James scowled.

"After meeting the two of you, I can honestly state that your participation would not matter either way. However, I would like to leave you with this thought," Somervell paused. "When Keiondre's army takes that wall, overwhelms that air force base, and captures the cache of weapons, where do you think that will leave your groups in the aftermath?" At that hurling of his chutzpah, Kellas Somervell turned, followed by Sam Wolfe, and walked away.

As the white and Hispanic tribes did not on this particular morning have any societal deviant to execute—for their individual cases had resolved themselves before arriving at A.B. Won Pat—both of their delegations stood at attention as the six political prisoners of the black tribe took position upon the blocks in the middle of Execution Alley and prepared to meet their ignominious fate. The night before, Kellas Somervell had convinced Keiondre and Charla to allow Sam Wolfe and himself to conduct the executions. He felt it would help the thousand-man army to see the solemnity of their leaders observing but not committing the heinous act of execution. Though the killings seemed inevitable, Keiondre and Charla needed to manifest a level of compassion, according to Somervell, that would allow them to separate themselves from their predecessor, Chenoweth. Somervell assured Keiondre that the Machiavellian manifestation of force could also be utilized as a pathway to a greater hold over his own tribe, along with a potential sway over the white and Hispanic tribe.

Hoffman, Hoffart, Brennan, Greco, and Sanders, followed by Huffer leading the irascible Erbskorn, marched their doomed prisoners to the blocks. The hooded men, with the exception of Erbskorn, trudged to the blocks in front of the massive audience. Erbskorn the entire march cursed at his captors with a level of vitriol that Somervell felt relieved that his aides were well out of earshot. Kellas Somervell, attired in his Celtic uniform of gladius and scutum only, approached the blocks containing the doomed convicts. Following closely behind, Sam Wolfe, armed with his Isherwood and clawed shank, kept in mind all of the lessons that he had learned about discipline, leadership, and determination. He had read over the past nine months countless tales of statesmanship concerning men like Shackleton, Washington, Lincoln, Lawrence, and Patton; he had been counseled by Kellas Somervell about the mélange of military and political leadership books he had acquired over the forty years on the island. The night before, after all had bedded down, the two had discussed the course of action regarding Erbskorn and his five cronies. Kellas hung the scutum around his neck and shoulder in order to free up his left hand as he stood on Erbskorn's right hand side and addressed the enormous crowd.

"The Lord works in mysterious ways," he bellowed, "He kept me alive for forty years on this island. He provided me with a task and the assistants with which to make it happen. Finally, sending me this man, Sam Wolfe, I had finally received the vision of my destiny and the fate of this island. My mission here on Guam must be to vivify a level of civilization on this island. To combat the heinous denial of the eighth Amendment." He paused, turned, and pointed to the giant eight blazoned upon the tarmac. "This island has been overwhelmed with violence, death, and destruction for far too long. Chenoweth, with his henchman, helped to maintain a level of anarchy on this island, which prevented the establishment of any form of civilization. Barbarism, cannibalism, and hedonism will no longer be practiced upon L.O.F.I. This man, Erbskorn, through his vile leadership and partnership with Chenoweth, perpetuated the violence upon this island. For those crimes, I say, an eye for an eye!" With that statement, Kellas Somervell grabbed Erbskorn by the head of hair, yanked it back, stood on the tips of his toes, raised his gladius, and thrust it downward into Erbskorn's neck all the way to the hilt—the blade emerging from the upper back. Blood ebulliently exploded in all directions, splattering Somervell's naked body. Kellas ripped the gladius out. Erbskorn's head, almost completely severed, fell to his left side and dropped to the ground as his lifeless body flopped with a thump to the block.

Somervell nodded to Sam Wolfe who then walked over to the second prisoner being held by Hoffman. Wolfe ripped off the hood and the doomed man looked over at Erbskorn's distorted head and body lying in the pool of blood still spilling over the edges of the block. The concrete blocks, flat surfaces stretching along the tarmac, were large enough for three or four men to stand upon. Erbskorn's block now continued to be caked in a stream of blood and gore. As Somervell approached, the second man that stood beside Wolfe and Hoffman leaned forward and vomited copiously upon the block. At that, Sam Wolfe walked toward the third man, whose hood Hoffart removed before backing away. The sick man doubled over in fear, grief, and vomit; Kellas mysteriously passed by him, moving toward the third man. As Kellas raised his gladius into the air, the third man clinched his eyes shut and began to urinate profusely which spilled from his shorts and pooled around his knees. Somervell spared the third man, then he and Wolfe advanced toward the fourth man who in turn had his hood removed by Brennan. As soon as the light hit the fourth man's eyes, he blinked, saw the mark of destruction wrought by Kellas on Erbskorn, and immediately began to ball and cry, begging for his life. Somervell moved toward the fifth man, who, as Greco removed the hood spit upon Somervell and uttered a correspondingly disgusting phrase. At that moment, as Sanders removed the hood of the sixth condemned guard of Chenoweth, Kellas Somervell thrust his gladius into the abdomen of the spitting man and let go of the weapon. As the man fell to his knees, Greco held him up by the shoulder as Wolfe took his clawed shank and slit open the belly of the impaled man on both sides. Having discussed the possibility of a contentious rebel, Somervell planned out the method of execution with Wolfe the night before. After Wolfe slashed the abdomen open, Kellas removed the gladius, stuck the sword into the soft ground, then as Greco continued to hold the expiring man, Somervell plunged his hands into the unruly rebel and began to pull out his large intestine. The sixth man puked and urinated himself. The other three whimpered in a most horrifying and childlike cry of mortal fear. Somervell continued to eviscerate the fifth man until his head and body slumped to the point where Greco could hold him no longer. Sam Wolfe stared over the shoulder of Kellas into the void of nothingness as he had been taught in karate when challenging a combatant—look at nothing, see everything. He did not want to see the gore.

"You four who are left," Kellas paraded in front of the quartet of surviving men, "I ask you here and now, where do your loyalties lie?" A long pause filled with stifled whimpers and cries. Another man puked. "Are you still loyal to Chenoweth or are you willing to serve and defend the new king of the black tribe, Keiondre? Are you willing to protect, fight, and die for his queen?" He turned his bare back upon the men and nakedly stood akimbo facing the black army, cognizant that the Hispanic and white contingent looked on and analyzed his actions. "What shall it be men? Chenoweth or Keiondre? Speak and pledge."

"Keiondre!" A uniform response arose from the four surviving Praetorian Guard. The second man bellowed, "We live to serve Keiondre!"

"Ha-ha, indeed gentlemen, indeed." Somervell appeared satisfied. "Hoffman, Hoffart, Brennan, and Sanders, untie these men, clean them up. Put them in charge of a platoon. We have God's mission to complete."

CHAPTER 22

"As the horns blew, the people began to shout. When they heard the sound of the horn, they raised a tremendous shout. The wall collapsed, and the people attacked the city straight ahead and took Jericho."
Joshua 6: 20

Hamilton stood sentinel atop the bell tower of Barrigada Catholic Church as she had done every day since the departure of Kellas Somervell. Since her orders from her mentor were simple, "Hold until relieved," she had scarcely departed her post except for a brief respite provided by Mikayla so she could sleep. She nervously watched as an army of black and brown men advanced upon A.B. Won Pat Airport the two days before and conducted summary executions on the Alley. She alerted Mikayla for fear because she could identify neither Sam Wolfe nor Kellas Somervell from that distance. However, this particular morning proved to be an existential crisis for Hamilton, one of many she would have in the final push for the wall. She now saw the black tribe's army of one thousand warriors scouring the ruined neighborhood of her childhood exposing, flushing, and putting to the sword every odd drifter, zombie, or loner in the area. Gathered with her atop the church bell tower, Lauryn and Mikayla sat stupefied as they watched potential impending doom head their way like locusts capable of slaughter.

"What do we do Hamilton?" Lauryn asked.

"Kellas told us to hold until relieved. Not fight. Not run. Hold." She paused. "We will hold; meaning we will hide."

"Where? The church?" Mikayla, Keeper of Faith, inquired.

"I am afraid not. The church could be vulnerable. So could the undercroft. We need to lock down the access to the library and church. We need to go dark and hide back by the MRE storage. We can wait it out a few days."

"Then what? I don't want to abandon our church."

"I will sneak back over here, scan the horizon, and see if the army has departed. I can't think of anything else. Kellas wants us to hold this place as best as we can." The herd of soldiers appeared to be a half mile to a mile away. The soldiers moved in fits and starts, spotting zombies or loners periodically, then chasing them down and quickly dispatching them. This type of carnage had been witnessed from atop the church tower for years; however, this seemed more demonic, more brutal, and more organized.

"Look at that man!" Mikayla observed. "He appears to be naked!"

"Indubitably," Lauryn responded. She watched as the man next to the nude warrior—presumably Kellas—saw a zombie emerge from the rubble, flee, run into other warriors then head back in the direction he originally came. Lauryn saw the clothed man swing with his right hand; a blunt object then crashed down on the zombie, followed by a slice with a hook–like implement in his left hand. At this, she knew that Kellas Somervell and Sam Wolfe had returned to Masada.

———

The girls abandoned their plan to hide in Masada's storage area as Kellas Somervell marched his army to the front door of the church, which had been barricaded for decades with old cars, trash, debris, and any other manner of island flotsam and jetsam sent by wind or planned by vandals. Kellas orchestrated warriors from the black tribe to clear the pathway and open the door for the Lord's house would now be open for business. Keiondre had his military flush the remaining elements of danger out of hiding and put them to the sword, and the next day he sent all but one hundred of his soldiers home, leaving a small contingent to guard Masada and escort him back to

Agat following the convening of the revolutionary council. Somervell proudly waltzed Charla, Keiondre, and Whatley through the church and library, showcasing the art and perusing the books. With the aides having finished a tearful reunion, Kellas instructed for a banquet table to be set in order to feast in the nave. Here, with Sam Wolfe, Collins, James, the aides, and the royalty, Kellas set the plan to assault the walls and revolt against their incarceration and conditions.

"Mr. Wolfe," Keiondre began, "Mr. Somervell has informed me time and time again that he wants me to instruct my tribe to wage war against the military with the Hispanic and white tribes while you attempt to get on the wall and if I may" he paused, "confront your teacher. Really?"

"Stated that way sir, it does sound absurd."

"First, refresh for me as to why your teacher would be on the wall this July and then tell me about last July. I am still somewhat confused; I came through the Naval Gate."

"Didn't any of you present get expelled from Hadrian's Wall?"

"Hadrian's Wall?" Charla inquired.

"Yes. The wall system protecting Andersen Air Force Base consists of two walls which stretch across the neck of the island, bend at a forty-five degree angle, and extend into the sea to block out the base." Wolfe scanned the room as if an expert on the topic. "I mean we learned about the walls in school; my history and language arts teachers loved this island. Always talked about how Guam helped America maintain a Utopia at home by shipping the offal of America here."

"Offal?" Charla bitterly chimed in.

"My teachers loved the word, especially Mr. Moore. He called everyone he hated offal." He glanced around the crowd then confirmed, "Leftover, inedible parts of a slaughtered beast."

"Hater, I see."

"Well, Mr. Moore had a certain view of the world. That explains why he became a principal."

"Okay. Again, explain why I should ask my tribe to raid this wall." Keiondre seemed less than convinced as the task came nearer—as if he agreed early on thinking the attack would never come to fruition. "Cause if I get this right, you want to confront him."

"Look, Mr. Keiondre, along with you two, James and Collins, this mission of revolution has two parts. The first follows Somervell's plan, which happens to be the only idea that matters. Kellas wants an armed insurrection to demand civility and rule of law. All of you should be interested in living on an island without cannibalism, incessant violence, and all the suffering endured here."

"Indeed, my boy!" Somervell interjected. "You are progressing wonderfully on your explanation here. If I may though, I would like to add that I also want to instill education and ethics. We may have been rightfully banned from America for our criminal behavior, but I believe with the establishment of civility, we can turn our perpetual banishment into something fulfilling. An island of our own destiny."

"So what about this idea of you getting on the wall to your teacher? Why?"

"Well, my plan, secondary of course, if it goes wrong will be immaterial to your cause. You are revolting, asking for basic rights that the Constitution, before they took it away, guaranteed we not be cruelly or unusually punished. I would say that has been violated."

"Okay, now what about your teacher?" Charla inquired.

"Well, he pushed me off the wall last July. When," Wolfe could not finish.

"That don't make sense. Teachers pushin' convicts off walls? Why not use the naval gate?"

"Well, Charla, this appears to be the part of the system kept from you all since you have entered en masse. The other wall apparently only gets used for ceremonial banishments, or expulsions."

"Man, what can I say? Crazy!" Charla seemed out of touch. "Why do that?"

"Well, I didn't get it at first either. I had been convicted of my third felony, and knowing the three strikes law and that I would automatically be sent here, I began to study how to survive. I learned all about this island my senior year prior to dropping out of school when I got mixed up in the drugs and all of that."

"Again, why are teachers on that wall tossing, did you say, former students off of the wall? Seems bizarre."

"Well, I agree. But last year, when they brought me up on the first wall, the Great Wall of Guam, they walked me down a plank to the other one called Hadrian's Wall. In this peculiar ceremony they strapped convicts to a bungee cord and individually tossed them into the interior of the island." Wolfe checked his audience. "Well, being strapped with two others, I had time to figure it out. Teachers had to push former students off of the wall to their doom."

"Why?" Charla continued to inquire.

"Well, if I may?" Somervell interrupted, "Sam and I surmised that the whole entire outlandish ceremony proved to be no more than an elaborate initiation."

"Exactly. The people pushing in convicts were all teachers. I also heard that the dignitaries present were all teachers last year who had tossed in former kids. These dignitaries, I heard the military men say, had completed their first year as principals and were preparing to head the mega-schools of America and all of that the job entailed."

"For what reason would school teachers and principals be visiting this island?"

"Well, Keiondre," Somervell conjectured, "it would appear that the American government utilizes the public school for nefarious public control. If they are ritualistically initiating principal candidates using their former students, it would appear the principals of the United States must be engaged in some clandestine secret society which controls or helps control the society. A pedagocracy if you will."

"Why do you think that?" Keiondre inquired.

"It only stands to reason," Kellas offered.

"Also," Wolfe interjected, "Kellas and I decided that it only makes sense based upon all of the testing, the rigidity of schools, the quick disappearance of juvenile delinquents. Heck, I can't tell you how many of my schoolmates have disappeared, been convicted or just died in high school. We get away with nothing. In our opinion, the teachers on the wall becoming principals, tossing off their former students, only confirms some sort of secret program."

"I didn't get tossed off no wall. Why?"

"Well, likely because none of your teachers were being promoted. You were just general population without a connection to a promoted teacher. So you were dumped here like many."

"Fascinating," Keiondre commented, "So principals and schools not only control the minds of the youth but also control elements of education far greater than my understanding."

"It appears so."

"So why do you want to get on top of this wall and get at a teacher?"

"Well, when I got arrested going back to see Mr. Moore, I never thought I would see him again. At the ceremony I wanted to talk to him, to tell him all that I needed to see him about. But he didn't let me explain myself; he just shoved me off the wall, rather coldly, I might add. I want my time with him. He owes me that much."

"So you would like us to attack the wall and risk death so you can talk to a teacher?"

"No, I want you to attack the wall and risk death to reclaim your Constitutional rights which have been stripped from you. While you liberate yourself, I will surreptitiously attempt to get my tête-à-tête."

"You realize we could all be killed attempting this?"

"We could," Kellas intervened, "However, I have faith based upon all that I have experienced on this island that the Lord, who works in mysterious ways, has sent Sam Wolfe to Guam to help lead the people here in claiming what they deserve."

"Speakin' of deservin'," Whatley unexpectantly responded. "Your girls don't deserve to risk bein' hurt."

"I agree," added Sam Wolfe, "Kellas and I have a plan to shelter them a bit during the battle."

"Ha-ha, indeed, all, indeed." Somervell joined in, "I believe the good Lord put me upon this rock to protect and save the innocent born upon this island. My aides will be isolated during the battle. The criminals of this island need to fight for their rights. The criminality needs to sacrifice for the innocent born here."

"Mr. Somervell, your girls ain't the only ones born on this island. Many others born on this island. How about them?"

"Well Whatley, I do believe you are absolutely correct. Could I put you in charge of rounding up the innocents of the black tribe so that they could be given at an alternate mission? Also, James and Collins, we need you to gather the innocents of your tribes. They too should have this protection." Somervell offered.

"Yep. I tell you who born here from the black tribe."

"Good. Whatley, you will lead that group." Kellas took on the air of a general. "Keiondre, I need your troops to be the head of the bull. Collins and James, your tribes will be the horns."

"Head of the bull?" Keiondre inquired.

"Horns?"

"Zulus gentleman! Do you know the Zulus?"

"Zu what? Bull horns, hell!" Collins struggled to articulate himself.

"Yes, the African Zulus, gentlemen, would attack like a bull. The horns would take the left and right flank to distract and engage the enemy, but the main force would penetrate and pummel with the forehead of a charging bull."

"What does that mean, man?" Again Collins ignorantly asked.

"Easy. Collins and James, you will lead your troops around the walls into the sea. Your men can wade out along the first wall, then moved beyond the second coming up onto the open fields of both flanks." Kellas paused, "Hamilton, please retrieve the model."

Hamilton rose, walked over toward the bookshelves, and picked up a crude but accurate model Somervell had constructed the night before out of children's toys that he had kept from when his aides were much younger. After setting the model on the table, the group could see the two walls extending into the sea—fifty or so yards for Hadrian's Wall and a hundred or so for the Great Wall of Guam. "Behind the walls, Collins and James, your respective tribes would have a straight run up to the shore and the base."

"What about my tribe attacking the wall head on?" Keiondre asked.

"Indeed, Mr. Keiondre, indeed. Your men have the most formidable task. Right now, I have Lia and MacNeil constructing grappling hooks and rounding up all the rope I have stored in Masada for the past forty years. We will be able to charge the wall, deploy the hooks up and over the wall, then quickly scale it."

"Won't my men be exposed?"

"Only briefly. Sam will cut off the firing with a move the Zulus only wished they had. Ha-ha!"

"Yes," Wolfe started, "I will take a small team of innocents, the aides, Whatley, Kellas, and some others born on this island, and enter the tunnel system. Though small and cramped on that side of the island, Kellas informs me that the base can be accessed through a little-known hatch in an abandoned storage area which empties into an old boiler room."

"Indeed. And my team of aides, led by Mr. Wolfe and myself will infiltrate from the rear. We will come up the back wall and surprise the delegation. We will prevent or stop any firing. As they stand atop the wall in relative security, we will assault them simultaneously from all sides. Brilliant eh?"

"Yes, we will signal you; Kellas found old flares here. Of the few we have, surely at least one will work. Furthermore, as a backup, one of the girls will carry the conch. When you see the flare or hear the conch, you attack! The walls of Guam will fall!"

CHAPTER 23

"When Gideon led the soldiers down to the water, the Lord said to him: Everyone who laps up the water as a dog does with its tongue you shall set aside by himself; and everyone who kneels down to drink raising his hand to his mouth you shall set aside by himself."
Judges 7: 5

July had arrived and Sam Wolfe's best-laid plans would not go awry. The final months had passed hurriedly. The herculean effort needed to mobilize the tens of thousands of L.O.F.I. inmates to the cause required arduous diplomacy and innumerable meetings between Keiondre and Charla with the other two incompetent and nefarious tribe rulers, Collins and James. Being convinced of the necessity to participate by Somervell in order to maintain the balance of power, the Hispanic and white tribes agreed to serve as the horns of the bull in the attack on the walls of fortification blocking off Andersen Air Force Base. Somervell himself took to teaching the tribes the rudimentary skills of swimming in case the water went above their heads as they swarmed out into the surf in order to circumvent the dual-walled system.

Keiondre and Charla had split their army into ranks to be hurled against the wall in waves as designed by Sam Wolfe. Kellas helped the nine loyal guards of the king and queen pick second lieutenants to lead the various elements of the black army to allow Keiondre's coterie to remain in the rear with the final company of two hundred of the black tribe's most trustworthy warriors. Wolfe and Somervell instructed Keiondre to send the most ruthless and violent criminals to the wall first with the grappling-hooks knowing their ferocity would propel them to move quicker—also being promised the spoils of all female teachers and soldiers captured. It had been agreed that Somervell and Kellas would lead the covert operation, with Whatley, the twelve aides, and a small contingent of other innocents born upon the island, through the tunnels to emerge on the air force base side of the walls in order to serve as the catalyst of the battle. The squad would capture a couple of uniformed soldiers, commandeer their clothes, fall in with the others on the wall, take hostages, then fire the flare. The four-point attack plan, as the leaders understood when presented by Wolfe and Somervell, appeared upon the surface, foolproof and prudent. All were in agreement, for if no flare fired, the hordes hidden in the woods would dissolve back to their respective camps.

Knowing that the dignitaries, teachers, and principals would begin being shuttled to the island via helicopters from the naval base, or a direct flight from a retired Air Force One, Kellas Somervell had Hamilton, Lauryn, Bailey, and Ashleigh stand watch in pairs at two abandoned church towers—one in Yigo, the other a few miles northwest. At the first appearance of the retired Air Force One, the girls' job would then be to rush a message to an outpost at the south end of Yigo. From there, Somervell had set up a simple, but ingenious, domino method of communication, which had men in groups posted every four hundred yards along the road to fan out as they travelled to hail that "The principals were coming!" Wolfe helped Collins, Keiondre, and James set up and space out the myriad camps so that upon the arrival of the dignitaries for the expulsion ceremony on the wall, the three armies could mobilize and be at the edge of the woods—thus the battlefield—in less than one hour. Spying by the aides provided ample time to assemble, for activity on Hadrian's Wall with expulsion devices and more than usual air traffic with helicopters alerted them that the ceremony would be imminent. Somervell had Whatley posted in an abandoned farmhouse north of Yigo, south of the old Highway One, the closest structure to the field brushing up against Hadrian's Wall, which through fortuity or faith provided access to an old Japanese tunnel, which would deliver the squad on the north side of the wall and into the heart of the revolution.

Kellas Somervell and Sam Wolfe sat in the antiquated barn that contained a hurricane bunker and access to the tunnel. The group, containing Whatley, Lia, Kayla, Megan, Nicole, Becky, and Sarah, had been patiently waiting after creeping through the jungle the night prior due to the arrival of the decommissioned Air Force One. Aware that the ceremony would be performed in the morning hours, Wolfe knew the aides had to be mobilized that evening in case the expulsions took place early the following morning. As the plane touched down, the mechanisms of communication established for the mobilization of the makeshift trinity of armies earnestly went into action. With stunning rapidity, due to the tutelage of Kellas, the three tribes moved into position spread out through abandoned towns and jungle overgrowth to conceal this unprecedented move of belligerence against the Guam security wall and military establishment. Since the U.S. military could certainly track the movements of the inhabitants of Guam utilizing drones and satellites, Kellas attempted to disguise the massing of people as nothing more than the normal gathering for inter-tribal war. Furthermore, knowing how the government sociologically studied the convicts, as explained to Kellas by Wolfe as lessons in his high school, Somervell felt confident that if the government had been observing the mass movements, it would have only piqued the scientists' interest.

In trees around the farm, a few other aides diligently watched for the moment a clear manifestation of ceremonial activities began. Wolfe had instructed the girls to look for soldiers with musical instruments, a band of soldiers with weapons, high-ranking looking military brass, and most importantly, a mess of well-dressed people who appeared to be out of place. Knowing that his former teacher-turned-principal would be on that wall filled Sam Wolfe with a sense of relief that his personal mission would be fulfilled along with the completion of Somervell's holy endeavor.

"Sam!" Lia charged into the barn area, "MacNeil says the activity has begun."

"Like what?"

"Just what you said. Helicopters landing one after another. People piling on top of the wall. Very busy."

"Good Lia. Good."

"Can we go?" Lia unsheathed her cutlass. "I am ready!"

"Easy, Lia, easy." Sam Wolfe took stock of his arsenal. His clawed shank hung from his neck. Isherwood rested by his foot along with the flare and a small pipe and rope. Kellas Somervell, wearing his cloak, picked up his gladius and scutum. "Whatley, gather your boys please."

"Yessir." He moved out of the barn to the house to gather his small posse.

"Alright ladies," Sam Wolfe waited until all of the girls fluttered into the barn before recapping his plan. "we will go down this rabbit hole, traverse under the wall, then emerge into an abandoned boiler room. You must do everything, and I stress everything, when I tell you. This little adventure could get a few of us killed."

"Exactly, aides. Do what you're told, when you are told, and every time you are told. I want to see you come out of this endeavor alive." Somervell offered. "Remember the plan!"

"Yes," added Sam Wolfe, "Kellas and I will exit the boiler room with Becky, Megan, and Kayla. You three slings will snipe a couple of soldiers, preferably sentries, so we can drag them in, incapacitate them, take their uniforms, then repeat the process until we can clothe a small squad to take the wall and hostages."

"When we have the situation in hand on the other side of the wall, we will fire the flare and the revolution will have begun. Like paratroopers we shall cause chaos on the other side." Somervell summarized.

"Any questions?" Sam Wolfe perused the aides and Whatley's crew. "Okay, none. Into the hole; let's go." Wolfe and Somervell assisted all into the aperture and down into the tunnel.

"Sam?"

"Kellas."

"Does it really need to be this way?" Somervell solemnly gazed upon Wolfe with hurt in his eyes.

"I am afraid so, Kellas. You put me in command of God's work on this island. I believe the Lord has spoken to me. Thy will be done!"

———

Traversing the tunnel proved dank work but Kellas, who had travelled this way a number of times before Sam's arrival and recently reconnoitered the area to verify a clear path, easily worked the squad to the paneled hatch, which would allow the group to emerge onto the Air Force grounds via the abandoned boiler room. Pushing open the hatch, Kellas Somervell, ever the intrepid one, boldly stepped out into the stale air next to rusted, archaic machinery. Kayla and Megan followed to cover the perimeter with slings in case of discovery. Sam Wolfe and Becky brought up the rear. As the squad moved toward the door at the top of three steps, Sam Wolfe examined the handles on the hatch. Two bar-like handles, one on the wall, the other on the door, offered the base for a locking mechanism to be attached which had vanished long ago. He leaned in, told the rest to remain silent, then closed the door. He moved toward the others as Kellas pushed open the rusted door out into an open storage area. Still in use for supplies, the group fanned out through the room, fearful that it could meet someone here.

Kellas had the girls crouch as he headed toward a window looking out onto the Air Force base. A flurry of activity could be seen from every angle, including a lone sentry standing in front of the very door the squad needed to move through in order to get to the wall. Somervell, not wasting a moment, waved to Wolfe and skulked to the door with the soldier on the other side. Carefully whispering, he informed Sam of the plan. Then without further ado, they both sprang into action. The door, posing a problem for it opened out, had its knob turned by Kellas and gently pushed open. It bumped into the soldier, who absent-mindedly pushed it shut. Kellas, exhibiting his level of equanimity, repeated his action. This time the soldier shuffled his feet, turned, and attempted to open the door to identify the door's mysterious ways. As soon as he poked his head around the edge of the door, Sam Wolfe grabbed him by the collar, yanked him down, and thrust his knee into the soldier's face. The crushing blow shattered the soldier's nose, and before he could call out, Somervell struck a blow to the back of his head rendering him unconscious. With stealth and speed, they disrobed the soldier and Sam Wolfe put on his uniform. After they dragged the soldier out of sight of the door, Kellas bound and gagged him, all the while considering how he might acquire a second uniform.

Without wasting a moment, Kellas Somervell and Kayla headed towards the door as Sam Wolfe stepped out on to the green plaza looking out onto the tarmac and the backside of the Great Wall of Guam. Wolfe stood still, much like the sentry prior to him, waiting for the opportunity to snatch another soldier's uniform. As the five minutes of waiting seemed to drag into infinity, Sam Wolfe noticed a soldier—nearly Somervell's build—walking alone. Wolfe waved toward him then gently cracked the door. He kept waving toward the soldier insisting that he needed his help. The soldier, who had stopped, began to walk in Wolfe's direction. Sam Wolfe, knowing that the cracked door behind him had Kayla crouched and loaded for bear, turned and walked toward the door when the soldier got closer. Seeing the glint of steel as they neared the door to within ten feet, Sam Wolfe stepped sideways, heard the snap of rubber, followed by a sickening thwack. The soldier, instinctively grabbing his head and doubling over, found himself hurled headfirst into the now thrown open door where he found Kellas Somervell's hilt end of his gladius too blunt for his head. He neatly fell unconscious. Somervell quickly gathered his uniform.

"Quickly girls, back into the hatch." Sam Wolfe followed the aides back toward the hatch in the wall, held it open, then peered in. "Quiet. Not a word. We will knock in code—one, two, one. Don't open unless you hear that. We will go and fetch a few more uniforms. Kellas and I can move more quickly alone."

"Alright." Kayla offered only one word.

"Be careful." Megan followed.

"Move back away from the hatch out of ear shot so you aren't discovered till we return." Sam Wolfe closed the hatch and took the pipe he had brought and slid it gently through the two bars. Fumbling on the ground, he found his rope he had brought, cut it in a length for a hitch, then secured the bar to the handles, thus protecting the girls from the ensuing fight. The rest of the cordage bound and gagged the second soldier and both were quickly hidden amongst the myriad boxes of supplies.

"You sure Sam?"

"Kellas, your faith led you to place me in charge. If you want to bring faith to this island along with civility and order, you must trust me. The Lord has shown me the way. Now let's go." Quickly, the pair move toward the door, peered out to see if anyone could be watching, then walked out onto the open field. Seeing a small shed across the field but away from the masses moving toward the wall, the pair walked in that direction.

"We need to split up. When I get to the group of soldiers and begin to move up the wall's elevator, you fire the flare." Sam Wolfe had informed Kellas Somervell that the plan concerning the flare had to be modified and so did the assault team. Playing on Somervell's undying and unflappable faith, Wolfe assured him that God had manifested this twist into the plan to fulfill his divine purpose. Kellas would not question after his forty years of success upon the island with only faith in God to guide him. More than the dignitaries on the wall would be surprised this day. "You ready?"

"Morituri te salutant!"

"Do it Kellas." Sam Wolfe briskly moved out from behind the shed, drifted with purpose toward a crowd of dignitaries, then headed towards an open spot as if standing guard. He scanned the crowd of teachers and principals hoping to recognize his former instructor, the man he wished to confront. As he perused the elevator, he spotted the antediluvian bow tie his instructor had loved so much. Mr. Murray Mallory Moore, now heading up the wall, had indeed arrived upon the scene as expected. Sam Wolfe began to move in the direction of the elevator to catch it when it returned from the heights of the Great Wall of Guam. Within minutes, Moore's crew had departed the elevator allowing it to return and Sam to board. On his ride up the side of the wall, Sam Wolfe could perceive Kellas Somervell behind the shed. As he stepped onto the open-air elevator, he raised his pinched hand and thumb to his forehead in the old British naval salute, then watched Kellas Somervell drift out of sight. The flare shot up into the air high over the wall. When Sam Wolfe stepped up onto the Great Wall of Guam, he noticed not only the myriad teachers, the downed plank crossing to Hadrian's Wall, and the plethora of soldiers and dignitaries, he also noticed a horde of men from three different starting locations emerge out of the woods, first at a trot, then a dead sprint. The revolution had begun.

CHAPTER 24

"The sun had risen over the earth when Lot arrived in Zoar, and the Lord rained down sulfur upon Sodom and Gomorrah, fire from the Lord out of heaven. He overthrew those cities and the whole plain, together with the inhabitants of the cities and the produce of the soil."
Genesis 19: 23-25

The crowd atop the wall stood dumbfounded. In all the years since the dawn of the expulsion process and the initiation of soon-to-be principals, no such morning had been met by anything more than a small collection on the edge of the clearing. This indoctrination of young principals culminated with the ritualistic ceremony of hurling one of their former students turned criminal onto the island of exile. This hands-on approach, along with all of the other training beforehand, served to weed out the weak-kneed and leave the schools of America in the hands of determined and dogmatic educators who knew when they labeled a student as a persona non grata, they doomed the aforementioned student to a life of government spying, surveillance, and at times, assassination. Though the program largely took credit for America's stellar public schools, low crime, and freed up government money (for prisons and jails were gone), the queasy and liberal minded of society often protested the island—the end result for most of these students. Sam Wolfe had come to grips, through Kellas Somervell's assistance, with the understanding that the key to America's prosperity and civility started with an apparent secret society of principals, which had obviously evolved into a high-level, top secret, society of educators who bore the weight of America's prosperity upon their shoulders. Sam Wolfe had returned to confront the man who hurled him into this cauldron of murder and mayhem without so much as listening to his reason for returning to school that fateful day twelve months ago.

Upon the wall, Sam Wolfe observed the panic in everyone's eyes as an unexpected army of savages and barbarians, murderers and rapists, extortionists and thieves, all exploded effulgently from the jungle with every manner of crude weapon in their hands, bent upon the destruction of the walls and the people who manned them. Wolfe looked over the edge of the wall as Kellas Somervell approached the base, told all to back away from the elevator, then rode it halfway up, pulling the switch to stop it, thus trapping all on top of the Great Wall of Guam. Wolfe moved toward the edge of doom as he shouldered up with other soldiers who began to push the teachers and principals, including Murray Moore, to the back of the wall. The soldiers began to move down the plank toward Hadrian's Wall as they removed their weapons from their shoulders. Below, on the flat plain stretching out from the wall, tens of thousands of inmates, screaming and yelling an insidious howl, charged the wall and its flanks extending out into the sea. Wolfe, down on Hadrian's Wall, shoulder to shoulder with the contingent of Marines, observed the flanking hordes slow down as they thrashed through the surf and down the wall that extended out into the ocean nearly fifty yards. Their progress further slowed as the dredged channel around the wall began to approach their chest. Grappling hooks began to fly up, hurled by trained men to elevate them upon the wall in hopes of catching the backside edge. A few landed quickly, one hit a Marine and impaled him, causing him to be pulled off the wall to his unfortunate death. The amount of grappling hooks sailing through the air quickly became an untenable hazard, for the Marines could not safely shoot down off the wall without risk of being hooked and pulled in. The lead Marine shouted for all to retreat back up the plank. With military precision and calm, the Marines retreated, then regrouped—along with Sam Wolfe—back to the Great Wall and prepared to set up a firing line to pick off inmates as they scaled the barrier. The lead Marine sergeant began calling for air support and instructions. The inmates had risen.

Shouts and screams reflecting terror could be heard all around Sam as the scores of inmates began to pour over the forward wall. The Marines fired repeatedly, killing numerous climbers, toppling them back into the abyss. Sam Wolfe peered into the two story gap between the walls as the Marines raised the plank to cut off access between the two barriers. Wolfe recalled learning in school that no human could survive the weaponry and murderous anti-personnel devices lining the walls. As Wolfe wildly shot, he glanced to the left and right waiting eagerly to see the hordes of flankers moving out in the ocean from the edge of the first wall to the edge of the second. Once they reached the inner wall, the Great Wall of Guam, a human chain made with hands or rope, would use the mass of people to pull the hordes from the first wall up to the second thus avoiding the no man's land between. Then, once the walls were sidestepped, they would advance up across the plain and overrun the air base. Sam Wolfe marveled as every element of the plan had fallen into place. As the inmates breached Hadrian's Wall on the frontal assault, and the flanks began to circumvent the sides, Wolfe knew that his plan had achieved perfection, the Lord's work would be complete, and every inhabitant currently attacking the installation would be dead within moments.

———

"Tell me, Mr. Wolfe," Kellas Somervell inquired a few nights prior to the culminating attack on the wall. "What makes you feel that the Almighty's work requires the annihilation of the inhabitants on this island?"

"Kellas, you have always felt that your mission from God on this island lay in the reconstruction of civilization, the re-institution of education, and the development of a new society. Like Noah, with Masada as my ark, I must deliver the only potentially good human beings into the next phase of this island's existence. The Lord said that the next time he cleansed the world it would be by fire. I assure you, when those animals attack that wall, they will be swept from the earth by fire."

"And who shall survive?"

"Keiondre and Charla, along with their nine loyal lieutenants and their company of soldiers; they will survive. Also, the innocents shall be spared."

"So, like babes in the womb, you plan on locking them in the vaulted tunnels under the earth." Kellas pensively gazed off into the distance.

"Remember Kellas, you told me months ago, that the reins needed to be handed to me. The Lord delivered me to you in order to complete his work. His work on Guam consists of the immolation of those that need to be cast into the everlasting fires of damnation. My year of studying in the church with you and reading the Bible, along with the many revelations I have had upon this island, solidified this plan in me. You were right; God provides signs if we choose to believe." Sam smiled. "God willing, I will stand on that wall soon much like the Archangel Michael and orchestrate the casting of these lost souls into perdition."

"Tell me then," Kellas interupted as he set down a glass of Bailey's finest concoction, "what led you to this violent epiphany?"

"All of the studies with Mikayla."

"Explain."

"Look how God delivered the Jews into the Promised Land. Or how the Judges defended the Israelites." Sam paused to contemplate, "Furthermore, God's wrath on Sodom and Gomorrah. The Torah, the Bible, and the Koran are full of examples where God punished the wicked when a prophet led his people."

"Ha-ha! Indeed, Mr. Wolfe. Your faith, merely a mustard seed upon your arrival, has blossomed into a divine fullness."

"Yes. You have shown me the signs. Masada! Your forty years here! Your John the Baptist ways in preparing my path! I see it fully! I am ready to do the Lord's bidding. If that means culling the herd, then so be it."

"And how will you convince Keiondre to follow this plan? He will lose some of his people."

"Keiondre has already agreed to the plan. Like David before, a man will gladly sacrifice others if it means he ends up on the throne. We discussed it together over wine and Machiavelli. He exhibits pure pragmatism in the matter of this island's conquest and his potential power."

"How do you plan for the island to operate afterwards?"

"Keiondre's warriors will be the gatekeepers of a new and better world here on Guam. We will run this island much like a medieval monastery. We will regiment schedules, introduce faith, and save the new inmates' souls. Just like you did with your aides."

"This all seems drastic but profound." Kellas acquiesced.

"The Lord moves in mysterious ways."

———

"Ladies and gentlemen!" A colonel bellowed from atop the Great Wall of Guam. He glanced around at the huddled masses yearning to be free of this onslaught. "Have no fear. Mission control has been observing this mob for days. Though we weren't sure of their intentions, we have planned for every contingency!"

"Colonel!" An excited lieutenant barked. "They are within range."

"Fire at will, lieutenant. Fire at will!"

Pop, pop, pop, pop, pop, ping! The repetitive staccato of the Marines' weapons fully discharging and ejecting their clips broke Sam Wolfe's reverie. The two dozen or so Marines, including Sam, had fired their archaic and ceremonial guns until they had run out of ammunition. Wolfe felt sure they only carried a clip in the ritualistic weapons, which were close to one hundred years old, in order to dispense with any minor incident. They were more for pomp and circumstance than practicality; furthermore, their close range effectiveness happened to be geared for unruly and incorrigible inmates who were being tethered to the cord for their final expulsion into the abyss of anarchy. The size of the Marine squad, along with the weapons assigned, had not been meant to repel legions of inmates scaling the wall. Pop, pop, pop, pop, pop, pop, ping! Another Marine ran out of ammunition. By now, hundreds of inmates had climbed the wall as the Marines did their best to kill as many as possible. Scanning the wall back and forth, Sam Wolfe saw Marine after Marine run out of ammunition. Wolfe's gun pinged as he fired wildly. Looking down into the troth or pit between the two walls, Wolfe could see the human chain working from Hadrian's Wall, near the shore, to the Great Wall of Guam which required them to extend out into the sea another twenty-five yards. A roar of panic rang out among the teachers and principals, frantic about their fate. Pop, pop, pop, pop, pop, pop, ping! The last Marine had discharged his antediluvian weapon. The delegation upon the wall looked like lambs preparing for the slaughter. Sam Wolfe gratifyingly smiled on the inside, for he knew, based upon all he studied and understood of the island's defensive system, it would all be over in a minute.

As the convicts poured onto Hadrian's Wall, they pulled up their grappling hooks and began to sling them across the great divide in hopes of hooking into the back edge of the Great Wall, pulling them taut, and crossing the void with a Tyrolean traverse. Zoning out the din of battle and panic, Sam quickly prayed that Kellas Somervell would be able to maintain the possession of the external elevator on the side of the wall until the time had arrived for the grand finale. As the trepidation reached a fevered pitch, Sam Wolfe heard the thumping and thwacking of approaching helicopters. He fully expected this response to the revolution but the very next moment ushered in the surprise that would allow the repulsion of this assault force to be finalized. He briefly remembered his teacher, who unbeknownst to him stood a mere fifteen feet away, telling his class that no manner of assault could penetrate or overtake the walled defense system of Andersen Air Force Base. Mr. Moore referred to it as impenetrable, and he even joked that, "God couldn't knock that wall down."

As the helicopters soared in, the latest form of American warfare, descendant from the decades old Apache attack helicopters, this new gun ship, the Sioux, referred to by pilots as a "Crazy Horse" would unleash upon these murderers, rapists, extortionists, pedophiles, and all other manner of human offal, a barrage of anti-human weaponry that hadn't been seen since the British rose from the trenches and stormed No Man's Land in the Battle of the Somme or in the town of Ypres. To add to the human misery and carnage, the surprise— for Wolfe knew there had to be a defensive barrier between the walls—manifested itself in full force. Just under the noise of the four approaching Sioux helicopters, a whirling din could be ascertained from under the water between the inner and outer wall. On each side, buried in the sea, an elephantine hydroelectric pulsating wave machine began to toss all of the inmates who had just completed the human chain across the aperture between the two walls. As the machines revved up, the tidal surge flooded into the sandy area between the walls, flushing men onto the beach which resembled a dry moat. Wolfe smiled. The end would come quickly. The Sioux helicopters now split into pairs and like the horns of the bull, flanked the walls in an arc. As they did, their nose cannons unleashed anti-personnel, fifty caliber machine gun fire— a veritable bullet hose—which cut the men on top of the wall in half. A mere ten seconds of fire from the four Sioux nose cannons had reduced a couple of hundred inmates into what appeared to be the wasted remains of animals in a slaughterhouse.

Sam Wolfe glowed inside for his plan had come to fruition. Relief overcame some of the dignitaries on the wall, for it appeared that the inmates' chance of surmounting the wall had disappeared. The Sioux gunships arced out at a wide angle. Then, a thunderous cacophony of murder erupted from the sandy trench between the two great walls when the inmates, belched up onto the shore, had to move inward toward each other as the tidal machine pushed hundreds and hundreds of men up on top of one another. The sand, loaded with late 21st century "Bouncing Betties," anti-personnel mines, popped and boomed, discharging burning phosphorous and razor-edged shrapnel. As the men pushed in, the mines popped into the air, exploding and dicing the assailants. Those being pushed in attempted to force their way back to the sea to no avail. The hydroelectric wave machines churned waves so high that men began to wash all the way into the center area of the two walls, setting off hundreds and hundreds of mines. By now thousands of men had landed between the walls, all being cut to shreds. Any chance of the convicts retreating from the sea had vanished. Moreover, a Sioux gunship spun and decimated the beach with cannon fire, annihilating and shredding all forms of humanity. The inmates had one fatally simple choice to make: die on the beach or die between the walls. The amount of men pushed between the walls proved so great that every surface mine had exploded. Still hundreds more men washed in only to find a bed of human body parts on which to lie. As the water drained, the command set off high explosives buried a few feet under the "Bouncing Betties." At this moment, Sam Wolfe thought he might be sick.

The powerful explosions hurled both living and dead into the air in a violent amalgamation of gore. Raining down upon the tops of the walls were limbs, chunks of meat and bone, intestinal tracks flung like parade streamers, and quartered carcasses thudding onto the rampart. At one point, a legless, decapitated torso with an exposed shattered backbone landed near Sam Wolfe as the spinal cord wormed and flapped about. Wolfe choked down his own stomach bile as two more Sioux gunships approached, hovering at each exit to the walled system. Looking down, he could see men, some barely hurt, some egregiously wounded, many in the agonizing throes of death. The fifth and sixth Sioux helicopters, which arrived on the scene, delivered the coup de grâce. Their nose cannons possessed a flame-throwing napalm weapon, which, as Sam Wolfe had planned for the Lord to do, destroyed the inmates by fire. A swell of heat bellowed out from between the walls. Sweat broke out immediately on those perched on high. The inferno below, besides the tremendous heat, hurled up the putrid and fetid stench of burning human flesh. The walls would not be breached. The walls would not tumble down.

CHAPTER 25

"God said to Noah and to his sons with him: See, I am now establishing my covenant with you and your descendants after you and with every living creature that has been with you. I will establish my covenant with you, that never again shall all creatures be destroyed by waters of a flood; there shall not be another flood to destroy the earth."
Genesis 9: 8-11

By now, the carnage had shifted toward the land, where the head of the bull attacked and had been repulsed at the foot of Hadrian's Wall. The hydroelectric turbines kept thrusting water between the walls, ensuring that any wounded would be drowned in a salty mash of gore. All inmates in the surf attempting to return to the shore had been cut down by a menacing fire from the Sioux helicopters. The horns of the bull were no more. After his meeting and revulsion of the Hispanic and white tribes' leaders, Sam Wolfe could think of no greater gratification than knowing that the dullard Collins and sexual pervert James along with all who followed them must be among the slaughtered dead. From the heavens, missiles rained down as the always-circling drones fired anti-personal weapons at the scene. Two fighter jets zipped in, dropping the newest versions of napalm, creating an impenetrable wall of flame near the edge of the jungle, trapping the insurrectionists between fire and stone. Not one living soul would walk from that battlefield. Keiondre and Charla, who kept their reserves well back in the jungle, melted away into the green abyss. Keiondre's careful assortment of reserves manifested a collection of proven friends, comrades, and trusted souls. Those who were lost would not be missed. As they retreated, Keiondre realized that Sam Wolfe's plan played out with such precision that it could only be the work of God. He resolved to pursue his new mission on earth under the direction of Sam Wolfe and Kellas Somervell without a single doubt in his mind. After all, within the span of a year, Wolfe rose to prominence, knocked off Chenoweth, mobilized an army and sacrificed the population of the island, a stupendous feat.

For the twenty minutes of shock and awe, Sam Wolfe stood on the wall in stunned silence, watching the fire and brimstone of his plan unleashed upon the unsuspecting heathens of the island. Around him teachers and principals stood, mouths agape; some wept, some whimpered, some vomited, and some did all three. Sam Wolfe turned to see the external elevator rise to the height of the Great Wall of Guam where Kellas Somervell stepped off. All around him lay the proverbial depths of hell as burning flesh, human carcasses, and blistered gore splattered every rock, plant, wall, and grain of sand on the beach. The whirl of the turbines stopped on the east side of the walls, allowing the rush of water from the northern section to flush all of the bodies out into the sea. Sam noticed the elevator heading down with a few unidentified dignitaries and a pair of Marines.

"Come on, son; we don't have much time." Kellas Somervell tapped Sam on the arm as the horrified group gazed out into the plain, attempting to estimate if twenty or twenty-five thousand inmates had just been massacred. Wolfe, coming to his senses, proudly exhaled as he observed his well-orchestrated holocaust.

"Yes, of course." Sam Wolfe bolted toward the plank, which had been raised to prevent the inmates from crossing to the Great Wall of Guam from Hadrian's Wall. The plank extended from wall to wall and had an expulsion device on the end that hung out over its ledge. He leapt onto the inside railing which served as a step at this angle and looked out at the crowd as he bellowed, "Mr. Murray Mallory Moore!" A shuffling tumult ensued as Murray Mallory Moore gazed upon Sam Wolfe, studied his face, then came to the realization that indeed the student he tossed into L.O.F.I. twelve months prior had somehow appeared upon this wall following this apocalyptic massacre.

"Sam Wolfe?" Incredulity blazoned upon his countenance, "What are you doing here?"

"Mr. Moore, I have returned; last year you did not give me the time to explain why I had fallen down and acquired my third strike." As Wolfe's teacher contemplated this statement, Marines stood dumbfounded as to whether to apprehend the uniform-clad Sam, for they were mystified by this surreal conversation in light of the carnage that surrounded them.

"Sam, how did you get onto the wall? Do you know why these inmates attacked?"

"Ha-ha, Mr. Moore!" Sam Wolfe imitated his mentor, Kellas Somervell, who surreptitiously commandeered the controls of the plank and began to lower it. "These inmates attacked the wall because I told them to attack the wall."

"What?"

"I have returned to see you, Mr. Moore, before I plunge back into L.O.F.I. I wanted to apologize, for I let you down. I returned to school last year to show you I had kicked the habit. When I first arrived on this island, I thought silliness drove me to school with real narcotics to prove that I stopped taking drugs, but it turns out that the Lord works in mysterious ways. My impetuousness proved to be His plan for me."

"The Lord? You mean God?" Moore stood dumbfounded at this revelation.

"Yes, Mr. Moore, I am now doing the work of God."

"What?" Moore inquired as the plank continued to lower and Sam Wolfe maneuvered himself so as not to fall. The crowd continued to listen in silence. With all they had just witnessed, they discovered themselves catatonic.

"Yes, Mr. Moore, my foolishness did not land me on the island of Guam; the Lord led me here. Like Noah, Joshua, Abraham, or Gideon, I am carrying out God's plan. I am to perform his work—the restoration of civilization upon this island, the introduction of faith, and most importantly, the punishment of the wicked."

"Are you kidding me?" Murray Mallory Moore appeared agitated. "What?! Did you see a burning bush? Did the Lord speak directly to you? Did he tell you to pick up the knife? Were you presented with the Arc of the Covenant?"

"Indeed Mr. Moore, indeed!" Sam Wolfe's conviction poured forth. "I have had numerous burning bush moments here. Now, I will...." Moore cut him off.

"Surely you didn't orchestrate this, this," he paused, "this annihilation of people in the name of God?"

"I looked, and there, behold a pale green horse. Its rider, named Death, and Hell accompanied him." Wolfe paused and raised his arms swaying, "I have been given authority by the Almighty over Guam to kill with sword, famine, and plague, by any means the beasts of the earth."

"My God, Sam, this illustrates insanity! Injustice!" Moore responded. "You are no better than Inquisitors! Or a jihadist. Slaughter in the name of God amounts to..."

"To what, Mr. Moore?"

"To terrorism. Religious extremism. Murder!" Moore searched for more modern historical precedent doubting that his former student would understand or necessarily know about the Spanish Inquisition. "I mean Sam, this act of carnage equates to flying planes into buildings in the name of Allah. Or putting truck bombs in front of governmental buildings. You have unleashed injustice here!"

"Injustice, ha-ha!" Sam Wolfe screwed on a stolid face. "I give you injustice! Sending women to this island knowing full well they will bear children represents injustice. We have innocent children born upon this island who should not pay for the sins of their fathers." Moore and the crowd stood quiet. "Your job, all of you dignitaries on this wall, from now on, will be to ensure that all women dumped upon this rock be sterilized for the sake of the unborn!"

"We must move," Kellas whispered into Sam's ear as he shuffled passed.

"Mr. Moore, I wanted you to know who I am." Wolfe held his arms up again. "I am not a jihadist or a terrorist. I do not work for heathens. I work for the Lord. Furthermore, I am a criminal. I deserve my incarceration upon this island. I am prepared to do my time. I willingly will do my time and serve the Lord's work."

"If you believe in your punishment, then why go to the pains to orchestrate this, this, this holocaust upon these poor souls?" Murray Mallory Moore fought to express his consternation.

"Mr. Moore, your teachings were correct. They are correct. I chose to ignore your warning. The country and its rules and laws concerning L.O.F.I. are just. I, like the thief crucified alongside Christ, accept my fate. From this moment on, I will serve as the gatekeeper of Hell for those dumped onto this island. We will serve as judge, jury, and executioner. Those who are of the benevolent form of criminality will be schooled in civility, given an education, and introduced to faith. Those violent criminals will be put to the sword."

"Why are you telling us this? Why are you doing this?" Moore seemed exasperated. Kellas, growing ever impatient, observed as more Marines mounted the wall and the fleeing teachers paused to listen to this bizarre dialogue. "Why not just kill them quietly? Why this elaborate slaughter? What do you want out of this?"

"I demand that all women sent to this island be sterilized, as I stated before." Sam Wolfe paused, knowing that all needed to hear his next demand. "Locked down in a tunnel, off a storage shed that accesses a 20th Century boiler room, you will find a group of innocents born on this rock. Offer them the chance to move to society. Finally, understand that we plan to stabilize this island. Make it a respectable community. We will implement God's laws and this island will become a 21st Century Australia." Kellas had moved toward the end of the plank and began to fasten himself to the bungee cord expulsion device. Sam Wolfe backed down the plank in his direction.

"Principals," Wolfe continued, "you are the gatekeepers of society. The cause and concept of the American Penal Colony System has manifested to me its level of propriety and justification. The inhabitants of this island deserve this incarceration. If a man can't live in accord with his fellow man in the richest, most powerful country in the world, then he does not deserve to live. There are no constitutional rights violated here. A pox upon those cries for justice! This island manifests justice. From now on, this community of criminality will learn that Guam represents their last pit stop in life. They will conform to our New Guam or be expunged from life. People will be educated, learn faith, and not live in fear if they can respect the rules and pursue our own level of happiness." Sam Wolfe noticed that Kellas Somervell had attached the bungee cord to his legs, ready to leap back into the island with the unpleasant task of weaving through the morass of carnage. He glanced back at the crowd.

"To L.O.F.I. I commend my spirit." Kellas Somervell leapt back into the island of Guam. Sam glanced around observing some of the aircraft returning toward the air base.

"Mr. Moore, work with these people and persuade them to give the innocents a chance at life beyond these walls. Their constitutional rights have been violated, for they never had a chance to embrace them. If they desire to remain with me and our civilization, let that be their choice." Sam Wolfe moved down the plank toward the expulsion device. He grabbed the deployed cord that Kellas had already detached from with his jump. He quickly pulled up the cord noticing a detachment of armed Marines forming on the wall. "Mr. Moore!"

"Yes, Sam?" Moore overwhelmed at the reunion with his troubled student, the smell of death, the horrific scene, and the surreal nature of the conversation, could not help but continuing the tête-à-tête as if it represented a normal reality.

"Now that you know who I am. I would like you to do the honors and expel me once again back onto the island. Would you do that for me?" Wolfe appeal to his former teacher.

"I reckon the authorities will want to talk to you about all of this."

"What will they do? Send me to prison? Ha-ha!" Sam Wolfe had pulled up the cord and started attaching it to his feet. "Mr. Moore, I have nothing but the utmost respect for you. Teachers were correct! America represents the greatest enterprise on the globe. With its abundant wealth, liberal society, racial acceptance, economic opportunities, and endless pursuit of happiness, I agree now; anyone who wishes to disrupt and disturb or destroy the utopia of America should be banished to this penal colony. Bravo statesmen! Bravo, politicians who devised this American structure. Just correct the injustice of the innocents born in this past generation and all generations to come. Rectify this issue." The marines stopped behind Murray Mallory Moore indecisive as to their next move due to the sudden placidity of the scene as the aircraft began to head home.

"Last year," Wolfe continued, "you pushed me into the abyss prior to my self-discovery at the very moment of yours. Now, our stars have aligned. I need you to throw me in again, this time both of us aware of the consequences." Sam Wolfe looked down as Kellas Somervell waded through the massive heap of smoldering corpses, which in the following days would be consumed by a tremendous mass grave.

"What do you mean Sam?" Murray Mallory Moore inquired.

"Quite simple, sir; this:" Murray Moore prepared to hurl Sam Wolfe into the abyss as Wolfe finished his thought, "from now on, you and the other teachers will rule in heaven and I shall serve America in Hell." At that the flummoxed teacher shoved his former student off the wall.

Sam Wolfe, consummated his actions, falling toward the earth after Mr. Murray Mallory Moore thrust him again into the abyss. He bounced, spun, settled, then dropped. This time, Sam Wolfe knew exactly the nature and capacity of his duty as gatekeeper of Hell. He bobbed up and down, then rather stoically disentangled himself and traversed the human carnage and gore, determined to rebuild civility. He followed Kellas Somervell having never felt more confident. L.O.F.I. would never again represent a failed Sisyphean experiment but rather a triumph of the Phoenix.

———

Sam Wolfe caught up with Kellas Somervell who had paused to allow his protégé to speak with him. Both men turned and look up to the top of Hadrian's Wall. Wolfe could see the expulsion device standing idle now with his former instructor standing akimbo. Next to Murray Mallory Moore stood a military man on a radio flanked by armed Marines. The smell of the burning flesh nauseated the men briefly who choked down their discomfort knowing that the plan, God's plan, had come to fruition. In the distance, the sound of a thumping helicopter could be heard.

"Ha-ha! Young Sam Wolfe, we have indeed achieved the goal of the Almighty."

"Yes." Sam Wolfe smiled.

"We have laid the foundation of a potential society."

"Agreed." Sam Wolfe looked off into the edge of the clearing where Keiondre and his army patiently awaited their new leader's return.

"All has been vindicated now young Sam." Kellas stepped over a decapitated corpse as Sam waded through the gore. "You have justified yourself to your instructor. The army has been established to secure the future of civilization here on Guam. And the unfortunate culling of the herd has been finished." Sounds of military aircraft continued to be heard, but the men discounted their actions as they moved across the plain of slaughter toward Keiondre and Charla. The band of soldiers began to move out from the protection of the forest. Wolfe identified the numerous lieutenants who had led the army through the jungle rooting out the enemies of civilization. Keiondre looked pleased, Charla relieved. Sam turned around. The top of Hadrian's Wall displayed a flurry of activity. He noticed the expulsion device had been removed.

"I suppose we just need to head back to the tunnel where we made our way under the wall."

"Indeed Sam. We need to make sure the aides are safe."

"I am hoping they are gone. Surely, the military will remove them from the island. The government owes them that."

"Indeed." As the men continued to make their way toward the black army, another group began to emerge from the cover of the trees. North of Keiondre and Charla, Kellas and Sam stopped in disbelief as a quick count proved this baker's dozen to be none other than Whatley and the other aides that the two had safely locked up in the tunnel. They had come back. Or had been forced back by the military. Either way, Kellas and Sam stood dumbfounded for this did not represent any part of their plan.

Sam turned around and checked out the wall. As he turned, he noticed Whatley waving his arms in the air in a near panic. Sam began to worry. Something seemed amiss. He scanned the wall. Now, Hadrian's Wall proved to be filled with soldiers. Some had binoculars fixed upon him, some on Keiondre's group, some on the aides, some in the air.

"Kellas."

"Indeed Sam, indeed." Kellas, gazing at the tree line, through his periph-eral vision could make out Sam's view, whose attention lay in the opposite direction. "Yes, Sam, I am worried about the emergence of the aides. You head to Keiondre; I will go check on my girls." Sam tried to process everything in his mind. A mind which had for the past year focused primarily upon a goal that quickly witnessed his meteoric rise to power. A mind which realized that in the grand scheme did not face a terrible opposition. A mind which saw everything piece together perfectly. Now, a nebulous cloud shrouded the mind for events seemed to be turning away from his control. In the year he spent on the island everything seemed to fall into place as part of Kellas's and the Almighty's grand scheme. He only needed to follow—not think so much, just do. Now, here in this moment, he began to conjecture about this plan. The aides were back, not on the other side of the wall in Anderson Air Force Base. The wall continued to fill with soldiers, along with more sounds of Sioux heli-copters. Kellas's cool demeanor had even faltered. Now, he stood questioning these events, the relative ease of their escape, and fact that the only inhabitants left on the island now stood on this open exposed ground as choppers rose from behind the wall.

"Kellas." Sam turned in a mild panic.

"Yes, Sam, I do believe I can read your thoughts." Somervell for the first time in the year Sam had spent with him upon the island had a wavering crack in his voice.

"I think we need to run." Sam turned back toward the wall. As he attempt-ed to force his body to move—to forget this faith that God's plan will deliver them all—Sam noticed a flash, heard a zip, then a grunt. He stared at the wall contemplating if they had just fired a shot.

"Sam!" Wolfe heard a pained voice followed by a thud. He turned to see Kellas kneeling on the ground holding a wound in his abdomen. "Sam. Run." Kellas gnashed his teeth, then rolled and fell on his back.

"No!" Sam shouted toward the heavens. Then he shouted toward the wall some two hundred yards off. He spun around, the aides had not yet noticed that Kellas had fallen, nor did Keiondre and his army.

"Sam." Kellas painfully exhorted as blood leaked through his hands gripped upon his belly. "Sam, we have been deceived."

"Can you get up?" Sam spun three hundred and sixty degrees in a panic, hoping against hope for a sign or guidance.

"Sam. I am finished. Save the aides." Kellas grimaced in pain. Crestfallen, he looked up toward the heavens, "I don't understand. Surely, we have not been forsaken." He coughed an agonizing cough. "Though I walk through the valley of death, I shall fear no evil." He trailed off.

As Sam Wolfe turned toward the trees to contemplate his next move, a brilliant flash blinded him and he fell to the ground next to Kellas Somervell. A palpable heat erupted from the island, and Sam could feel the scorch upon his exposed skin. The delayed scream of a fighter that had passed could be heard. Sam blinked to see a wall of flame rising from the trees. Suddenly another rush and explosion followed by another screaming fighter. The wall of flame rose nearly one hundred feet into the air; the heat proved vicious. Sam Wolfe lay on the ground indecisively stunned. More fighters could be heard screaming above as round after round of napalm hit the forest scorching and incinerating everything in its wake. Sam rose to a knee trying to formulate a plan, but all he could do proved futile.

Screams could be heard as he saw the aides fleeing the forest of flame and heading straight for Hadrian's Wall. Likewise, Keiondre and his men ran at him. Wolfe noticed that some of the men were already set ablaze staggering about in the throes of death. Sam stood on his feet; he could see in the distance burning warriors everywhere emerging from the trees. He looked to his right. The aides were screaming in terror. He spun around at the thumping audible from his rear. Sam realized what he had done as two Sioux choppers fanned out. He glanced down at Kellas.

"Kellas! What do we do?" Sam screamed above the din.

"Sam." Kellas choked out with tears of agony in his eyes. "We have been forsaken." At that word, Kellas Somervell's head exploded as the sniper perched upon Hadrian's Wall delivered the pinpoint quietus. The sound of Sam Wolfe screaming in profound fear and rage were drowned out by the

Sioux helicopters which settled above him and began to open fire on the last remaining and living inhabitants of the island of Guam. As he howled toward the heavens for justice, he witnessed the same wholesale slaughter that he had had wrought upon his enemies. Now that same death would be delivered unto his followers. The aides, Whatley, along with other innocents futilely ran towards Hadrian's Wall as they were cut to pieces in a flurry of gun fire. As the second gunship slaughtered the remnants of Keiondre's army, Sam Wolfe turned and ran toward the wall himself.

As Sam sprinted toward the wall yelling "Why" up to the heavens and the soldiers, he could hear the swoosh of fighters going overhead as they dropped napalm on the dying members of his tribe. He never looked back, knowing he'd only see the incineration of the shattered and bullet-ridden bodies of the island's last inhabitants. He did not wish to view the killing of twelve young innocent girls whom were now paying for his sin. He leapt over the carnage from earlier, running in a blind panic. Those upon the wall stood and gazed at his frantic run. Behind him nothing lived—not man, woman or beast. Flames and smoke, fire and brimstone rose toward the heavens in an apocalyptic scene the likes of which Dante Alighieri or Hieronymus Bosch could only have envisioned. Sam continued to run, contemplating the horrors he inflicted upon his friends and enemies. God's work. He felt sure that he had been carrying out God's work. Kellas, Masada, the twelve aides, how could all of those along with the various signs from the Lord prove to be for naught? How could all of that labor and planning only amount to the destruction of it all? Why keep Kellas alive for forty years on this desert of civilization only to allow him to be butchered outside the walls? What did it all mean? Did God really have a plan?

As he arrived at the foot of the wall and glanced up, he had forsaken the hope for a sign from the Almighty. Just as quickly as he became a believer, he became a non-believer. He realized all he had done had been in vain. His faith had only led to slaughter. He looked up the wall to see a contingent of Marines looking down upon him. He turned and noticed that the flame had died down, but the wall of black smoke continued to billow toward the heavens. The fighters had moved out to sea and the helicopters had moved off into the distance apparently scouring the forest for any survivors. Sam Wolfe stood apoplectic at the face of the wall and began to shout towards the heavens.

"Why! Why kill them all? Why kill the innocents? Why? Answer me you bastards!" Sam Wolfe could see a herd of men gazing over the edge of the wall, but none said a word. Sam looked left and right down the base of the wall; human gore littered the area in a scene straight from the trenches of the First World War. As he started to shout again, he saw a parting of the soldiers' faces atop the wall. He waited and saw the emergence of his instructor, Murray Mallory Moore.

"Mr. Moore!" Wolfe stepped back from the wall. "Mr. Moore, surely you didn't have anything to do with this!"

"Sam Wolfe, you are responsible for all of the deaths here today!" Moore shouted down from his perch. "Your juvenile blind faith has led to the slaughter of thousands today. Thousands!"

"Why kill Kellas? Why kill the aides!" Wolfe had nearly become hoarse with the screams of the last few minutes.

"They were complicit. You raised the army. You brought this all upon them. Now, all are punished."

"Why not kill me?" All stood atop the wall in silence. Wolfe bellowed, "Ahhhhhhhhh! Why not kill me?" Murray Mallory Moore looked about the carnage behind Sam Wolfe and extended his arms as if to gesture that the island now belonged to him.

"You wanted the island; you have the island. You can now have your island and your religion and live like the animal you have become." With that the soldiers began to disappear from the sight of Sam Wolfe as they moved up the plank toward the Great Wall of Guam. The last head gazing over proved to be Murray Mallory Moore's, "Goodbye Sam Wolfe. Good riddance."

"No!" Sam Wolfe screamed the word with all of the energy that he had left. He charged the wall as Murray Mallory Moore disappeared and began to pound his fists upon the base. "I am not an animal!" He continued to shout as he reflected upon his friend and mentor back up the beach dead from two sniper's bullets. "I am not an animal." He cried as he thought of the twelve young girls all in the blossom of life that he had led to their ignominious death. As he contemplated their purity and innocence then realized that as they ran in fear they were cut down and incinerated, Sam Wolfe vomited copiously upon the base of the wall. "I am not an animal," Sam gasped through the dry-heaves of his now emptied stomach. He thought of Keiondre, Charla, and all of the men he led to this battlefield. "I am not an animal." He dropped to his knees futilely smacking the wall with his fists reflecting upon all of the lives he had taken on this island in the name of God, the Almighty, and his perceived justification of it all. He gave up the thought and succumbed to whimpering and regret. He pressed his face against the wall in agony knowing that he had truly been forsaken. He sobbed; he gasped; he gave up the last remnant left of his spirituality.

"I am not an animal."

36755075R00123

Made in the USA
Charleston, SC
11 December 2014